gossip girl
the carlyles

gossip girl
the carlyles

Created by
Cecily von Ziegesar

Written by
Annabelle Vestry

poppy

LITTLE, BROWN AND COMPANY
New York   Boston

Poppy

Little, Brown and Company
Hachette Book Group USA
237 Park Avenue, New York, NY 10017
Visit our Web site at www.pickapoppy.com

First Edition: May 2008

The Poppy name and logo are trademarks of Hachette Book Group USA.

alloy**entertainment**

Produced by Alloy Entertainment
151 West 26th Street, New York, NY 10001

Cover design by Andrea C. Uva
Cover photo by Roger Moenks

ISBN 978-0-316-02064-0
10 9 8 7 6 5 4 3 2 1
CWO

Printed in the United States of America

Gossip Girl novels created by Cecily von Ziegesar:

Gossip Girl
You Know You Love Me
All I Want Is Everything
Because I'm Worth It
I Like It Like That
You're The One That I Want
Nobody Does It Better
Nothing Can Keep Us Together
Only In Your Dreams
Would I Lie To You
Don't You Forget About Me
It Had To Be You
The Carlyles

I do desire we may be better strangers.

—William Shakespeare, *As You Like It*

gossipgirl.net

Disclaimer: All the real names of places, people, and events have been altered or abbreviated to protect the innocent. Namely, me.

| topics | sightings | your e-mail | post a question |

hey people!

Surprised to hear from me? Don't be. Something's happened on the Upper East Side, and I can't keep quiet about it. There's a new threesome in town, and they're far too exquisite not to talk about. . . .

But first, I need to back up a little.

As we all know, this summer our beloved Avery Carlyle passed away. Benefactress extraordinaire, she gave away pieces of her fortune to museums, libraries, and parks the way other people donate last season's dresses to St. George's thrift shop. At seventeen, she made headlines dancing on tables at Elvis's first New York show. At twenty-one, she married (for the first time) and moved into the famous peach-colored town house on the corner of Sixty-first and Park. And at seventy, she still drank scotch and soda and was always surrounded by fresh-cut white peonies. Most important, she knew exactly how to get what she wanted—from husbands, society hostesses, heads of state, *anyone*. A woman after my own heart.

And why should you care? Keep your panties on, I'm getting to that. Avery Carlyle's wayward daughter, Edie—who ran away years ago to Nantucket to find herself through art—was called back to New York to sort through her mother's affairs. Judging by the bookcase of leather-bound journals (and the six annulled marriages) the elder Mrs. Carlyle left in her wake, that process may take a while. Which is why Edie recently shut down the Nantucket house and moved herself and her fatherless triplets into an infamous penthouse located on Seventy-second and Fifth.

Meet the Carlyles: **O**, ruggedly handsome, buff bod, golden blond hair, an ever-present Speedo . . . looks good so far. Then there's **A**, wheat blond hair, cobalt blue eyes, a fairy-tale goddess robed in Marni. And lastly **B**, which simply stands for Baby. *Aw.* But just how innocent is she?

Of course, our UES friends are up to some new tricks. There's **J**, last seen drinking Tanqueray gimlets on a yacht in **Sagaponack**. But why was she there, when she was supposed to be performing arabesques at the Paris Opera House? Did the pressure get to her, or was she just homesick for her tycoon-in-training boyfriend, **J.P.** . . . ? Don't forget the impeccably mannered **R**, swimming laps in the rooftop pool at **Soho House** while his mother filmed a piece on summer entertaining for her television show *Tea with Lady Sterling*. We all know Lady S can't wait to plan his fairy-tale wedding to longtime girlfriend, **K**, but will young love endure? Especially when **K** was seen in the confessional at **St. Patrick's**? They say confession is good for the soul.

What will the old crowd think of these three new additions to our fair island? I, for one, can't wait to see whether they sink or swim. . . .

your e-mail

Dear GG,
So, my mom went to Constance Billard like a million years ago with the triplets' mom, and she told me the reason they moved here is because **A** slept with the entire island—boys and girls. And then **B** is, like, this crazy, brilliant genius who's mentally unstable and never washes her clothes. And **O** apparently swims up to Nantucket on the weekends in a Speedo. Is that true?
—3some

a:
Dear 3,

Interesting. From what I've seen, **A** looks pretty innocent. But we all know looks can be deceiving. We'll see how brilliantly **B** does in the city. As for **O**, Nantucket's a long way away, so I doubt he can swim that far. But if he can . . . I've got one word for you: *endurance*. Exactly what I look for in a man.

—GG

q:
Dear GG,

I just moved here and I love New York!!!!! Do you have any advice to make this year the best year ever?

—SMLLTWNGRL

a:
Dear STG,

All I can say is, be careful. Manhattan is a pretty small place itself, albeit much more fabulous than wherever you came from. No matter what you do, and no matter where you are, somebody is watching. And it's not going to be gossiped about in your high school cafeteria—in this town, it's bound to hit Page Six or Gawker. If you're interesting or important enough to be gossiped about, that is. One can only hope.

—GG

q:
Dear GG,

I bet you're just saying you deferred college because you didn't get in anywhere. Also, I heard that a certain monkey-owning dude never made it to West Point, and I think it's pretty mysterious that he's still here and so are you. Are you really a girl?? Or are you even a senior? I bet you're just some nerdy thirteen-year-old with no boobs, so people can't tell if you're a girl or a boy. I mean you're definitely not the real thing. Even the site looks different.

—RUCHUCKB

Dear RUCHUCKB,

First of all, it's called a makeover! Get with the program. Second, I'm flattered that my continued presence is spawning conspiracy theories. Sorry to disappoint, but I am as feminine as they come, without a pet monkey in sight. My age? As the venerable elder Avery Carlyle would say: A real lady never tells.

—GG

sightings

This just in, from the newbies: **O** running in **Central Park**, without a shirt. Does he *own* any shirts? Let's hope not . . . ! **A** trying on a silver sequined YSL minidress in the dressing room of **Bergdorf's**. Didn't anyone tell her Constance has a dress code . . . ? And her brunette sister, **B**, in **FAO Schwarz**, clinging to a guy in a barn-red Nantucket High hoodie, putting stuffed animals in inappropriate poses and taking pictures. Is *that* what they do for fun where they're from?

Okay, ladies and gents, you all probably have to go back-to-school shopping—or, for those of you who've headed off to college, read Ovid and chug a PBR in your new eight-by-ten dorm room. But don't worry; I'll be here, drinking a glass of Sancerre in the corner booth of Balthazar, reporting on what you're missing. It's the dawn of a new era on the Upper East Side, and with these three in town, I just know it's going to be another wild and wicked year. . .

You know you love me,

gossip girl

welcome to the jungle

Baby Carlyle woke up to the sound of garbage trucks beeping loudly as they backed up Fifth Avenue. She rubbed her puffy eyelids and set her bare feet on the red bricks of her family's new terrace, pulling her boyfriend's red Nantucket High sweatshirt close to her skinny frame.

Even though they were all the way on the top floor, sixteen stories above Seventy-second and Fifth, she could hear the loud noises of the city coming to life below. It was so different from her home in Siaconset, Nantucket, better known as Sconset, where she used to fall asleep on the beach with her boyfriend, Tom Devlin. His parents ran a small bed-and-breakfast, and he and his brother had lived in a guest cottage on the beach since they were thirteen. He'd surprised Baby with a visit to New York over the weekend, but he'd left last night. When she couldn't sleep, Baby had dragged a quilt onto the terrace's hammock.

Sleeping alfresco? How . . . au naturel.

Baby shuffled through the sliding French doors and into the cavernous apartment she was now expected to call home. The series of large, cream-colored rooms, with their gleaming hardwood floors and ornate marble details, was the opposite of comfortable. She dragged the Frette duvet behind her, mopping the spotless floors as she wound her way to her sister Avery's bedroom.

Avery's golden-blond hair was strewn across her pale pink pillow, and her snores sounded like a broken teakettle. Baby pounced on the bed.

"Hey!" Avery sat up and pulled the strap of her white Cosabella tank top up on one tanned shoulder. Her long blond hair was matted and her blue eyes were bleary, but she still looked regally beautiful, just like their grandmother had been. Just like Baby wasn't.

"It's morning," Baby announced, bouncing up and down on her knees like a four-year-old high on Honey Smacks. She was trying to sound perky, but her whole body felt heavy. It wasn't just that her whole family had uprooted themselves from Nantucket last week, it was that New York City had never felt—*would never feel*—like home.

When Baby was born, her emergence had surprised her mother and the midwife, who thought Edie was only having twins. While her brother and sister were named for their maternal grandparents, the unexpected third child had simply been called Baby on her birth certificate. The name stuck. Whenever Baby had come to New York to visit her grandmother, it was clear from Grandmother Avery's sighs that while twins were acceptable, three was an unruly number of children, especially for a single mother like Edie to handle. Baby was always too messy, too loud, too *much* for Grandmother Avery, too much for New York.

Now, Baby wondered if she might have been right. Everything, from the boxy rooms in the apartment to the grid of New York City streets, was about confinement and order. She bounced on her sister's bed some more. Avery groaned sleepily.

"Come on, wake up!" Baby urged, even though it was barely ten, and Avery always liked to sleep in.

"What time is it?" Avery sat up in bed and rubbed her eyes. She couldn't believe she and Baby were related. Baby was always doing ridiculous things, like teaching their dog, Chance, to communicate by blinking. It was as if she were perpetually stoned. But even though her boyfriend was a raging stoner, Baby had never been into drugs.

It doesn't really sound like she needs them.

"It's after ten," Baby lied. "Want to go outside? It's really pretty," she cajoled. Avery took in Baby's tangled long brown hair and puffy brown eyes, and knew immediately that she'd been crying over her loser boyfriend all night. Back in Nantucket, Avery had done everything possible to avoid Tom, but this past weekend it had been impossible to escape his grossness, from the stained white Gap athletic socks he'd ball up and give to their cat, Rothko, to play with, to the one time she had caught him doing bong hits on the terrace wearing only a pair of Santa-print boxers. She knew Baby liked that he was *authentic*, but did authentic have to mean appalling?

Short answer? No.

"Fine, I'll come outside." Avery pulled herself out from under her six-hundred-thread-count Italian cotton sheets and walked barefoot onto the terrace, and Baby followed. Avery squinted in the bright sunlight. Below her, the wide street was empty except for an occasional sleek black town car whooshing down the avenue. Beyond the street was the lush expanse of Central

Park, where Avery could just barely make out the tangled maze of paths winding through its greenery.

The two sisters sat together, swinging in the hammock and looking over the other landscaped Fifth Avenue terraces and balconies, deserted save for the occasional rooftop gardener. Avery sighed in contentment. Up here, she felt like the queen of the Upper East Side, which was exactly what she was born to be.

Is that right?

"Hey." Their brother, Owen, six foot two and shirtless, stepped onto the terrace carrying a carton of orange juice and a bottle of champagne, wearing only a black Speedo bathing suit. Avery rolled her eyes at her swimming-obsessed brother, who could easily drink anyone under the table and then beat them in a 10K.

"Mimosa anyone?" He took a swig of orange juice from the carton and grinned at Avery's repulsed grimace. Baby shook her head sadly as her tangled hair brushed against her shoulder blades. Always tiny, Baby now looked absolutely fragile. Her messy brown hair had already lost the honey highlights that always showed up during the first weeks of a Nantucket summer.

"What's up?" he asked his sisters companionably.

"Nothing," Avery and Baby answered at the same time.

Owen sighed. His sisters had been so much easier to understand when they were ten, before they'd started acting all coy and mysterious.

He took a swig of orange juice, wondering if he'd ever understand girls. If they weren't so irresistible in general, he might have given them up and become a monk. Case in point: The only reason he was up so early was the semi-pornographic dream that had forced him out of bed and on an unsuccessful hunt for a pool.

Dream about *whom*? Details, please.

He placed the unopened bottle of champagne in a large, daisy-filled planter and took another swig of OJ before squeezing into the hammock next to his sisters. He glanced down at the mass of trees, not believing how small Central Park seemed. From up here, everything looked miniature. Not like Nantucket, where the expanse of dark ocean went on forever. Sconset was the nearest point in the country to Portugal and Spain, and Owen always wondered how long it would take him to swim there.

"Helloooooo!" The sound of their mother's voice and the jangling of her handcrafted turquoise and silver bracelets carried out onto the terrace from inside. Edie Carlyle appeared in the doorway. She wore a flowy blue-patterned Donna Karan sundress, and her normally blond-streaked-with-gray bob had been knotted into a hundred tiny braids. She looked more like a scared porcupine than a resident of Manhattan's most exclusive zip code.

"I'm so glad you're all here," she began breathily. "I need your opinion on something. Come, it's inside." She gestured toward the foyer, her chunky bracelets clanking against each other.

Avery giggled as Owen dutifully slid off the hammock and padded into the apartment, following Edie's long stride. For the past week, Owen had been acting as Edie's de facto art advisor. He had been to an opening almost every night, usually in an overcrowded, patchouli-drenched gallery in Brooklyn or Queens, where he'd drunk warm chardonnay and pretended to know what he was talking about.

The expansive, wood-paneled rooms of the penthouse that had once probably housed toile Louis XIV revival chaises and Chippendale tables were now barren except for a few castoffs

Edie had found through her extensive network of artist friends. Avery had immediately ordered a whole ultramodern look from Jonathan Adler and Celerie Kempbell, but the furniture hadn't yet arrived. In the interim, Edie had managed to find a moth-eaten orange couch to place in the center of the living room. Rothko was furiously scratching at it, his favorite new activity since moving to New York. Most of the Carlyles' pets—three dogs, six cats, one goat, and two turtles—had been left in Nantucket. Rothko was probably lonely.

Not for long. Sitting next to Rothko was a two-foot-high plaster chinchilla, painted aquamarine and covered in bubble wrap.

"What do you think?" Edie asked, her blue eyes twinkling. "A man was selling it for fifty cents on the street down in Red Hook when I was coming home last night from a performance. This is authentic, New York City found art," she added rapturously.

"I'm out of here," Avery announced, backing away from the plaster sculpture as if it were contaminated. "Baby and I are going to Barneys," she decided, locking eyes with her sister and willing her to say yes. Baby had been moping around in Tom's stupid sweatshirt all weekend. It had to stop.

Baby shook her head, pulling the red sweatshirt tighter against her body. She actually kind of liked the chinchilla. It looked just as out of place in the ornate apartment as she felt. "I have plans," she lied. She'd decide what those plans were just as soon as she was out of her family's sight.

Owen gazed at the statue. One of the chinchilla's heavily lidded eyes looked like it was winking at him. He really needed to get out of the house.

"I, uh, need to pick up some swim stuff." He vaguely remembered getting an e-mail saying he needed to pick up his uniform from the team captain at St. Jude's before school started tomorrow. "I should probably get to it."

"Okay," Edie trilled, as Avery, Owen, and Baby scattered to opposite ends of the apartment. School started tomorrow. It was the dawn of a new era.

Edie tenderly carried the chinchilla sculpture into her art studio. "Have fun on your last day of freedom!" she called, her voice echoing off the walls of the apartment.

Like they don't *always* find a way to have fun?

the best things in life are free

Avery couldn't help grinning to herself as she emerged from the apartment building and started walking south down Fifth. It was only ten o'clock in the morning, but the streets were already buzzing with tourists and families. The late August heat was laced with a cool breeze that made her shiver in anticipation. She couldn't wait to see the trees flanking the avenue turn brilliant orange, red, and yellow. She couldn't wait to snuggle up in a cashmere Burberry coat and sip hot chocolate on one of the benches lining the austere stone walls surrounding Central Park. She couldn't wait until tomorrow, when she would start school at Manhattan's exclusive Constance Billard School for Girls and her life would *finally* begin.

She turned onto Madison, pausing at the large plate-glass windows of the Calvin Klein boutique on the corner of Sixty-second Street to take in her reflection. With her long, wheat-colored blond hair wrapped in a Pucci print headscarf and a peony pink Diane von Furstenberg sleeveless wrap dress hugging her athletic frame, she looked like any Upper East Sider out for a stroll. In Nantucket, where fleece was party attire and a party was drinking a six-pack of

Molson on Sconset beach, Avery had always been out of her element. But this year it was all going to be different. Finally, she was right where she belonged.

Avery tore herself away from the shop window and continued to walk down Madison. Just past Sixty-first Street she reached the door to Barneys and smiled exultantly as the dapper, black-suited doorman held it open. She breathed deeply as she entered, the achingly familiar scent of Creed Fleurissimo hitting her along with the AC. It had been her grandmother's favorite perfume, and Avery could practically feel the elder Avery's spirit steering her away from an oversize apple green Marc Jacobs bag and toward the true designer purses.

Avery walked through the luxury handbag department, reverently touching the crocodile skin and soft leathers. Her eyes stopped on a cognac-colored Givenchy satchel, and she felt her stomach flutter. Its gold buckles reminded her of the antique chest she'd left behind in Nantucket. She'd always imagined some ancient blue-blooded great-aunt had lost the trunk in the Atlantic when her ship sank on her honeymoon, only for it to be recovered by a bearded lobsterman years after her romantic death. Avery had a habit of making things far more romantic than they actually were.

Well, that's way better than sucking your thumb and biting your nails.

"Exquisite piece." Avery heard a smooth voice over her shoulder. She turned around and took in the saleslady behind her. She was in her mid-forties, with gray-streaked hair pulled back into a sleek bun.

"It's beautiful," Avery agreed, wishing the saleslady would disappear. She wanted this moment to be pure: a moment between her and the purse.

And the imaginary lobsterman?

"Limited edition," the saleslady noted. Her name tag read NATALIE. "It was actually claimed, but we never heard back from the buyer. . . . Would you be interested?" Natalie raised her perfectly plucked eyebrows.

Avery nodded, transfixed. She glanced at the price tag—four thousand dollars. But she hadn't really bought that much since she had arrived in New York, and wasn't that what Edie's new accountant, Alan, was for? Besides, as Grandmother Avery had once reminded her when she'd admired a particular vintage Hermès Kelly bag in her namesake's extensive collection: *Handbags never die. Men do.* This bag was forever.

"I'll take it," she said confidently, her just-manicured petal pink fingernails reaching for the supple leather straps.

"Oh, there you are!"

Avery and Natalie turned in unison to see a willowy girl with cascading auburn hair and a freckled complexion sweep across the marble floor. Avery paused, transfixed. Even in a fluttery white Milly sundress with enormous D&G sunglasses perched on her head, the girl looked exactly like the ballerina in the Degas painting hanging in Grandmother Avery's library. "I came to pick up my bag. So sorry I didn't get your messages—I was in Sagaponack. My cell phone service is awful out there." She sighed deeply, as if a weak cell phone signal in the Hamptons were the most monumental handicap.

"Thanks again for holding it." The girl grabbed the satchel from Avery's hands, as if Avery's job had been to hold it for her. Avery narrowed her eyes as she firmly grasped the bag's strap.

"You must be Jack Laurent." Natalie pressed her lips into a tight line as she turned to the girl. "Unfortunately, because we do have a release policy and we have someone interested, I'm afraid that we'll have to put you back on the waiting list."

Avery smiled a *too bad* smile at the girl, feeling giddy. No one at Constance Billard could possibly have this bag. It seemed all the more valuable now that she saw how in demand it was. Avery tugged on the handle, but the girl made no effort to loosen her grip.

"I can see why you need a new bag." Jack glanced pointedly at Avery's worn Louis Vuitton Speedy purse. It had been her thirteenth-birthday present from her grandmother, and it was *well loved*, as Grandmother Avery would have put it. "There are some outside you might be interested in."

Avery narrowed her blue eyes at the girl and gripped the cognac-colored bag's shoulder strap. Outside? As in, the tacky knockoffs hocked by vendors on the street? She was speechless.

"Now that that's settled," Jack went on, tightening her grasp around the Givenchy's straps, "can we please take care of this?" she ordered Natalie haughtily, her green eyes flashing.

Natalie drew herself up to her full height of five foot two. She stood comically between the two girls, who faced each other eye to eye five inches above her head. "That's the only one we have," she began authoritatively. "It's a limited edition and rather fragile, so I'm sure you both will be able to work something out." She reached for their fingers, trying to pry them from the bag's leather handles.

"I don't think that will be necessary," Avery said, giving the purse a sharp tug that surprised Jack. She stumbled forward, losing her grip. *Take that, bitch*, Avery smirked.

Before Jack could regain her balance, Avery strode quickly away across the marble floor of Barneys, clutching the satchel protectively against her chest, like a football player headed for the end zone. She'd gotten there first, and she was going to leave here first, with the bag that was rightfully hers. Only ten yards separated her from the exit. Unable to help herself, she turned around to glare at Jack victoriously. It was the Carlyle equivalent of a touchdown dance. The girl's pale freckled face was drained of its perfect tan and her green eyes looked more confused than angry. Avery grinned, feeling giddy. But all of a sudden, a hideous buzzing sound erupted around her. She looked around in annoyance but couldn't see where the buzzing was coming from. Not daring to hesitate, she continued to walk, feeling a surge of victory.

"Excuse me, miss?" A burly security guard appeared in front of her. His name tag read KNOWLEDGE. Avery looked up in confusion. She tried to sidestep him, but he moved his bulk in front of her with ease.

She's not the first girl to make a run for it in Barneys!

"Give me the bag, baby girl, and it'll all be over," Knowledge said gently and quietly, holding on to Avery's thin arm. She could feel his gold-ringed fingers make an indentation on her tan skin.

"I was going to pay for it," she insisted, trying not to sound desperate. Wordlessly, she handed him the bag as her blue eyes widened in shock. Could they really think she was trying to steal it?

Natalie joined them, whisking the purse out of Knowledge's hands. Avery felt red splotches begin to form on her chest and face, which always happened when she was upset, a precursor to tears.

"I really think they should have an age limit for some floors, don't you?" Avery overheard one white-haired lady say loudly to her female friend with overly teased red hair, wearing a leopard print Norma Kamali shirtdress. Avery suddenly felt like she was five years old.

"I was going to pay for it," she repeated loudly. "The checkout counter wasn't clearly-marked." Even as she said it, she cringed. Checkout counter? She sounded like she had taken a wrong turn at Target.

She shook her head, trying to appear supremely irritated and reached into her own LV-monogrammed purse. She would pull her brand-new black AmEx out of her red and green striped Gucci wallet. Then everyone would see it was all an unfortunate mistake and apologize and give her loads of complimentary products for the inconvenience.

"Luckily, the exit *is* well marked," Natalie replied icily. She was enjoying this, Avery realized. She lowered her voice. "Don't worry. We're not going to call your parents." And with that, Natalie whirled around on her black Prada pumps and walked back to Jack, who was waiting with a steely smirk on her irritatingly freckled face.

"I just *had* to have it for the first day of school," Jack cooed dramatically. She took the purse in her hands, examining it as if to make sure Avery hadn't dirtied it with her sticky fingers.

"Your shopping trip is over, honey." Knowledge's soft voice interrupted her awful reverie, as two more security guards escorted her out a side entrance onto Sixty-first Street.

The door closed with a thud.

Avery's faced burned. She half expected an angry Barneys mob to follow her as she scurried away, but instead two thirty-something women pushed their black, tanklike Bugaboo strollers past her, chatting about nursery schools. White-gloved doormen stood outside rows of luxury apartment buildings. A red double-decker bus headed toward Central Park. Avery felt her heartbeat slow down. No one had a clue who she was or what had just happened. She readjusted her headscarf and crossed the street with her chin held high. This wasn't Nantucket, where everything was broadcast until infinity. This was New York, a city of more than eight million people, where Avery could do whatever she wanted to do—be whoever she wanted to be. So what if she hadn't gotten the Givenchy satchel? She still had the new patent leather Louboutin slingbacks she'd bought yesterday and her lucky pearls from Grandmother Avery. She could probably go back to Barneys tomorrow and no one would recognize her.

As she crossed Fifth, a cute guy in a gray Riverside Prep T-shirt and a Yankees cap jogged by, smiling at her. She smiled broadly back, batting her carefully mascaraed eyelashes. Tomorrow, Avery Carlyle would begin her brand-new life at her brand-new school and Jack Laurent would be a distant memory—some bitchy diva who had stolen her purse, never to be heard from again.

Maybe. The thing is, New York is a big city, but Manhattan is a very small island. . . .

this looks like the beginning of a beautiful friendship

Owen Carlyle stood in front of an imposing redbrick town house between Park and Madison and hesitantly rang the doorbell marked STERLING. He'd gotten an e-mail last week that he was supposed to pick up his swim team uniform from Rhys Sterling, the St. Jude's team captain, but he was still kind of embarrassed to stop by unannounced. It sort of felt like he was trick-or-treating.

Like anyone wouldn't give him a treat at any time of year.

He rang the doorbell again. Pretty blue flowers sprang from orderly white window boxes flanking the entrance. Idly he leaned down to smell one, thinking of a certain someone he wanted to give flowers to. As Owen inhaled the sweet scent, the door swung open, revealing a woman in a navy blue linen dress with striking, perfectly white hair, even though her face was completely unlined. She sort of looked like a white wig–wearing Nicole Kidman.

"Good day," she announced in a prim British accent, opening the door partway and glancing down her ski-jump nose at Owen quizzically. "May I help you?"

"Hi. I'm, uh, Owen Carlyle? I'm here to see Rhys. I'm new

to the swim team and wanted to pick up my stuff?" he began awkwardly. He really hoped he had the right house.

The woman's face broke into a warm smile. "Owen Carlyle! Of course, I knew your grandmother quite well. What a wonderfully unique woman." She ushered Owen into the expansive foyer. Owen awkwardly toyed with the blue flower he had snapped from outside. "You know she was on the show a few times?"

Owen furrowed his brow in confusion. In front of him was a grand, sweeping red-carpeted staircase like the one in *Sunset Boulevard,* one of Avery's favorite films. He had no idea what it was about, but Avery had probably watched it four hundred times.

"Tea with Lady Sterling," the woman said sternly, as if she was correcting him. "Tea with *me,*" she clarified.

Owen still didn't know what the fuck she was talking about. He seldom watched TV, and when he did, he made a point of not watching shows with the word *tea* in the title.

"Nice to meet you." Owen stuck out his hand awkwardly. The foyer walls were painted a soothing taupe color and were bordered by ancient-looking English foxhunting scenes. Suddenly, a preppy-looking guy wearing pressed chinos and a pristine short-sleeve blue button-down shirt bounded down the red-carpeted staircase. He looked like he was headed out to play golf. Owen tucked his hands into the pockets of his ratty Adidas shorts and hunched his shoulders inside his thin gray Nantucket Pirates T-shirt.

"Rhys! You have a guest." Lady Sterling smiled fondly at the two boys. "This is Owen Carlyle. Owen, darling, please do tell your mother I would love to see her. We've only met once, at a charity function, and you know how those things are," Lady Sterling trilled as she clicked down the hall.

"Nice to meet you, man!" Rhys gave Owen a firm handshake.

He was just a little bit shorter than Owen's six feet, two inches, and had dark brown hair and gold-flecked brown eyes. He opened a closet door and pulled out a maroon Speedo swim bag. "This is for you."

"Thanks, man." Owen pawed through it to find six Power-Bars, a maroon towel with ST. JUDE'S embroidered on it, and three tiny black Speedos. He held one up to his hips awkwardly. It was about five sizes too small. "Well, good meeting you." Owen stuffed the swimsuit back into the bag and turned to go.

"Wait up," Rhys called behind him. "You busy this afternoon? Want to go to brunch? Fred's is pretty good. It's on the top floor of Barneys."

"No!" Owen said quickly, one foot already outside. The last thing he wanted to do was run into Avery in the midst of some sort of fashion emergency.

Rhys looked crestfallen. "Oh, that's cool."

Owen shook his head. "I mean, can we just grab bagels instead? Go to the park?" he asked awkwardly. Despite the bevy of girls following him at all times, Owen had never really had close guy friends. In fact, it was *because* of the bevy of girls following him at all times. The guys at NHS had always been jealous of Owen's good looks and easy confidence, and knew they didn't stand a shot at scoring when he was around. Owen tried not to care, and he wasn't lonely or anything. But come on. It wasn't *his* fault he was a chick magnet.

It's not easy being beautiful.

"Fine by me." Rhys nodded in agreement and pulled down a pair of Ray-Bans as they made their way out of the town house and toward the park. On the way, they stopped at a deli for bagels and beers.

Breakfast of champions!

They crossed Madison and then Fifth, and when they entered the park Rhys guided them through several winding paths, heading farther and farther west. Finally they stopped at some castlelike stone structure sitting regally behind a small pond. It was about three stories high and looked like a medieval fortress.

"This is one of my favorite places in the city," Rhys said. "Belvedere Castle. When I was younger, I thought the castle was real and wanted to live in it. My mom has her own TV show, *Tea with Lady Sterling*?" He looked at Owen questioningly.

"Yeah, she mentioned that." Owen kicked at a pebble on the pathway. Girls in Malia Mills bikinis were tanning themselves in some big field, pretending they were in the Hamptons, and stoner guys were playing Hacky Sack or Frisbee. It was kind of sad: New Yorkers were so fucking starved for nature, they had to pretend a patch of grass was the beach.

"Since she's English, I figured we should have our own castle." Rhys shrugged sheepishly.

Owen laughed, settling onto the rock as Rhys cracked open a can of Olde English, careful to keep it concealed inside a paper bag. He passed the brown bag over to Owen. Owen took a sip and surveyed their surroundings. The pond's surface was covered with old leaves and greenish scum, but an endless array of girls with perfect late-summer tans were picnicking on the grass beside the imposing stone castle. Despite the flock of hot girls in loosely tied bikini tops, Owen found himself searching for a flash of butterscotch candy–colored hair. He sighed in frustration.

For the past few months, no matter where he was, all he'd been able to think about was Kat, the girl he'd hooked up with at a bonfire on Surfside Beach at the beginning of summer. He'd spotted the curvy girl with dancing blue eyes and hair the color of their golden retriever, Chance, and hadn't been able to tear his gaze from her. By the time she wandered up to him and asked for help opening her Corona Light, Owen was practically in love. And when she asked if he'd show her the lighthouse a few minutes later, they both knew what they wanted to do. There, in the sand in the dark, they'd lost their virginity to each other. It had been the wildest, most irresponsible and amazing thing Owen had ever done.

"What's your name?" he'd asked afterward, tracing his fingers down the curve of her shoulder. He'd felt like an asshole then. Sure, he was a player, but losing it to a girl without exchanging names was too much, even for him.

"Here's a clue." She'd pulled out a delicate silver bracelet that spelled KAT in loopy, careful letters.

They'd spent the rest of the night fooling around on the beach and running into the water whenever they got too sweaty. She was from New York, only visiting Nantucket for the day, she said, and knowing she'd be gone tomorrow somehow made it even more special, like it was his last night on earth. The next morning, Owen had woken up alone on the beach. It might have been a dream, except he had the silver bracelet as proof. Owen pulled the bracelet out of his cargo shorts now and ran his thumb over the uneven scratches on its surface. He held it up to his nose to see if he could somehow smell her.

"What is that?" Rhys asked curiously, snapping Owen out of his romantic reverie.

"Just . . . a good luck charm," Owen lied, slipping the bracelet quickly back into the pocket of his Adidas shorts. He wanted to ask Rhys if he knew Kat, but there were millions of people in the city and he didn't want to seem like some lovesick freak.

Too late.

"Oh," Rhys said, losing interest. "So, Nantucket, huh? What was that like?" he asked.

"It was cool," Owen said. "Small." There was no way he was going to tell the first person he'd met in Manhattan that all of the guys at Nantucket High sort of ostracized him for being a player. He took another sip of beer. The carbonation tickled his throat and the sun made him feel sleepy.

"It's pretty small here, too," Rhys told him. "I've been in the same school with the same guys since kindergarten."

Owen watched as two freckly girls walked past them, their shopping bags swinging in unison. He couldn't believe he was about to spend the rest of his school days surrounded by guys. What would he look at? "So, what's it like not having any girls around?"

Rhys squinted his gold-flecked brown eyes, as if he'd never really thought about it. "It's fine. My girlfriend goes to Seaton Arms, which is down the street, so it's not like it's all guys all the time."

Owen sighed in relief. He stretched out on the blanket, feeling the sun warm him through his thin gray T-shirt. A runner jogged by wearing skintight Day-Glo Lycra.

"So, one of the things I'm supposed to do as captain is to give some informal, end-of-summertime splits to Coach," Rhys said, breaking the silence. "Since I don't have any from you, let's just race each other across the pond, and I'll estimate your times off mine."

"Right here?" Owen asked skeptically, sitting up.

"Why not?" Rhys stood up on the rock, motioning for Owen to stand next to him. Rhys took off his shirt and revealed a sculpted six-pack and broad swimmer's shoulders. Owen shrugged and pulled his T-shirt off too. Two girls flipping through a French *Vogue* on a nearby bench looked up to stare over their magazine.

Hello!

"Ready? Go!"

Owen dove into the muddy pond without a moment's hesitation. He kicked through the seaweed and began to freestyle, startling the ducks in his path. He tore through the water with a smooth, strong stroke, his competitive instinct taking over.

He reached the other end of the noxious pond, breathing hard as he set his feet down on the squishy mud bottom. It felt like week-old oatmeal between his toes. Green gunk clung to his arms. Across the pond, Rhys stood on the rock, drinking out of his paper bag and laughing. Owen narrowed his eyes. What the fuck? The two girls on the bench giggled.

"Hey, dude, you're pretty fucking fast," Rhys yelled good-naturedly as he made his way around the pond toward Owen. A green-jumpsuited park ranger appeared from behind the castle, shouting.

"You can't swim there!" he yelled, charging toward Owen with a rake.

Forgetting about his shirt and shoes, Owen sprinted away. Rhys caught up with him on one of the winding paths out of the park. As they reached the exit, they stopped and doubled over laughing. Owen grabbed the still-open forty out of Rhys's hand. Maybe living here in NYC wouldn't be so bad. A cool guy friend, hot girls, and fierce swimming—what more could he want?

Hey, this is Manhattan. There's always more to want.

voulez-vous coucher avec j?

Jack Laurent stuffed her pointe shoes in her regulation pink School of American Ballet dance bag, ignoring the other dancers drinking Vitamin Waters and flirting with the Fordham freshmen gathered around the fountain outside Lincoln Center. This year, Jack was in the prestigious internship program, in which she would take several classes a day in hopes of being selected for performances with the company. She had been dancing for most of her life, and it came as naturally to her as breathing. But today, she'd been half a second behind the music. For the first time, ballet had seemed hard, and Mikhail Turneyev, the internship program director, had noticed every single one of her missteps.

As she walked across the expansive marble plaza, Jack noticed a spot of blood from a blister staining the powder-blue suede Lanvin flats she'd bought at Barneys just this morning.

"*Fuck,*" she murmured. Angrily, she pulled off her shoes and threw them in a trash can. *Thud.*

One man's trash is another's treasure.

She slid her feet into the faded blue J.Crew flip-flops she kept in her bag for when she got a pedicure and sat on one of the low stone benches flanking the reflection pond opposite the Vivian Beaumont Theatre. She glanced at her Treo and saw that her father had called three times while she was in class. She'd consented to bimonthly lunch dates with him at Le Cirque, where he would ask her about school and dance and pretend to care about the answers, but, as a rule, they never called each other just to chat. He wasn't even aware she'd left the Paris Opera Ballet School of Dance early, and she did not feel like getting into it.

Jack was the unplanned offspring of Vivienne Restoin, the celebrated French prima ballerina, and Charles Laurent, the sixtysomething former American ambassador to France. Vivienne had gotten pregnant when she was twenty-one, and, as she was so fond of reminding Jack, sacrificed her dancer's body—and her career—for her only daughter. They'd left Paris as a family when Jack was only a year old, but her parents had divorced after a few years in New York together. Her dad had later remarried (a few times) and now lived in a town house with his new wife and the stepbrats in the West Village. Jack pulled out her pack of Merit Ultra Lights, lit one, and exhaled with a dramatic sigh.

"I thought you were giving those up this year."

Jack whirled around to see her boyfriend, J.P. Cashman, strolling toward her. He was wearing a pair of khaki shorts and a neat, pink Brooks Brothers button-down. In his hand was a dog-eared copy of *An Inconvenient Truth*. He'd just come back from an expedition to the South Pole with his real-estate tycoon father, who was trying to ward off a slew of bad publicity by championing the environment. Jack quickly stamped out the cigarette with the heel of her flip-flop. J.P. hated that she smoked, and she usually tried to refrain in his presence, but how was she supposed to know he'd surprise her after class? And didn't she deserve a teeny-tiny break when it was technically still summer?

"Hi, beautiful." J.P. pulled her into him and she gripped his strong back as they kissed. He tasted like ginger candy. He rested his hand on her fleshier-than-usual hip.

While taking classes at the Paris Opera, she'd developed an addiction to the pain au chocolat from the bakery down the street from her dormitory.

"Want to grab lunch?" J.P. asked, easily snaking his arm around her waist. She stiffened under his touch, feeling like an extra-plump sausage in a pink leotard casing.

Moving from a size zero to a two is *such* a tragedy.

"As long as it doesn't actually include food," Jack agreed, leaning against J.P. They walked hand in hand down Broadway toward Columbus Circle. The streets were crowded with families soaking up the last weekend of summer, and the air felt thick and hot.

"So," J.P. began, gallantly slinging Jack's bag over his shoulder, "after the expedition, I was able to connect with this Columbia professor who's working on sustainability, and I'm actually interning—"

"J.P.?" Jack interrupted. "You didn't tell me I look pretty." She knew it might sound pathetic to someone else, but J.P. always told her she looked pretty when he saw her. It was always the first thing out of his mouth and what Jack loved most about him.

Self-centered much?

"Yes, I did. I said, 'Hi, beautiful.' That's the same thing," J.P. responded, hardly looking at her as he held open the gleaming glass door of the Time Warner Center.

True, Jack reasoned. She hated to demand a compliment, but

ever since she'd been kicked out of the Paris Opera program for drinking muscadet alone in her dorm room, she'd been feeling a little shaky. She'd come home early and spent the last two weeks at her friend Genevieve's sprawling Maiden Lane compound in the Hamptons. Drinking Tanqueray gimlets on the beach hadn't been a bad way to end the summer, but feeling off during class this morning had brought back the memory of her Paris embarrassment and left her feeling raw.

They took the escalator up to Bouchon Bakery, the casual bistro on the third floor, and sat at a table overlooking Columbus Circle. Cars were backlogged in the traffic circle, and tourists lounged around the fountain at its center. Now that she was back with J.P., Jack felt her old confidence returning. So she'd have to eat salads for a few weeks and spend a few extra hours a week in the studio. Who cared? The most sought-after boy in New York loved her. They were all but destined to get married, live in one of his dad's luxurious buildings, and take fabulous vacations to rest up from their equally fabulous lives. And in the meantime, maybe this year was finally the year they would do it. *It* it.

That'd be one way to burn calories.

The sound of Tchaikovsky's *Nutcracker Suite* erupted from Jack's pink ballet bag. She pulled out her phone and looked at the display. Her father again. Jack grimaced and pressed ignore.

"Who's that?" J.P. asked, taking a bite of the grilled cheese sandwich a skinny, goateed waiter had just set down on the table. Jack could feel her stomach growling.

"Charles." Jack shrugged and grabbed a fry off his plate. One wouldn't kill her.

"When was the last time you talked to him?" J.P. frowned.

Jack wrinkled her freckled nose. Just because J.P. was close to his own father and had gone on a freaking summerlong father-son Antarctic expedition, he assumed everyone should have the same type of jovial cross-generational relationship. J.P. was per-petually positive, which Jack loved, because it balanced out her tendency to freak the fuck out if someone got her order wrong at Starbucks. Now, though, she wanted his enthusiasm directed toward *her*. They could start by sitting in one of the luxurious leather seats in the screening room of the Cashmans' apartment, watching *The Umbrellas of Cherbourg* or some other ridiculous French film and taking off one article of clothing every time someone lit up a fresh cigarette.

She grabbed another fry. Just thinking about J.P.'s hands on her body made Jack hungry.

Um. Doesn't she mean *horny?*

"Let's get out of here," she whispered across the table, drag-ging her fingers across his tanned upper thigh, pleased when she saw his brown eyes widen excitedly.

Check, please!

r's enchanted evening . . . or not

Rhys dove into the tiled twenty-five-meter pool in the basement of his parents' town house on Eighty-fourth between Madison and Park. He propelled his body through the blue water, slicing it with his strong arms in a desperate attempt to sober up after an afternoon spent drinking with the new guy, Owen Carlyle.

Aren't you supposed to *drink* water to sober up?

Rhys felt seasick as he stopped to take a break at the other end of the pool. It didn't help that the pool was decorated with distracting hand-painted Italian folk art tiles depicting starfish, kelp, and octopus. He felt like he was drowning in some developmentally delayed five-year-old's finger painting.

He glanced at the large, fogproof clock above the teak doors that separated the pool from the rest of the basement fitness center. Seven thirty-five. His girlfriend, Kelsey, was supposed to come over at eight, and they hadn't seen each other since June. He'd been in Europe all summer, visiting the Welsh estate that had been in his father's family for generations and spending most of his time at the local pub with his cousins or heading to London via private jet to watch soccer games. Kelsey had been at her Orleans home on the Cape. They had talked on the phone, but less frequently than Rhys would have liked. Between their different schedules and the time difference, they'd kept missing each other—she'd always call when he was asleep; he'd always call when she was at the beach or sitting down to dinner or just not *there*. Now that they finally had the chance to be together, Rhys really didn't want to be drunk.

He ducked his head under the water and began a fast butterfly. As his strong arms knifed into the water, he got into a rhythm and began to feel better. Butterfly was his favorite stroke because it was both powerful and tender. You had to work with the water and against it at the same time. He'd always thought it was kind of similar to sex.

Not that he would know.

For the whole summer, all Rhys had been able to think about was his and Kelsey's end-of-year promise: as soon as they saw each other again, they'd make love for the first time.

Make love? Oh brother.

Rhys and Kelsey had known each other since they were in the same highly selective kindergarten class at All Souls on Lexington. Even then, he'd asked her to be his Valentine, a moment Lady Sterling had caught on tape and replayed every February 14 on her show. They'd begun dating seriously at the beginning of ninth grade and now, like jazz music and red wine, they belonged together.

Tonight, he sort of hoped he wouldn't have to say anything. They'd be so excited to see each other it would just . . . happen.

"Anyone here?" a voice called out through the steamy air. Rhys stopped mid-stroke, surprised to see Kelsey standing in the doorframe. She was early. She was beautiful. Just seeing the way the delicate gold Me&Ro anklet he'd given her hung from her tan ankle made him feel like he was about to burst.

"Hey." Kelsey stepped toward the side of the pool, her tan arms wrapped around her chest. Rhys pulled himself up from the ledge and grabbed her in a huge bear hug. Her hair smelled like apples.

"Rhys! You're all wet!" she giggled, her face breaking into a sunny smile that showed her slightly crooked teeth.

"Sorry about that." He stepped back and picked up a towel from a nearby bench, knotting it right below his slim hips.

"It's okay," Kelsey conceded as she wrinkled her slightly upturned nose and planted a delicate kiss on his lips. She stepped back and wrung out the hem of her knee-length dress. "How are you?"

"Good," Rhys murmured. "I mean, now I am." Or at least, he would be soon. He had two bottles of Cristal chilling in his bedroom that he had taken from his banker father's large stash. And he knew it was cheesy, but he had also gotten two dozen Sterling roses from the florist shop on the corner as he was coming home from the park.

Nothing like drinking forties to bring out a guy's romantic side.

"Race you?" She raised her eyebrow suggestively, like she knew a delicious secret. Rhys had forgotten how infectious her enthusiasm was. He hated those girls who pretended to be too cool for everything, and Kelsey was the total opposite: everything from *The Starry Night* at MoMA to a Jacques Torres caramel made her smile.

Kelsey bounded up the wide stairs to the main floor of the Sterling town house, which was built with broad, oak beams that made it seem more like an Old English manor house than a mansion on the Upper East Side of Manhattan. All of the furniture was heavy and dark and utilitarian, rescued from various castles throughout Europe, making it look blandly austere, even in the daytime.

As they raced up the wide, red-carpeted stairs at the center of the living room, Rhys couldn't tear his eyes away from Kelsey's athletic, freckled calves and the easy swish of her dress. He said a silent prayer that his mother wouldn't hear them. The last thing he needed was to get into a lengthy conversation about teen trends that would invariably be part of the back-to-school segment on *Tea with Lady Sterling*.

Teen trend: losing your virginity on a bed of rose petals from the bodega on Seventy-ninth and Madison.

He beat Kelsey up the stairs and catapulted into his bedroom suite on the third floor. Quickly he lit the white Bond No. 9 candles he'd bought for the occasion and cued Snow Patrol on his Bose iPod SoundDock. He had just dimmed the lights as she slid through the doorway.

Down boy!

"God, no wonder you're such a good swimmer. Those stairs are a workout," Kelsey sighed dramatically, pretending to wipe sweat off her high forehead. Rhys nodded, but was too distracted to smile. Normally he loved her goofiness, but now he wished she could be a little more serious. She surveyed the dim room.

"What's going on?" Her blue eyes darted from the petal-covered bed to the sound dock to the candles on the windowsill. Rhys quickly pulled the curtains so the summer sunset didn't peek in. It suddenly seemed a little too over the top to try to have a romantic night together when it was still so light outside. "What's all this for?"

"I missed you." He ran his hands through his still-wet brown hair, then awkwardly let them fall back to his sides, as if he didn't know what to do with them. It was weird just standing there in his bathing suit while Kelsey was fully clothed. It felt dirty, somehow. He wished that his brain didn't still feel so foggy, and that he hadn't gotten so drunk when he was hanging out with the new kid.

"I want to show you how much I love you," Rhys continued, pulling her to him and kissing her. As his lips brushed against hers, the line replayed in his head. *I want to show you how much I love you?* Was that totally cheesy? He suddenly noticed that the water from his bathing suit was puddling on the walnut floor. He hoped it didn't look like he'd peed himself.

Nothing's sexier than a good set of Depends.

"That's sweet." Kelsey pulled away and sat on the king-size sleigh bed. She pulled her knees tightly to her chest. "Remember when we used to have sleepovers in first grade and your mom would always pull the curtains and pretend it was midnight when it was really only like six o'clock?"

"Let's talk about that later," Rhys whispered, kneeling next to her on the bed. He gently kissed her bare shoulder blade as he inched the strap of her dress down her shoulder. Maybe the setting *was* a little too over the top. It was sort of nice with the sunlight pouring in. Kelsey smiled mysteriously and Rhys felt his insides flip-flop. He moved to kiss her collarbone and then her neck, and finally her lips. It was happening. It was finally happening.

There was a loud tapping noise on the door.

Rhys pulled back a little, but he could still feel Kelsey's hot breath on his cheek. "Hello?" he yelled cautiously.

"Rhys, darling, is Kelsey here? I thought I heard her voice." It was the strident voice of Lady Sterling, complete with a touch of an English accent, even though she'd been born and raised in Greenwich, Connecticut, and not Greenwich, U.K. Rhys wondered if she knew what they were doing, or about to do.

"Yeah, Mom," he mumbled, pulling the towel back around his waist and shaking his head. His mom adored Kelsey. Luckily, the feeling seemed to be mutual. If it wasn't, Kelsey never complained. It was one of the many things he loved about her.

"How lovely!" Lady Sterling's voice went up an octave in the actressy way it did when she was in front of the cameras. "Well, I would love to see you both in the solarium for tea. I'm anxious to hear your thoughts for the back-to-school component of the show tomorrow," she trilled from behind the door.

"Sounds great, Lady S!" Kelsey called back. She smoothed her sundress and hooked her wavy, butterscotch candy–colored hair behind her small ears.

Lady Sterling's heels clicked away, growing softer as she made her way down the staircase. "We should go down there." Rhys shrugged helplessly. "I'm sorry. Are you mad?"

"No," Kelsey said, getting up from the bed. "It's okay. Another time." She swooped over to the recessed window and blew out a candle. "I'll go entertain your mom. You can meet us when you get changed," she added, kissing Rhys on the nose.

Rhys blew out the remaining candles as Kelsey shut his bedroom door. Was it just him, or did she not seem that upset at the interruption? He walked into the adjacent bathroom, turned on the water, and let the steam overtake the room. Maybe it was all in his head. He *was* still sort of drunk, after all.

Maybe. But you know you're in trouble when there's more steam in the bathroom than the bedroom.

gossipgirl.net

Disclaimer: All the real names of places, people, and events have been altered or abbreviated to protect the innocent. Namely, me.

| topics | sightings | your e-mail | post a question |

hey people!

For some of you less-fortunates, tomorrow is D-day, or should I say S-day: back to school. After a summer of partying till 5 a.m. and sleeping till 4 p.m., it's time to set those alarms and pack those satchels. As you pull on your new TSE cardigans and strap on your oh-so-studious Miu Miu patent leather Mary Janes, remember: it's not *all* work.

After all, here on the Upper East Side we work hard and play hard. Here's a *real* to-do list for the first day of school:

1. Book a massage at Cornelia Day Resort on Fifty-third and Fifth—waking up early to walk to school is hell after a late night dancing at Hiro Ballroom.

2. Get your tutors lined up—the cute premeds from Columbia are in high demand, so don't procrastinate! There are plenty of terminally unemployed and tragically overeducated losers out there, but don't you want someone nice to look at?

3. Get ready for your close-up—the candid shots for the yearbook are always taken in the fall, and we've all seen what the *E! True Hollywood Story* digs up. And aren't we all destined to be famous?

Some of you are veterans by now, and have your BTS essentials already in hand. The seniors certainly know the drill. But for you incoming juniors, let me remind you: this is the year people begin to pay attention. It's when your fake ID doesn't look quite as fake, when college doesn't seem that

far off, and when a wild Friday is no longer stealing a bottle of your dad's
Bombay Sapphire gin and watching old movies. It's time to establish your
reputation. Just don't let people know how hard you're trying.

sightings

A walking to Constance Billard in the dark, wearing her uniform, practicing
the route. We know you're excited, but seriously . . . **B** taking inappropriate pictures of herself on the terrace, using her camera phone. Um, it's
not as private as you think up there. . . . **O** shirtless on Fifth. And Madison.
And in my dreams . . . **J.P.** with his dad at the site of dad's new green
building in Tribeca. Way to go, Captain Planet! . . . **R** tossing rose petals
out his window, onto Eighty-fourth Street . . . **J** packing her *Elements of
Calc* textbook into a limited-edition Givenchy satchel that I heard was only
available in Europe. Is there anything she *doesn't* have?

your e-mail

Dear GG,
So, I heard that they're now, like, doing full body searches at Barneys
because the chick who moved into the Waldorfs' old apartment has
some type of major shoplifting scam going on. Apparently, she was,
like, totally trying to set **J** up. Do you know what happened?
BARNEYBABE

Dear BB,
Well, we all know girls can get a little sticky-fingered and sneaky at
Barneys. But would a newbie really be bold enough to try to steal
something *and* get on **J**'s bad side?
—GG

q: Dear GG,

I was hanging out in Central Park today and I saw this totally hot guy swimming through the duck pond. I want to hook up with him, but do you think there are any weird diseases in the water?

—Germ Phobic

a: Dear GP,

If you want to hook up with him so badly, imagine how many other people want to hook up with him, too. I would be more worried about competition than about radioactive pond scum.

—GG

q: Dear GG,

My parents are forcing me to go to a stupid single-sex private school, even though I just came back from a month trekking around Europe, where people are so free and in touch with their sexual sides. I am so freaking depressed and have no idea what to do about it. Seriously, teen alienation has been done to death; I am so not the young druggie girl cliché, and I certainly do not write poetry or create weird films. But what can I do to minimize the pain?

—Disaffected Girl

a: Dear DG,

Um, you sound like a lot of fun. You're right, though—teen alienation *has* been done to death. So, you're young, you're rich, and hopefully you don't look like too much of a disaster, although maybe a quick wax session is in order, since I know how the European guys like the natural look. My advice is the same as I'd give to any self-respecting five-year-old on her way to the first day of ultra-exclusive kindergarten: find a friend! And don't hit the boys on the playground—unless you're into that sort of thing.

—GG

Time to get some beauty rest—and you should too. Remember, tomorrow is the first day of the rest of your life. Use it wisely.

You know you love me,

gossip girl

all about a

"Are you sure you're going to be okay?" Avery asked her seven-minutes-younger sister, Baby, who was clutching her home-made extra-large chai and staring fixedly down at her dirty white Havaiana flip-flops. They turned onto Madison and walked toward the redbrick building on East Ninety-third Street that housed the Constance Billard School for Girls.

"Yeah," Baby responded, annoyed. Her sister was the one who had been freaking out and had made them leave their apartment at 7 a.m., a full hour before school began. "I don't think I'm going to stay too long, anyway," she added mysteriously as she pulled her wavy brown hair into a messy ponytail and knotted it into itself. Baby had the type of hair that looked better the less she brushed it. Or washed it. Which meant she didn't do much of either. If Avery didn't ambush her once a week with Bumble and bumble detangling mist and a Mason Pearson boar-bristle brush, she'd have dreadlocks by now.

Paging Doctor Fekkai. If only he made house calls.

"Can you take off that sweatshirt? It stinks." Avery glared at the red Nantucket High sweatshirt Baby had refused to take off since Tom left. Avery loved romance, but why couldn't Tom have left something normal, like a Tiffany necklace, for Baby to remember him by? "Please?" Avery asked again, more sweetly this time, seeing that Baby had no intention of taking off the sweatshirt.

Baby crossed her eyes and stuck her tongue out at Avery as she pulled the hoodie off to reveal a tie-dyed Grateful Dead T-shirt, a relic from their mother's hippie days. Avery sighed in frustration. Was her sister really that determined to make all their couture-wearing classmates hate her? Baby rooted around in her oversize neon green vinyl Brooklyn Industries messenger bag and found her blue Constance blazer.

"I'm only doing this for you." Baby smiled sunnily at Avery as she pulled the blazer on and stuffed the sweatshirt into her bag.

"There, that's so much better," Avery sighed, satisfied. Thankfully, the blazer obscured the dancing bears on Baby's shirt.

Together, they turned the corner on Ninety-third and approached the three-story redbrick building. "Here we go," Avery said under her breath as they walked through the massive royal blue double doors of Constance Billard. She looked around nervously at the sea of girls in seersucker skirts with their gleaming, freshly high-lighted hair. How could she possibly know which girls to befriend? Her confidence fell for a second, and she almost wished she were back at Nantucket High, where last year she'd been voted best dressed and most likely to succeed in the senior superlatives section of the yearbook—even though she'd only been a sophomore. How could she possibly stand out here?

Where there's a will, there's a way.

"Okay, freshwomen! We have a tour in five minutes!" a large woman with a round, flat face like a Raggedy Ann doll boomed as she grasped Avery's shoulder and shepherded her over to a group of short, nervous-looking girls huddled in a corner.

"I'm a *junior*," Avery protested. Did she look that young? With a black leather Coach headband perched neatly atop her blond head, new navy blue kitten-heel Louboutin slingbacks, and her lucky pearls from Grandmother Avery, she certainly didn't *think* she did. As she looked around, she saw that each girl was carrying the exact same Louis Vuitton Speedy purse she'd tried to replace yesterday at Barneys. It practically screamed *clueless*! She blushed.

"Welcome to Constance Billard. I'm the headmistress, Mrs. McLean," the woman boomed, the purple buttons of her pant-suit straining against her voluminous chest. "A student guide will be with you shortly for first-year orientation." She patted Avery's head distractedly and turned on her heel to follow a diminutive dark-haired teacher with a short haircut.

"Do I look okay?" Avery whispered anxiously to Baby, once she was a safe distance away from the group of younger girls.

"Yeah, sure," Baby said distractedly, stopping to examine the trophy case that sat in the middle of the main hall.

"I'm going to run to the ladies' room," Avery decided. She needed to make sure she wasn't having some type of makeup crisis and wanted to redo her lip gloss, re-brush her teeth, and make sure her hair didn't have any of those weird blond flyaways. "We have French in five minutes!" she added with a nervous screech. Baby just waved in the direction of the bathroom.

Avery stood in front of the mirror above the row of sinks and washed her hands even though she didn't need to. To the left and right of her were girls she guessed were her classmates. She smiled in the mirror at one girl with straight brown bangs who was applying way too much Nars blush in Orgasm. It was a flattering color on everyone—but not if you caked it on.

"Hi, I'm Avery," she blurted, surprised by her boldness. But there was something sort of friendly in the girl's brown eyes.

"Jiffy." The girl smiled briefly, but then returned to frowning at her reflection. Avery quickly dried her hands with a paper towel, unsure whether the girl was being nice or had totally blown her off.

As she emerged from the bathroom with only a minute to spare, Avery glanced down at the schedule taped into her pink leather Filofax. ROOM 125, AP FRENCH WITH MADAME ROGERS. One twenty-five was just down the hall. She walked in, passing Baby, who was sitting by the exit. Avery wanted to sit front and center.

"So, Jack left Paris early to hang out in Sagaponack?" Avery overheard Jiffy ask as she walked into the room. She sat down next to a large-chested girl wearing a cream-colored puff-sleeve Calvin Klein blouse.

"Yeah," the busty girl said in a bored voice, playing with the two chunky Hermès enamel bangles pushed past her elbow. "I was only in the Hamptons for a few weeks. I'm kind of over the whole East Coast thing."

Avery smiled. Everyone sounded so sophisticated. But Jack . . . wasn't that the name of that bitch from Barneys? Avery calmly smoothed her blond hair. It was probably just a really common Upper East Side name, like Chloe or Madison.

Or Baby?

The bosomy girl looked in her direction expectantly. Avery smiled back, feeling giddy.

"Steal any more bags yesterday?" Avery heard a voice behind

her. As she turned around, she found herself face-to-face with her own reflection, winking back at her from the brass buckle of a Givenchy satchel. She slowly looked up. Standing there, smiling down at her, was Jack Laurent, wearing beige Christian Louboutin pumps and a perfectly worn-in seersucker uniform, looking even taller and bitchier than she had yesterday.

"Um, hi," Avery mumbled, avoiding eye contact, as two words—*oh* and *shit*—ran through her head.

"Next time, you might want to check out the Barneys outlet in New Jersey," Jack announced, smiling at the two girls behind Avery. "Also, you're going to have to move, because you're in my seat." Jack unpacked a notebook and a sleek silver Montblanc pen from the satchel and spread them territorially across the desk. "You can sit over by the door, in case you need to make a run for it," she suggested in a syrupy fake voice. "After you steal Madame Rogers's purse or whatever."

Her face flaming red, Avery picked up her bag and looked around for another seat. The classroom had filled up quickly, and the only place available was right next to Baby, who hadn't taken off her sunglasses and was carving something into the wooden desk with her pen. With her wrinkly blazer, tousled hair, and dark shades, she looked like Kate Moss in the rehab years. Avery slowly walked over to join her. She loved her sister, but there was something undeniably dorky about sitting next to each other on the first day of school, like they had no other friends.

Do they have any other friends?

"Hey." She slid into her seat.

"Who was that?" Baby asked, pushing the sunglasses off her face and onto her head so she could examine the pretty, freckly-faced girl glaring at both of them. Baby smiled fakely at her and waved. The Upper East Side was so full of bitches, she thought. "What's her problem, anyway?" she asked loudly. Avery could practically feel all eyes on the two of them. This was *not* the way she wanted to meet her new classmates.

"I don't know," Avery whispered back. She hadn't told Baby about the Barneys debacle yesterday, knowing Baby would never let her live it down. She pulled her black TSE cashmere cardigan on and buttoned it, just in case her hives began to flare up. Madame Rogers walked in wearing an elegant black Tocca pantsuit. She was in her sixties, but had aged well, like Catherine Deneuve. She put her books on the desk and surveyed the roomful of girls. "Welcome back," she said. "Jacqueline, as always, a delight to have you here," she added, noting Jack seated front and center, practically on top of her desk. It was impossible not to notice whomever was in that seat, Avery thought bitterly. "Since we have some new girls in the class, we will begin by introducing ourselves in French. Jack, can you take notes on the board?"

Jack stood up. "Of course. Is there a piece of chalk I can *steal*?" she hissed in Avery's direction as she gracefully sashayed to the front of the room, her auburn hair swinging. Madame Rogers spotted Avery and Baby and clapped her hands together as if seeing them was the most thrilling thing she had ever experienced.

"Nos nouvelles étudiantes!" she cried. *"Peut-être voulez-vous vous présenter?"* Our new students! Perhaps you'd like to introduce yourselves?

Avery cleared her throat, trying not to look too eager. She knew exactly what she was going to say; she'd been running the introduction through her head all morning. *My name is Avery Carlyle. I just moved here from Sconset, Nantucket, and am so excited to be living here. My hobbies are—*

"Peut-être pourraient-elles commencer par nous parler leurs choix interessants vestimentaires?" Jack suggested innocently, before Avery or Baby could get a word out. *Maybe they could begin by telling us all about their interesting fashion choices?* She held the piece of chalk up to the board as if they might not notice the sarcasm in her tone and actually respond.

"Quelle bitch!" Baby burst out, partially covering her words with the tail end of a very fake sneeze. Avery's head whipped around to glare at her sister. Did Baby just swear?

"Excusez-moi?" Madame Rogers's aristocratic face grew red.

"Excusez-moi." Baby smiled.

Très apologetic.

"Mais, comment dit-on bitch?" Baby continued, speaking in perfect French. *"Parce que je pense que c'est le meilleur mot pour décrire cette fille."* She pointed at Jack.

Avery quickly parsed the words. Baby had spoken rapidly, like a true native speaker, which was impressive. Except that she had just announced that Jack Laurent was a bitch.

"Je m'excuse." Avery quickly broke the shocked silence, not even looking at Baby. What the fuck was her sister doing?

"Sortez!" Madame Rogers demanded. "To Mrs. McLean's office, please," she added more softly, obviously trying to maintain her composure and regain control of the class.

"Au revoir." Baby grinned and collected her enormous messenger bag. Winking at Avery, she sauntered out of the classroom.

Avery looked over at Mrs. Rogers, frantic to fix the mess her sister had made. "It's her first day of school and she gets nervous. It's sort of a disorder. Like, French Tourette's syndrome," Avery announced in desperation.

"That was your sister?" Madame Rogers asked, looking at the roster and dropping any pretense of speaking French. Avery nodded, even though she was ready to disown Baby at this point.

"And you are?" The room was silent. Jack was still standing with her chalk poised, waiting to write down the proceedings like a court transcriber.

"Avery Carlyle. Again, I apologize. It's not her fault," Avery lied. Let Baby sound like a freak. At least the other girls would feel sorry for Avery for putting up with a *challenged* family member. Out of the corner of her eye, Avery saw a broad smile creep across Jack's face.

"I apologize, Madame Rogers," Jack said primly. "I didn't realize I would upset her so much. I met Avery the other day, and if I had known they were sisters, I would have been a little gentler. I know Avery has some issues, too," she finished, frowning in concern, like the Carlyle sisters were the saddest girls she'd ever encountered.

The rest of the glass giggled and turned to stare at Avery.

"Attention!" Madame Rogers tapped her ruler against the wooden desk at the front of the classroom. "I do not want to hear another word from anyone this morning. We're going to have a verbs quiz instead."

There was a collective groan as blue books were passed down each row. Avery could feel twenty sets of angry eyes on her. The girl in front of her thwacked a pile of blue books on her desk; some fluttering to the floor. As Avery bent down to pick them up, she spotted a hastily scribbled note stuck inside one of the books, obviously intended for a girl down her row. *Is the new girl ON something? Think the blonde is as much of a freak?* The answer was underlined twice in purple, bubbly script: *YES.*

Avery crumpled the note and dropped it to the floor. So much for making a good impression. Her life at Constance was already very over.

Avery: 0. Jack: 2. But it's only the first day. There'll be plenty of time for a rematch.

all's fair in love and war

Owen slouched down at his desk in Ms. Kendall's small, blue-carpeted art history classroom at St. Jude's School for Boys. It was his last class before lunch, and he couldn't wait to bolt out the door and undo the tight top button on his pressed white dress shirt. He squirmed in the worn wooden chair, his overly starched khakis rubbing against the backs of his knees.

"Has anyone felt like that?" Ms. Kendall, their young, disappointingly mousy art history teacher looked rapturously at a slide of Caravaggio's *Conversion of Saint Paul.*

Owen studied the painting and imagined explaining it to Kat. He'd had a dream about her again last night, and now he couldn't get her off his mind. He examined the picture again, looking at how the light was streaming in the window and onto Saint Paul. That was how it had felt. One moment he had been just himself, and then he had seen her and . . . God, he was horny.

"Mr. Carlyle, would you like to come to the front of the room and explain some of Caravaggio's most prominent techniques?"

"I think Duke's got it," Owen mumbled as he glanced over at super-scrawny Duke Randall, whose hand was wildly waving in the air. Already he'd heard that most guys had crushes on Ms. Kendall. There was even a rumor that she would invite her favorites back to her office for some "extra studying." He couldn't believe these guys were so desperate they were fantasizing about their teachers. She had about six coarse black hairs sticking out of a pear-shaped mole on her chin.

Hot.

As all five feet, five inches of Duke walked up to the large white screen at the front of the room, the bell rang, signaling the end of class.

"Okay, gentlemen. Remember, in art, as in life, it's all about desire!" Mrs. Kendall clapped her hands and blushed furiously.

Rhys paused beside Owen's desk as he was packing up. "How 'bout we get some grub?" he asked companionably.

"Sure," Owen answered as they walked out of the classroom together. The hallway was packed with guys in identical blue, gold-buttoned blazers.

"Okay, I'm going to head down to my locker. Back in a sec." Rhys turned right and headed toward his locker. Owen continued down the hall and glanced at the two short guys on either side of his own freshly painted gray locker. They looked like they were headed to meetings on Wall Street rather than calculus class. His cell beeped and he slid it out of his pocket, hoping that Kat could have somehow found his number.

How about his name?

WORST DAY OF MY LIFE, the text from Avery read. He grinned at his sister's propensity to exaggerate. She'd probably found out there were no hair dryers in the locker room or something. He leaned against the cool metal of the locker and glanced down the hallway. His eyes landed on a pair of legs. Girl's legs. He traced their familiar bend, up past a freckled thigh, over a plaid pleated knee-length skirt and white starched oxford shirt. And then he saw her.

Kat.

The illusion walked closer to him and Owen yelled out, despite himself, "Kat!"

She looked over in confusion and then broke out into a sunny smile. Her caramel-streaked hair was effortlessly shiny, her blue eyes animated and bright. Even in the drab fluorescent lighting of the school hallway she looked radiant.

"Rhys!" she squealed. Owen whirled around. Rhys was just turning the corner behind him.

"Hey!" Rhys pulled Kat into a hug while Owen looked on, feeling like he was witnessing a car crash. "Owen, this is my girl-friend, Kelsey," Rhys said, resting his arm on her slender shoulder. Owen stared at the girl. It was Kat. *His* Kat.

Or, uh, *Kelsey.*

Rhys looked back and forth between Owen and Kelsey. Kelsey looked like she'd seen a ghost.

The ghost of summer's past?

"Do you guys know each other?" he asked.

"I don't know him." Kelsey stepped away from Rhys as if she had been slapped. "I wanted to surprise you and he pointed me to your locker. What was your name again?" She looked at the linoleum in front of Owen.

"Owen," Owen choked out. He felt like he was trying to talk under water. What the fuck was going on?

"It's nice to meet you," Kat said to his feet.

Owen knew he couldn't look at her. He didn't want to see her silvery-blue eyes looking at Rhys the way she'd looked at him that night on the beach. Had she been lying when she said it was her first time?

"So, I guess Kat and I are just going to hang out during lunch. Sorry to bail on you," Rhys said, completely oblivious to the fact that both Owen and Kat were staring at the same spot on the ground. Rhys pulled Kelsey's hand up to his lips and kissed it, as if he wanted everyone to see how in love he was. Owen had already gotten the picture.

"Hey, can we get out of here?" Kelsey whispered urgently. Rhys could feel her hot breath in his ear. It reminded him of last night, and he found himself getting a little excited, even though it was only twelve thirty and they were in the austere, gray-lockered hallways of St. Jude's.

"Sure," he replied eagerly, then noticed how pale her face was. "Are you okay?" He reached out and touched her forehead in concern. Maybe she was getting sick.

"Yeah." Kelsey shrugged her shoulders, and her heart-shaped mouth curved into a smile. "Just, you know, first-day-of-school jitters."

Or two-timing stress?

"Nice meeting you, Owen," Kelsey said purposefully, not making eye contact.

"You too," he muttered, shuffling down the hall and resisting the urge to kick something.

Rhys and Kelsey walked down the concrete steps of St. Jude's and turned toward East End Avenue. Without asking, he stopped by the vendor on the corner and bought them each a cup of coffee, black for him and two Splendas with 1 percent milk for her, from a metal cart on the corner. Rhys always felt a little manly when he could take care of her, even in little ways.

What more could you want in a guy?

Wordlessly they walked to a wooden bench in Carl Schurz Park and sat down, facing the East River. The park was empty except for one elderly lady shuffling along the promenade with her red sweater–clad Yorkie and a few Rollerbladers noisily skating back and forth. Normally, the river looked totally gross, and you really could imagine bodies floating downstream. But with Kelsey by his side, it was almost romantic. Rhys sighed in contentment as he draped his arm around her slim shoulders. He wondered if he could reserve a suite at the Mandarin for after school on such short notice.

"I was thinking about yesterday," he began. "I was thinking—"

"I was thinking too," Kelsey interrupted. The steam rose up from her coffee cup, and he could see red tints in her caramel hair. He couldn't wait until later, when they would pour each other glasses of champagne and toast the first night of the rest of their lives. "I was thinking that I need to tell you something," Kelsey continued.

"What is it?" Rhys asked. She sounded so serious. The Yorkie had sat down on the ground, but its oblivious owner was still shuffling along. He poked Kelsey, hoping she would laugh. She didn't notice.

"I don't think we should see each other anymore," Kelsey told him flatly, staring straight ahead at the river.

He furrowed his tanned forehead and brown eyebrows.

"I'll always love you," she continued. She put her coffee cup on the ground, balancing it awkwardly on a patch of grass.

"What happened?" Rhys demanded. His eyes were stinging, and he could feel blood rushing to his ears.

"There's someone else," Kelsey said in a rush of words.

"What?" Rhys dropped his coffee cup. The brown liquid formed a pool that began seeping toward her vintage black and white Prada flats. Someone else? Someone besides him?

"Oops!" Kelsey said as she pulled her feet up to her knees and laughed nervously. Rhys caught a glimpse of tan thighs under her skirt, but they weren't his to look at anymore. They were . . . someone else's. He couldn't think of any words to say. A tear trickled down his face, followed by another, and he angrily brushed them away.

"If you cry, I'm going to cry," Kelsey whimpered. "This is really hard for me, too. I didn't want to hurt you, but then you were in Europe and I was on the Cape all summer, so . . ." She trailed off, looking at the water, and then turned to face Rhys, tears in her silvery-blue eyes. Rhys realized he had never seen her cry before. "I'll always love you, but it would be dishonest if we stayed together." With that, Kelsey got up and walked out of the park.

Rhys stayed put on the worn wooden slats of the bench. He looked at the ground, noticing for the first time how sparkly the pavement was if you kept staring at it. He wasn't sure whether he was going to cry or faint. He closed his eyes and saw stars.

Good thing he's got a new friend with broad shoulders to cry on.

if bad girls have more fun, then why is *b* miserable?

Baby opened the heavy oak door to Mrs. McLean's office, glaring at the word HEADMISTRESS embossed on the gold plaque that hung from it. It sounded so over the top, like Constance Billard was some sort of nineteenth-century finishing school. She slid onto one of the rigid wingback chairs in the waiting area, across from the secretary, who was pretending to be busy on the computer. She couldn't stand the pretension that seemed to ooze out of every corner of Constance, from the French professor who looked like she had been sent from central casting to the dark-oak everything. Before they'd moved, Baby had begged her mother to be allowed to stay in Nantucket, but she'd said no. Edie had even been talking about moving permanently into their grandmother's peach-colored town house once the lawyers were finished. Baby had never felt more desperate to be back in Nantucket and with Tom, who never demanded anything of her, who just let her *be*.

"Mrs. McLean is ready for you," the skinny, stringy-haired, middle-aged secretary nodded at the walnut door that led into the headmistress's office.

"Thanks," Baby said fake sweetly, standing and walking through the door.

"I'm Mrs. McLean." The intimidatingly large headmistress stood up and squeezed out from behind her enormous mahogany desk, casting a shadow over Baby. "And you must be Baby."

Baby nodded and flopped onto a stiff blue velvet love seat in a corner, tucking her legs underneath her. The whole room was decorated in shades of red, white, and blue. Baby wondered if maybe Mrs. McLean thought she was the president.

Mrs. McLean looked pointedly at Baby's thin legs, motioning with her eyes for her to move them. Baby swung her feet back to the floor and sighed. For the past sixteen years, she'd only ever received praise from her teachers. She'd always gotten straight A's in everything, without even having to try. But now, everything was just so different. Sure, she could spiritedly explain that she'd simply been demonstrating situationism—the 1960s avant-garde European movement to restore authenticity in life. Back in Nantucket, she might have even gotten extra credit for her outburst. But sitting in Mrs. McLean's rigid office, she felt the energy drain from her body, and she didn't at all care to explain what she was feeling.

"Madame Rogers just called down and is quite distraught by your outburst," Mrs. McLean began, taking Baby in with her muddy brown eyes. "I think we got off on an exceptionally bad note here, didn't we?"

Baby grimaced. She hated when teachers used the pronoun *we* when they meant to say *you,* as in, *You really fucked up, now didn't you?*

Which was exactly the point.

"Before we get to that, though, you do have an unusual name,"

Mrs. McLean said, shuffling through Baby's file. "Is there anything more appropriate you would be comfortable using?"

Baby narrowed her blue eyes. "That's my name," she said slowly, enunciating each word. This school was all about conformity. It was one thing to be forced to wear a uniform, but they wanted her to change her *name*?

"Okay, then. I just wanted to let you know it was an option if you wanted something more academic." Mrs. McLean coughed, and Baby glanced at a wooden-framed photograph of a farm that stood out amid the red and blue cups of pencils. "But of course, it's your choice. And now, on to the matter at hand. I know it's your first day and things may be overwhelming for you and your sister. Nevertheless, we expect students to adapt to our way, the way of Constance Billard."

Mrs. McLean smiled at Baby in an almost motherly fashion, and for a fleeting moment Baby felt a flicker of affection. Mrs. McLean looked a bit like Doreen, the lady who ran the pie shop back in Nantucket. Doreen would always give Baby a slice of rhubarb on the house when she forgot her wallet. "I know you and your sister have had a rather untraditional upbringing. Is there anything you want to tell me about?" She folded her hands expectantly, as if waiting for some tear-filled confession.

"Nope." Baby shook her head. *Except for the fact that I hate everything about New York.*

"All right, then. I'm willing to overlook this incident if you are willing to participate in a week of Constance community service. This will be after school, and it's not a punishment. I'm going to design a schedule that will help you become familiar with Constance Billard traditions. I want you to feel like Constance is your home."

Baby imagined herself polishing the trophy case in the lobby as girls trampled over her to get to a sample sale or to Barneys or to wherever they went after school.

"So, what do you think?" Mrs. McLean pressed. "Do your community service and give us a month of good behavior, and we'll put this incident behind us."

"That sounds fucking awesome." Baby yawned. A thrilling tingle shot up her spine as Mrs. McLean's small Raggedy Ann mouth formed an *O* of surprise.

"Excuse me?" Mrs. McLean's tenor voice turned into a growl, but Baby didn't stop staring straight into the headmistress's eyes.

"Give me manual labor." Baby yawned again. "That sounds exactly like the type of out-of-the-box thinking that makes Constance Billard *exceptional*." She almost giggled at the last sentence. "Can I go now?" Baby asked.

"No." Mrs. McLean pursed her lips. "I've seen your grades, and you're smart, but here, that's not enough. Last year a girl who'd succumbed to bad influence had to find a more appropriate educational situation—at *boarding school*."

Sounds familiar.

Mrs. McLean plucked a slim blue booklet from a file cabinet and handed it to Baby. *Constance Billard Code of Conduct* was printed on its cover.

Baby stood up and smoothed out her skirt. It was so stiff it felt like it could stand up by itself.

"One last thing." Mrs. McLean leaned back in her chair and locked eyes with Baby. "At Constance, we have a tradition of excellence, which includes a three-strikes rule—no exceptions."

A smile played on Baby's lips. This was going to be even easier than she'd thought. If she got kicked out of Constance, Edie would have to admit that she didn't fit in here and would have no choice but to send her back to Nantucket. A few more days of mumbling French swears and she'd be on the ferry, the ocean breeze ruffling her hair.

"Did I say something amusing?" Mrs. McLean looked her sharply up and down.

"No." Baby moved toward the door.

"Okay then." Mrs. McLean didn't look entirely convinced. "Read the booklet. And remember, Baby, this counts as your first strike."

Baby strode out of the office smiling triumphantly. She'd never really been into baseball, but now she had a new appreciation for it.

For it's one, two, three strikes you're out at the old ball game!

how to win friends and influence people

Avery was relieved when the bell rang after AP English, meaning it was time for the all-school assembly. She followed the mass of girls making their way to the lobby, their shiny ponytails bouncing and their Chloé flats clicking against the polished floors.

Nervously she patted her hair in place and followed two of Jack Laurent's bitches-in-waiting into the crowded auditorium.

"I heard she was kicked out. Apparently she's, like, a total Winona-style klepto and was banned from the supermarket in Nantucket for stealing, like, Triscuits," Jiffy Bennett told a small blond girl as she tossed her wavy, long brown hair over her shoulder. Jiffy was freckly, with severe, blunt-cut bangs that framed her round face, and the other girl was carrying around a salmon-colored newspaper and wore black Prada glasses, as if she'd just stepped out of an editorial meeting at *Vogue*.

"Really? I didn't hear about her. I heard about the one who never washes her hair. Like, she believes her natural scent is an aphrodisiac. Can you imagine taking gym class with her?" the glasses-clad girl remarked loudly, pushing her glasses up further on her button nose.

"Well, you know they're triplets, right? My mother went to school with their mother, and I heard from her that the brother is gorgeous! He was supposed to be a Valentino runway model, but he decided to stay in the United States. Also, he's supposed to go to the Olympics, and he wears a lucky Speedo under his clothes all the time. The same one, apparently," Jiffy finished importantly. Avery felt her heart stop—they were definitely talking about her family. No one but Owen wore Speedos instead of boxers.

Jiffy glanced in Avery's direction, a wave of recognition flashing across her dark brown eyes. Avery turned abruptly away and walked quickly to the back of the auditorium, ignoring the butterflies in her stomach and wishing she could be anywhere but here.

"Is anyone sitting there?" Avery motioned to one of the only seats that hadn't been taken, next to a tall, thin girl with shaggy, chin-length brown hair pulled back in bobby-pinned twists.

"You are, aren't you?"

Avery wasn't sure if it was a question or an order. She hovered awkwardly over the empty seat as the girl stared up at her. Her blazer was unbuttoned and she was wearing a sheer white tank top and ridiculously tall, six-inch stripper-style platform boots. Avery wasn't sure, but it sort of looked like her nipples were pierced. She averted her eyes before the girl caught her staring at her chest.

"Go for it." Nipples patted the seat impatiently and turned back to her book. As soon as Avery sat down, she heard the girls in the row behind her giggle and exchange whispers. She shifted uncomfortably and glanced at the book the girl was reading. *Look Both Ways: Bisexual Politics*. Avery scanned the room to see if she could move somewhere else without seeming rude, but there were no more empty seats. She sighed and sat back, hoping the assembly would start quickly so she wouldn't be roped into a conversation about the politics of nipple piercing or something equally gross.

"Are you new?" the girl asked, closing her book. Avery didn't look over. "I'm Sydney Miller." She held out her hand.

"Avery," she mumbled, shaking the offered hand. The girl nodded knowingly.

"That's a great name. My parents named me Sydney because it was where I was conceived. Then, of course, they got divorced three years later. I'm the only reminder of their stupid Australian sexfest." She cocked her head in anticipation, like she was waiting for Avery's own conception tale.

Avery tried not to stare in disbelief. She wasn't about to share the fact that her mom had gone to some hippie sexfest at a gross outdoor concert in New Hampshire and ended up with triplets. She forced her eyes back to the elegant calligraphy on one of the hymnals in front of her.

"Just as an FYI, this place sucks," Sydney confided. "I can't wait to get out of here. Seriously, two years until graduation." She sighed tragically, and then coughed a raspy smoker's cough. "I was hoping my parents would send me somewhere downtown so I could at least hang out with NYU kids. Here, it's like Bitch City, don't you think?"

"Not really," Avery whispered, self-conscious about how loudly Sydney was talking.

Maybe she'd had a bad first day, but she still intended to get to know people here and fit in. So far she loved everything about Constance, from the buttoned-up headmistress to the elegant views of the Ninety-third Street town houses out the large, arching windows of the auditorium to the rickety, moth-eaten blue velvet seats. Avery pulled out her MAC compact from her purse and looked critically at her cheekbones and the side-swept bangs that complemented her high forehead. What was it about her that was alienating all the girls except this overfriendly bisexual with the pierced nipples? As she leaned down to put her compact back into her bag, she noticed a large, misshapen black star on Sydney's forearm.

You can't be alternative unless you have a tattoo that looks like it was drawn with a Sharpie.

Sydney followed her gaze. "Yeah, I got that tat back in Spain this summer. My stupid parents got together again and wanted to have a middle-age rediscovery-of-sex fest, so they sent me to Europe. Some guy I met on the beach in Barcelona did it, so of course it came out fucked up. Are you into body art?"

Does a reverse French manicure count?

"No." Avery shook her head and smiled slightly, trying to be polite.

"Oh." Sydney looked disappointed. "Sometimes it's the really buttoned-up girls who are totally the kinkiest on the inside."

Just then, Mrs. McLean marched in, with Baby shuffling behind her, looking comically tiny behind Mrs. M's bulk. Whispers flitted up and down the aisles as she was escorted to a seat in the first row. Avery felt the familiar red flush rising in her chest. What had Baby done this time?

Jack glanced back and saw Avery sitting next to Sydney Miller, a girl whom everyone had ignored since she came out as an "academic lesbian" in eighth grade and had insisted on spelling *woman* w-o-m-y-n. Jack pulled a pack of gum out of Genevieve's bag, wondering idly if Genevieve's chest had gotten even larger. It looked bigger than it had last spring.

Not that she was about to measure it or anything.

Mrs. M strode onstage and stood in front of the girls in her all-purple Talbots pantsuit she only busted out on special occasions. She glared out at the crowd and Jack rolled her eyes. Everyone knew Mrs. M was in a pissy mood on the first day of school because she hated to leave her Vermont farm and her domestic partner, Vonda. She would much rather be baking casseroles and riding a tractor. It was common knowledge that Mrs. M was hoping to retire early so she and Vonda could start an alpaca farm upstate and open a made-to-order-yarn business.

Anyone want to join their knitting circle?

"Now, ladies, it's a pleasure to have you all back, despite some rough transitions." Mrs. McLean glanced at Baby, and Avery's heart thumped against her ribs. "We're pleased to welcome all our new students to the Constance Billard family." A smile spread across Mrs. M's large, doughy face as she looked down upon the rows of well-scrubbed Upper East Side girls.

A few rows ahead, Jack poked the skinny blond girl with the large chest who had been in French class with them. Both giggled, then looked stageward in rapt attention when they saw Mrs. M glaring in their direction.

Mrs. M began to discuss policies for the upcoming school year. *Extra-long hours at the guidance office for those seniors needing assistance with early-decision college apps, no smoking on school grounds.* Blah, blah, blah. Avery zoned out and began thumbing through her pink Filofax. She refused to use a PDA, because she loved the elegant simplicity of writing down dates and events. So far the whole school year loomed ahead in rows of empty pink boxes. What could she possibly do to make her mark here?

Hasn't she already sort of made her mark?

"Now, ladies, I'm pleased to announce a new board position in addition to that of class president," Mrs. McLean droned. Avery perked up. "The student liaison to the board of overseers. As you know, we have a very good relationship with our overseers, some of whom have been with Constance since its founding, and, as such, are very invested in its future. The elected student will represent the student body and will be involved in all decisions regarding the governing of our school."

Jack felt Jiffy's pointy index finger dip into her toned bicep. She shrugged her off. Who cared about a stupid school leadership position when she had so many more important things to think about?

Like J.P. with his shirt off, taking *her* shirt off, followed by his pants and her skirt . . .

"Can they *please* remove the mirrors in the cafeteria?" Elise Wells, a tall sophomore asked, her arm waving wildly in the air, her thick, bluntly cut hair bobbing. Two more girls whooped in affirmation, as if they had just heard about a surprise Prada sample sale, and suddenly, all sides of the room erupted in flurries of discussion. Everyone hated the mirrors, which not only made you feel fat while you were eating lunch but made it impossible to hide from anyone.

"Quiet down, ladies!" Mrs. McLean gestured for order. "This is not the time to discuss the design of the school. The student liaison to the board of overseers would have a say in any structural decisions, as well as a say on discipline and school-sponsored events. It's a one-year commitment that I'm pleased to open up to the junior class. If you're interested, please see me after the assembly for an information packet. The elections will be held at the annual mother-daughter Tavern on the Green brunch on Sunday." Mrs. McLean clapped her hands together, and the room was filled again with excited whispering.

"What a fucking waste of time," drawled Sydney lazily as she twirled a silver skull ring around and around her thumb.

But Avery was only dimly aware that Sydney was still at her side. She couldn't believe her luck. Becoming the student liaison would be the perfect way to get noticed at Constance. She'd been on student council at NHS and had organized a fundraising benefit for the coast guard that had even been written up in *Boston Common*. This couldn't be any harder, could it? She'd get involved, show her school spirit, meet people, and add a cool new extracurricular activity to her transcript, all in one fell swoop.

"The events-planning part sounds sort of cool—Jack will totally get elected, so we should start thinking of some parties," Jiffy whispered loudly to the blond girl she was seated next to.

"See what I mean about the Bitch Brigade?" Sydney gestured to Jack, who was busy typing on her Treo while whispering to her large-chested blond friend. "This whole school belongs to Jack Laurent," Sydney snorted. Ignoring her, Avery stood up and power-walked her way down to Mrs. McLean at the podium. She wanted to be the first in line for the information packet so the headmistress would know how serious she was about the position.

At the front of the auditorium, Jack rose slowly from her seat, flexing her calf muscles and noticing appreciatively how toned they were. She was glad she'd woken up early and gone to the studio for Madame Walters's Rise and Shine barre class.

Leisurely she made her way to the stage. Mrs. M was standing behind an embossed oak dais holding a stack of grape jam–colored folders that perfectly matched her suit. This student liaison thing sounded sort of boring, but it would be a good extracurricular to have on her college applications, and she'd be able to use the Constance budget to plan some cool parties. Besides, her friends had practically forced her to sign up.

As Jack strolled among the groups of girls streaming out of the auditorium, she noticed Elisabeth Cort, a junior who'd run for and lost practically every leadership position since she'd wet her pants during seventh-grade student council elections, sprint up to the front. Jack was about to tell her not to bother, but then thought better of it. She approached Mrs. M and smiled, picking up an application packet from the pile. Then she noticed that obnoxious Avery Carlyle marching up right behind her, a determined glint in her bright blue eyes. Jack bit her lip knowingly. Elisabeth Cort didn't stand a chance, and neither did the shoplifting island girl with the French Tourette's sister. How lame of her to even try.

Hey, never underestimate the New England work ethic.

gossipgirl.net

Disclaimer: All the real names of places, people, and events have been altered or abbreviated to protect the innocent. Namely, me.

hey people!

The bell hasn't even rung, and yet so much has already happened today! I may need to start thinking about a news ticker. . . .

first impressions

You can reinvent yourself over the summer, but it only takes a second to make an impression for the year. And those triplets have certainly established themselves as the ones to talk about on Manhattan's Golden Mile. First off, can we please discuss the wonder that is **O**? The rumors are true and he is beyond gorgeous, but he seems to be too busy making guy friends to even give a second glance to the ladies. Don't worry, I'll fix that. **B** is anything but innocent. Exhibit A: her expansive knowledge of French curse words. But why so angry? French is the language of love—maybe that's all she needs. And **A**'s style is admittedly impeccable. But as we all know, looking perfect just means you've got more to hide. . . .

the tragic breakup of a UES golden couple

She was whimsically artistic. He was painfully polite. They were childhood sweethearts. The affair was given a seal of approval by Lady S herself. So what happened? Did someone get cold feet? Or was someone looking for more heat?

the girl who needs a bang trim

Ladies, I know thick bangs are in, but when your hair is hanging a centimeter above your eyes, you look like someone threw a Missoni centerpiece bowl over your head and began to snip. Guess what? You don't need to spend two precious hours at Elizabeth Arden Red Door Salon to get a trim. They're called scissors. Snip away! The DIY look is *very* in right now.

the almost-married power couple

Have they or haven't they? They spent a summer apart, where he developed a social conscience and she developed a taste for pastries. Are they still as close as they were at the end of last year, when he would greet her outside ballet class with flowers? Or are they *closer*?

sightings

J dragging on Merits during double photography. Didn't she give those up . . . ? **A** cowering in the back of AP English, not looking at anyone. That's not the way to make friends . . . ! **R** calling in an order of roses to be delivered to **K**'s apartment . . . **O** fidgeting and tapping his foot in American history, looking like he's about to burst out of his skin. Why so agitated?

Okay, I'm off to **Elizabeth Arden Red Door** salon. All this speed typing has just about ruined my reverse French manicure. Sigh. It's a tough life, but somebody's gotta live it. . . . Over and out!

You know you love me,

swear to dog

Baby frowned. Her sister hadn't even acknowledged her when she snatched the information packet from Mrs. McLame after the all-school assembly was dismissed. Baby didn't bother to stop by her locker and instead sprang out the royal blue doors and tore off her stupid, itchy navy blue blazer. She pressed 1 on the speed dial of her slim red Nokia, excited to hear Tom's voice.

"Oh my God, so I had to go to Brazil on this exchange program my parents signed me up for, and I thought it would be, like, hanging out on the beach and partying in Rio. Instead we were supposed to build houses. Hello, who the fuck knows how to build a house? I'm from fucking New York," Baby overheard one girl say to another as they strode down the steps. She had stick-straight brown hair and kept bumping into her friend as she walked.

The phone continued to ring, and Baby imagined Tom at his dented red locker in the crowded hallway of NHS. After school, everyone would be heading out to get a snack at the diner or to hang out at the beach a few blocks away. She counted ring number five as she flopped down on the school's stone steps facing

Ninety-third Street. Girls streamed out of the royal blue doors on either side of her. One almost clocked her with a silver Balenciaga bag as she flipped open her phone.

"'Lo?" Tom's voice sounded warm and lazy and reminded her of summer picnics and rainstorms and Wilco playing too loudly on the stereo in the muddy brown 1988 Mercury Cougar he'd bought from his grandfather. He'd added leopard-print sheets to the back and had wedged a George Foreman grill under the hood for impromptu beachside barbecues.

Talk about pimping a ride.

"It's me," she said in a small voice and glared down at the blue and white seersucker skirt spread out over her knees. If she were in Nantucket, she'd be wearing one of the hippie dresses from her mom's closet, which always felt like a second skin. Here, she felt so stifled. The last time she'd worn a knee-length skirt that buttoned at the waist had been when she was five and had gone to tea at the Plaza with Grandmother Avery. "How was school?" she asked, trying to ignore the loud conversations going on all around her.

"I got fucking Funkmaster Smith for English again, which is going to blow, but at least I have a double study."

Baby giggled, remembering Mr. Smith's potent BO. She even missed that. Tom felt so far away. She wanted him close to her so badly it hurt.

She heard a rustle in the background. "I want the phone!" a girl's voice whined impatiently. It was Kendra, one of the peripheral hangers-on whom Baby had known since kindergarten. They used to be friends, but ever since Kendra had become a raging stoner, her interests were now exclusively pot and the college guys who came to Nantucket to work at the restaurants for the summer and never left. "Hey, Ba-ay-bee." Kendra drew out Baby's name into three syllables, and Baby knew she must be pretty baked. "So, is there crazy shit going on down there? What's it like living in New York?"

"Yeah, um, it's fine," Baby lied. "I'll probably be back next weekend for the beach party, though." *Make that definitely,* Baby silently amended as she saw a girl yelling at the driver of a sleek town car that had pulled up in front of the school.

"So soon? I'm sure there are much better parties in New York, right?" Kendra drawled lazily.

"Hey, can you put Tom back on?" Baby said shortly. She wasn't in the mood for one of Kendra's pot-induced hypothetical conversations.

"Sure," Kendra agreed. "But don't worry if something comes up. We'll get by without you." Baby heard laughing in the background. They were probably already piling into Tom's car by now. Baby kicked at the stone step with her heel in frustration and jealousy.

"So, you think you really might be able to come on Friday? Don't you have to go to a cotillion or an opera or something?" Tom asked in his sleepy-stoner voice.

"It's New York, not the Deep South!" Baby smiled. She loved Tom's utter lack of pretension.

And regional knowledge?

"Of course I'll come. I can't miss the first beach party of the school year." Baby was counting down the hours. She couldn't wait to sleep with Tom outside in her hammock, only a few steps from the ocean.

"Cool." Baby could almost imagine him nodding in agreement. "Anyway, we're all heading down to the dock, so I better get going. I miss you," he finished.

"I miss you too," Baby echoed, and hung up the phone.

She stood up and crossed the street, unsure of what to do with herself for the rest of the afternoon. She considered waiting for Avery, but her sister seemed to be intentionally ignoring her, so Baby decided to intentionally ignore her right back. She determinedly stepped off the curb.

"Watch where you're going, baby!" a bike messenger yelled as he took a tight turn onto Madison and almost ran into her. Hearing her name yelled in a voice so angry and hard instead of warm and soft, Baby felt a red-hot surge of rage—at her mother, at her new school, at all of New York City—shoot up through her tiny frame.

"Fuck you!" she yelled angrily. A group of elderly ladies standing by the bus stop began whispering among themselves. Baby seethed. She hated New York. Everyone was the same. Those ladies were exactly like Jack Laurent and her bitch crowd, except two hundred years older.

Mad at herself for even caring what they thought, she ducked into a nearby Starbucks and bought an iced chai from the over-caffeinated barista who shouted out every single order. As soon as she took a sip, she wanted to spit out the ultra-sweet liquid. Back in Nantucket, they would have already had her chai waiting for her by the time she walked down to The Bean, her favorite coffee shop. Chains like Starbucks had been banned on her beloved island.

Hello, they also don't have Barneys. Or pretty much anything else anyone who's anyone cares about.

As she pushed open the door to Starbucks and reemerged in the bright sun, she saw a huge yellow labradoodle pulling on its Gucci leash and dragging its owner, who was also trying to manage two small puggles in matching red and blue Marc Jacobs coats. She shook her head, feeling bad for the dogs, who looked as uncomfortable in their outfits as she was. Their owner was a nice-looking teenage boy with closely cut brown hair, brown eyes, and broad shoulders. Baby zeroed in on his shorts. The claylike color was Nantucket red—something no one, not even Islanders, would ever wear. No one normal, anyway.

As she watched, the labradoodle deliberately arched its back and unleashed a large brown coil of poop on the guy's leather sandal. It was almost like he was doing it for Baby's viewing pleasure.

"Nemo!" the guy cried, looking down in disbelief. Just then, the dog broke free and took off, bumping into a woman's stroller and excitedly weaving through streams of pedestrians on the sidewalk.

Without thinking, Baby abandoned her chai on the sidewalk and dashed down the street, desperate to catch up with the puppy before it got run over by an MTA bus or an errant town car.

"Get a leash!" Baby heard a woman cry behind her.

Finally she caught up with the dog just as it was about to bound into oncoming traffic on Fifth. It blinked dolefully at her with its warm brown eyes.

"You're okay," Baby whispered to the dog and firmly clasped its collar. She picked up its leash, reminded of the scene in *Annie* where orphan Annie befriends Sandy, the cute stray dog who becomes her best friend and follows her everywhere.

At least she's made *one* friend.

"I know you wanted to get away from him, but I have to bring you back to your owner, okay?" She pulled the dog around the corner to Starbucks. Standing outside was the dog's owner, hopelessly trying to scrape the crap from the top of his foot with a black plastic bag. The puggles had wrapped their leashes around his legs and were sniffing the flower boxes outside the coffee shop.

"Here's your dog. Except I really don't think you deserve him," she said self-righteously as she handed over the leash.

He blushed the same tomato red shade as his shorts. He *would* be cute, she thought, if she went for that handsome, privileged, Upper East Side spoiled type.

And didn't have a boyfriend?

Nemo sat down next to his owner with his head cocked expectantly. The guy held out the hand that was holding the bag of dog poop, then thought better of it and pulled it back. "Sorry. Normally I would shake hands but . . ." He shrugged. "I'm J.P. Cashman. And these monsters"—he glanced down at the dogs, who were now sitting obediently in a neat row, blinking up at Baby and looking not at all monstrous—"are Nemo, Darwin, and Shackleton. I promised my mother I would take care of them for the next few weeks."

"I'm Baby." She held out her small hand. She didn't want to add to the general New York City rudeness.

Clearly.

"Baby," he repeated, raising his eyebrows. Baby narrowed her eyes at him. Her name had been challenged enough today.

"Better name than Shackleton," she said, nodding at the puggle in the blue coat.

"My dad's really into explorers. Real and imaginary."

"Cute." Baby petted the dog's coffee-colored fur. It drooled in appreciation.

"I think maybe we started off on the wrong foot." J.P. looked down at his shit-encrusted toes and laughed, surprising Baby.

She'd thought he would be more upset about his soiled mandals. Maybe Mr. Red Shorts wasn't so uptight after all.

Well, you know, shit happens.

"So, you must go to Constance." J.P.'s brown eyes flicked down to her skirt. Baby blushed and nodded, feeling like a walking advertisement for Upper East Side snobbery.

"I go to Riverside Prep. On the West Side. I'm a junior." J.P. glanced up expectantly.

Darwin squirmed toward her. His eyes were bulging so much he looked like a cartoon dog silk-screened on the front of an Urban Outfitters T-shirt.

"Hey, puppy, it was nice meeting you, too," Baby patted the dog and gazed into his huge trusting eyes. If only people could be so simple. "Good luck," she told the guy dubiously, and started to walk away.

"Hey, wait!" J.P. yelled to her retreating back. "So, all the dogs really seem to like you, and I need some help. Our dog walker ran off with our gardener."

Baby stopped walking. Was he kidding? She turned to face him again, curious.

"No, seriously. It's sort of sweet, actually. They got married last week and are on their honeymoon in Niagara Falls. So, anyway, now the dogs are my responsibility, but would you want to help out?"

Baby opened her mouth, ready to say no. Talk about typical. He wanted her to do his dirty work?

"We'd pay you, of course." J.P. smiled broadly, as if that solved everything.

Baby considered it. Okay, so this guy's outfit was totally lame, but his dogs were adorable. Besides, it had to be better than moping around feeling sorry for herself.

Or embarrassing her sister in front of their new classmates.

"Sure," Baby agreed. "But I don't need your money. I'll consider it charity work."

J.P.'s face lit up. "I'll find a way to make it up to you," he continued, all business. "If you could meet me tomorrow at three at my house? I'm at Sixty-eighth and Fifth." He pulled a thick ivory card out of his pocket and handed it to her.

This guy had *business cards*? She glanced at it briefly, expecting some ridiculously fake-sounding title, but it simply listed his name and address in neat black block lettering. He lived in the penthouse of the Cashman Complexes. Of course his building would share his last name.

But of course.

"I'll see you tomorrow," she said crisply, turning on the heel of one flip-flop and stuffing the card into her seersucker skirt pocket. Behind her, one of the dogs let out a low-pitched whine.

Sounds like someone's got a case of puppy love.

sometimes you need to go into the closet

Avery didn't bother looking for Baby after school. If Baby wanted to act like a freak, she could do it all by herself. Instead, Avery hailed a cab and immediately commanded the driver to bring her to her grandmother's town house on Sixty-first and Park. The house was a four-story pale-peach Italianate-style building that looked more like it belonged in Charleston or San Francisco than on the Upper East Side. Avery loved how it stood out from the other redbrick buildings surrounding it, like a reminder of how unique and one-of-a-kind Avery Carlyle the First had actually been. Avery the Second hoped she had inherited some of that je ne sais quoi. She'd need it, especially after today's rocky start.

She pushed open the heavy iron door and groaned when she saw Karen, the mousy-looking paralegal with a penchant for mismatching Ann Taylor separates from the clearance rack. She had been sent by Meyers & Mooreland, the law firm that was handling the Carlyle estate, and had set up a makeshift office right in the middle of the front room to manage the cataloguing and appraisal of Grandmother Avery's valuables. Avery hated the way the lawyers had taken over the house. When she'd first found out her family was moving, she'd begged her mother to let them live here, instead of the penthouse on Fifth, but the lawyers and Edie had agreed that it would be easiest and most efficient if the Carlyle family lived elsewhere until the house had been properly catalogued. No matter what, their present penthouse, with its vague smell of cat pee clinging to the bedroom and the tacky, impossible-to-remove Yale sticker on the inside of the medicine cabinet, didn't feel like home the way Grandmother Avery's house did—at least when Grandmother Avery's house was devoid of lawyers. The first time she'd stopped by with her mother, Avery had rescued a dozen vintage French *Vogue*s from the trash.

A true Samaritan. Until she sells them on eBay in exchange for that vintage Hermès Birkin she's been yearning for.

"Hey!" Karen called cheerfully, not looking up from her laptop. Avery ignored her and tromped up the stairs and into her grandmother's large bedroom suite. She headed straight into the expansive walk-in closet, breathing a sigh of relief as she turned on the muted lights. Row upon row of Chanel suits hung before her, lined up according to color and length. The eighties had been all about tight leather minis and silk halter tops by Valentino and Nina Ricci, but in her later years Grandmother Avery had never left the house in anything but a knee-length suit and Ferragamo pumps, her wrists and neck adorned with tasteful jewelry. Avery closed her eyes, wishing that when she opened them Grandmother Avery would be there. She'd always known what to say to make Avery feel better. But when she opened her eyes, all she saw was a closet full of lifeless clothing.

"Can I borrow these when I grow up?" five-year-old Avery had asked once, holding up a handful of diamond-encrusted pendants and bangles that were a gift from the Count of Lichtenberg.

"No," her grandmother said as she firmly removed a particularly large diamond and ruby dinner ring from Avery's finger. "Diamonds like that are only for women over thirty. And the only diamond that looks better than the one a man gives you is the one you purchase yourself." With that, Grandmother Avery had brought young Avery on her first trip to Tiffany & Co., where she'd been allowed to hand over the platinum AmEx herself after picking out a simple rose drop pendant in a platinum setting.

Avery touched the buttery linen of a pink suit and sighed. She wished Grandmother Avery were here so they could have a cup of tea and plan the best way for Avery to win the position at school. Ever since the assembly today, she knew she *had* to get elected as student liaison to the board of overseers. But the liaison would be chosen by the student body, and all the girls seemed completely biased against her. Not only that, but she had less than a week to win them over. "What should I do?" she whispered, running a finger down the sleeve of a powdery gray suit.

Throw a fabulous party! she practically heard the Chanel suit whisper back.

Avery stepped away from the Chanel jacket and wandered into Grandmother Avery's expansive dressing room. She picked up a Tiffany silver picture frame that housed a photo of Grandmother Avery when she was in her twenties, before her love affair with Chanel. She wore a boxy Yves Saint Laurent ensemble with Dior pumps. With her thick, long hair and wide eyes, she looked eerily familiar. Avery turned to the full-length antique mirror, trying to mimic the elder Avery's confident *I can get anything I want* look. Not bad. She looked glamorous and competent—clearly the right person for the position.

But is it the right look for *making friends*?

Avery wandered back into the bedroom. Two stuffed bears sat at the small pink and white hand-painted table set up in the corner. A china tea set was displayed on the table's surface. It was silly and sentimental, a fixture in the nursery that both Edie and the triplets had played in as children. When Grandmother Avery had become bedridden this past spring, she'd asked for the toy to be placed in her room as a reminder of her own tea parties. She regularly entertained Anne Hearst and Senga Mortimer and had won over all of New York's best hostesses by out-hostessing them. Avery picked up a teacup. What better way to introduce students to her—and her past—than by holding an updated, totally cool and unique tea party?

Practically skipping with glee, Avery ran down the stairs and into the dining room, flinging open the glass doors to Grandmother Avery's china cabinet.

"What are you doing?" Karen snapped, holding a handful of files and squinting her lopsided blue eyes at Avery. She was wearing Nine West pumps. Avery wanted to slap her.

"I need these. Can you give me some packing materials?" Avery ordered, thrusting a bone-thin china cup at her.

"I'm not sure. . . ." Karen hesitated.

"My mother asked for them." Avery felt like stomping her foot. After all, the teacups belonged to *her* family, not to Karen. "They're ours," she added insistently.

"Okay." Karen relented, scurrying off to find bubble wrap. Even though she knew it was childish and completely inappropriate, Avery stuck out her tongue at Karen's retreating backside. The position at Constance was all about being a leader, not a follower, exactly like Grandmother Avery. When she was voted in, Grandma Avery, wherever she was, would be so very, very proud.

When? Cocky much?

the poor little rich girl blues

Jack leaned back against the steps of the Metropolitan Museum of Art as she sucked down the Splenda-sweetened dregs of her iced coffee. Jiffy Bennett, Genevieve Coursy, and Sarah Jane Jenson were perched around her, smoking Merits and occasionally glancing down at the shirtless skater boys performing tricks on the steps below. This was where they always ended up hanging out when there was nowhere else to go, and even though it was kind of boring, Jack felt totally at home. This was her junior year, when she would get the lead in *The Nutcracker*, be the toast of New York City, maintain an A-plus average, and *finally* have sex with J.P. It was all too perfect, and it was all about to come true.

"So what was up with that girl in French?" Jiffy asked as she turned her freckled face to the sun and exhaled a cloud of smoke in the direction of the skaters.

"Baby Carlyle?" Sarah Jane looked over and readjusted her glasses. "I don't know. My mom knew the Carlyles' mom in school, though, and apparently she's a total freak, too." Sarah Jane had practically white eyelashes and eyebrows, giving her a permanently startled expression. "But their grandmother was *the*

Avery Carlyle, so, you know, they can't, like, ban Avery and Baby from Constance. . . ." She trailed off, sighing.

"*The* Avery Carlyle? What does that mean?" Jack asked. Talking about the Carlyles was so boring. She'd rather talk about something interesting.

Like herself, for instance?

"You don't know who Avery Carlyle is?" Sarah Jane looked even more surprised than usual. "She was, like, one of those old lady philanthropists. She hung out with Brooke Astor, Annette de la Renta . . . all them. One of my aunts was friends with her. Apparently, she had affairs with at least one royal in every European country. My aunt said it was her goal or something." Sarah Jane nodded summarily.

Thank you, Miss *Town & Country*.

"Whatever," Genevieve said loyally. She leaned back on her elbows so that her boobs stuck out for the viewing pleasure of the gaggle of Frisbee-toting St. Jude's guys walking past.

"It's not like she can win that election thing anyway, right? You're going to do it." Genevieve shaded her eyes from the sun and squinted over at Jack. Last year, Genevieve had been Jack's best friend. But Genevieve had spent the summer with her producer dad in L.A., where she'd had a less-than-five-minute fling with Breck O'Dell, the star of some stupid summer movie. Now she was completely full of herself. Not like Jack was jealous or anything. Having a fling with a B-list movie star was bordering on tacky.

"You totally should do it. You'd get to do something about the auditorium and the mirrors and the uniforms, and you'd be responsible for social events—we could totally have a huge, school-funded party with the Riverside Prep boys. Or maybe St. Jude's. What do you think?" Jiffy asked eagerly as she pawed through the purple information packet detailing the position's duties. She wore two ponytails on either side of her head in some sort of farm girl look that was an attempt to be Anna Sui edgy but actually made her look like a poodle. "You'd probably want to do a party with Riverside Prep because of J.P., right?"

"Probably." Jack smiled. For the first time, the position didn't sound like some sort of lame, résumé-padding activity. Getting the school new uniforms and planning parties could actually be pretty cool. And since she was competing with Elisabeth Cort, that weak-bladdered, unfortunately truck-shaped girl whose breath always smelled like tuna fish, and the klepto Avery Carlyle, she doubted there'd be much campaigning necessary. Bagging the SLBO position would ensure an absolutely sparkling high school transcript, as well as allow her to be even more socially active than she already was, without lifting a finger.

"Oh my God, Breck just messaged me! He said he's going to be in the city this weekend!" Genevieve squealed, pulling out her Treo and blushing as Sarah Jane and Jiffy crowded around the screen's tiny display.

Jack rolled her eyes. "Okay, I'm out." She stood up, brushing the back of her seersucker skirt. She would go home and change, and spend the afternoon with J.P. Unlike Genevieve, she had a *real* boyfriend.

Jack walked home to Sixty-third between Fifth and Madison, smiling as she caught sight of the stately ivy-covered town house with window flower boxes and an artfully curving front entrance. But as she approached, she paused. Two moving trucks stood outside. Her mother gripped the wrought-iron railing that bordered the front steps, chain-smoking Gitanes as if her life depended on it.

"Mother?" she asked, a terrible suspicion gnawing at her. Vivienne's eyes were as red as her hair, and mascara streaks had dried into awkward rivers down her pale face. Jack walked closer and stood below her mother on the stoop. "Mom?" she said again, and looked around. Had they decided to redecorate? Three overweight men without shirts were sweating onto the polished surface of their George Nakashima turned-leg dining room table as they heaved it out the entranceway.

"Your father . . ." Vivienne sobbed noisy, racking, French-accented sobs as if she were auditioning for *Phèdre*, the French tragedy they had read last year in Madame Rogers's class. In it, a Greek queen plots revenge on her ex-lover before completely going off the deep end. "He has sold the house and the furniture. All of it. All is gone." She blew into her red silk handkerchief and sniffled. *"Bâtard!"* Her face clouded ominously.

Two more movers were smoking Marlboros dangerously close to Jack's walnut four-poster canopy bed. Her bed always made her feel like royalty. Its pristine white eyelet bedspread had slipped off and was now lying in a heap on the cracked pavement.

"We're . . . *homeless*?" Jack exclaimed in disbelief. Maybe her mother was overreacting. It wouldn't be unusual. Whenever she spoke to Jack's father she threw the phone against the wall. She'd been through six silver Bang & Olufsens this year.

"We will live in the upstairs garret," Vivienne said. "It will be like when I was a girl, living in the cinquième arrondissement and going down the hall for water. It is what we must do. An artist must always suffer," her mother finished dramatically as she gestured with her still-burning cigarette.

Jack narrowed her eyes. The garret was a collection of rooms on the top floor of their town house. In the past, her father, who now worked as an investment advisor at Citigroup, had threatened Vivienne with living up there if she didn't stop spending money. It had become a sort of joke between Jack and her mother: they used it as storage space for some of the more extravagant and rarely used items they purchased on shopping binges with Charles's credit cards.

Hey, sheepskin-lined lizard-skin Gucci boots need to go *somewhere* in the summer.

"Your father said he tried to warn you, but you never returned his calls. He said I had my chance. He never saw that I was an artist! An artist cannot just *work*. What, he wanted me to go to an office, answer phones?" Vivienne wailed, wringing her small hands. Her tiny dancer's body had once been limber and elegant but now looked positively frail. One of the moving men raised his eyebrows at the other, who was pulling up his butt crack–revealing pants.

"You knew he was going to do this?" Jack cried. She thought of her ancient father, his much younger wife, and the stepbrats living in the Perry Street town house. Assholes.

"Well . . . yes," Vivienne admitted. The smoker's lines on her forehead creased.

"And what am I supposed to do?" Jack screeched, gripping the iron railing for support. She felt like she was going to throw up.

"Ah, cherie." Vivienne stood and enveloped her in a hug. Jack could feel every one of her vertebrae and the cloying smell of far too much Chanel No. 5. "It will be good for you to learn how to suffer." Vivienne pulled away and disappeared up the ivy-covered service entrance with a grand flourish.

Jack watched her mother's unnaturally delicate frame retreat in disbelief.

One of the movers huffed as he carried a ruched bergère chair from the living room out of the doorway. How could they be so nonchalant? Didn't they realize they were moving away her *life*?

Jack tried to compose herself. In dance class they'd once had a meditation session where they learned to calm audition nerves by choosing one word and repeating it in their heads. She tried to do that now by imagining her spine in alignment, and her one word: *perfect*. The instructor had wanted her to choose another word—like *fight* or *focus*—warning her that perfection was impossible to achieve. She'd chosen it, anyway.

"Hello!"

Jack turned to see a tiny blond girl bound down the steps. She looked about five years old and wore a pink tutu and matching wings from FAO Schwarz. Jack narrowed her eyes at the innocent little girl. A new family was already living in her house? Her parents could have as many dramatic fights as they wanted, but how could he just put Jack up in the attic, like some antique castoff?

Or some lizard-skin boots?

Jack closed her eyes and massaged her temples, hoping that when she opened them the little girl would be gone and her life would be back to normal.

"My name's Satchel! I live here now!" Jack's eyes flew open. The little girl danced above her on the steps. *Her* steps.

"Satchel?" Jack croaked in disbelief. She glanced down at her Givenchy purse. The sight of the buttery leather comforted her, and she was thankful she had some dignity left. She straightened her shoulders and elongated her neck. *Perfect.*

She would just book a room at the St. Claire. Unless . . . unless . . . unless her father had also canceled the credit cards?

Quelle horreur!

at st. jude's, it's all for one and one for all . . .

"Okay, guys! I know it's the first day back but you're looking slow," Coach Siegel yelled from atop the rickety metal lifeguard stand at the Ninety-second Street Y, where the St. Jude's team practiced every day at 3 p.m. He blew his shrill-sounding whistle while he discreetly checked out his abs in the stand's reflective surface. He was twenty-five, had graduated from Stanford only a few years before, and still had oats to sow, as he mentioned to his swimmers at every opportunity.

In lane three, Rhys was listlessly swimming the crawl. He felt Owen pass him, leaving him in his wake as he charged toward the pool wall. Even though he was used to being the fastest, Rhys couldn't get himself to care. Instead, he glided leisurely toward the end of the lane.

"Sterling, stay behind a second." Coach hopped off the stand and walked over to Rhys, his Adidas slides making a squishing sound against the wet deck. He had a square jaw, skinny legs, and a buff chest that he claimed the ladies loved.

Rhys dragged himself up on the damp pool deck with a sinking feeling in his stomach.

"Sterling." Coach Siegel ran his hands through his shaggy reddish-brown hair. "You were late," he stated.

Rhys nodded and glanced down at the water pooling on the tiles. One puddle looked sort of like a heart. Rhys put his foot in it, and the water scattered across the blue tile in runny droplets.

"Sorry, I just had some things to take care of," he said, not looking Coach in the eye. In fact, he had spent the first fifteen minutes of practice crying in the rarely used bathroom near the upstairs science labs while he looked through all the camera-phone pictures he'd taken with Kelsey last spring. She'd looked so thrilled to have his arm around her shoulders. What had gone wrong?

"Oh-kaaaaay," Coach Siegel said slowly, drawing the word out to several syllables. Rhys winced. It wasn't enough that his girlfriend had stomped all over him, but now he was getting heat for it at practice? "I know it's the first day of school and stuff comes up, but it's not just you missing the first few minutes. You were off the whole practice. The new kid, Carlyle, clocked you!" Coach Siegel narrowed his mouthwash-blue eyes at him, waiting for more of an explanation.

"Sorry, I'm dealing with some personal stuff," Rhys mumbled. The phrase *there's another guy* kept banging around his head. Was that true? Who could it possibly be? Some Cape Cod kid? A Riverside Prep guy Kat had met at a party?

"Lady trouble?" Coach perked up.

"No, just . . . school stuff," Rhys said quickly.

"Okay, well, hopefully this was just a rough start, because I can't have my captain perform like you did today." Rhys nodded and Coach clapped him on the back. "And let me know if it's lady trouble. Girls can kill you," he said knowingly.

Yeah, but we're so worth it.

Rhys trudged to the locker room, where Jeff Kohl and Ian McDaniel were passing around a silver flask of Maker's Mark. The room was super-humid and smelled like chlorine, BO, and feet.

"Is *niiiiiiice*." Ian did a ridiculously bad Borat impression as he offered the flask to Owen. Owen shook his head. Just then, Rhys stormed through the door and tore open his locker.

"So, dude, I sucked." Rhys pulled a Vitamin Water from the side pocket of his overstuffed Speedo swim bag and took a long swig.

"You seemed fine." Owen wrung out his towel distractedly. Now that he was out of the pool, he found it impossible to stop thinking about Kat or Kelsey or whatever the hell her name really was. How long had she and Rhys been dating? Were they in love? Was that why she hadn't even told him her name? Did Rhys have any clue she'd been unfaithful to him this summer?

"No, I really sucked," Rhys repeated.

"Hey, dude, you need a beer," Hugh Moore, a muscley junior, yelled. He threw a Budweiser over from the next row of lockers. The can hit the floor, sputtering as it released a hiss of carbonation and foam.

"Not now, man," Rhys said, knowing that, as captain, he should give some half-assed speech about how they weren't supposed to drink in season, let alone in the locker room. Except he really couldn't get himself to care. Instead, he wanted to cry.

Again.

"So, you know the girl I introduced you to at lunch? Kelsey?" Rhys asked, his face contorting as he sat down heavily on a worn wooden bench.

Owen nodded and pushed his wet blond hair out of his eyes. How could he forget? He pretended to root around in his Speedo bag, not looking at Rhys. On the other side of the locker room Hugh, Ian, and a few other guys grabbed Chadwick Jenkins, one of the freshmen. "We're going to shave off your eyebrows, man!" they shouted gleefully, pulling the terrified ninth grader over to a row of sinks.

"So, she broke up with me right after you left," Rhys said woodenly, not even caring who heard. "She said there was another guy."

Owen dropped his Speedo bag on the floor and sat down next to Rhys. Kat—*Kelsey*—had broken up with Rhys? She was single again? *There was someone else?* Did that mean . . . ?

"Wait, your girlfriend broke up with you?" Hugh repeated in disbelief, releasing Chadwick. Hugh sat down next to Rhys on the locker room bench. "Lay it on me." He draped a companionable arm around Rhys's shoulders and opened another can of Bud, unleashing a stream of spray that landed at Owen's feet.

"I don't know what to say. It was out of nowhere. She said there was someone else . . . and I don't know who it could be, unless it was some asshole she met on the Cape. Whoever it is, I'll break his fucking face," Rhys muttered.

Owen had to stop a smile from spreading, feeling elated and guilty at the same time. Had Kat had broken up with Rhys because she wanted to be with *him*?

And guys are supposed to be so clueless.

Hugh nodded supportively. "This is serious." Droplets of water from his arm cascaded down Rhys's chest. "Hey guys? Come over here." Owen glanced around at the collection of guys, most still in their Speedos, some with newly shorn eyebrows.

"Okay," Hugh said, standing up on the bench and waving the open beer can around in the air. His ribs stuck way out, giving his chest an almost concave appearance. "I just learned that Rhys Sterling, our captain and all-around good guy, has gotten his heart stomped on by a Seaton Arms girl." A collective groan echoed across the locker room. "Now, I know as well as you that it happens to the best of us. And we know that Rhys will find another girl. But until he gets one, I propose a challenge in the name of solidarity." He looked around grandly and cleared his throat. "Until Rhys gets action, we won't get action. And we will prove it by the beard." He stroked his chiseled chin with his free hand and looked around.

"What the fuck?" Ken Williams yelled. He weighed more than two hundred pounds and looked more like a linebacker than a distance swimmer.

"We'll all grow facial hair until Rhys gets lucky with a lady. Until then, none of us are going to hook up, either. And Jenkins, that means no playing with yourself," Hugh yelled. "Who's in?"

One by one the swim team guys hooted and high-fived Rhys, who sat on the bench, staring forlornly at the damp floor.

"You don't have to do that," he mumbled. The guys' support was sweet and all, but shouldn't he be galvanizing them to do well at Conferences, not showing what a pussy he was about a girl?

"If Rhys doesn't get any, neither do we!" Hugh yelled. Owen scrutinized the guys, taking in Chadwick's scrawny arms and Ken's thicket of chest hair. He wondered if any of them actually *could* get any. Either way, he hoped this was more a hypothetical gesture of devotion and not an actual pact. Owen had never gone more than a week without kissing a girl.

And we love him for it.

"Thanks," Rhys muttered to Hugh.

"No problem." Hugh smiled. "Besides, my girlfriend is in France this year, so I'm in blue ball city with you, my friend." One by one, the guys walked off, rubbing their prepubescent chins, as if they could massage stubble into being.

Rhys mustered a weak laugh and then turned to Owen. "I'd just feel so much better if I knew who the guy was," he confided as the locker room emptied out. It was so quiet Rhys could hear the hollow hum of the flickering fluorescent lights overhead. They made his arms look weirdly blue. "If you find the dude, can you just pull off his nuts for me?" He tried to laugh, but it came out as a horrible choking sound.

"Sure," Owen said, guiltily. "I don't really know anyone. . . ."

"Yeah, I know, just if you hear anything. Or if you see her, maybe she'd talk. Just let me know if you find out anything. It's all this guy's fucking fault." Rhys stood and kicked his locker. It made a sharp clanging sound that echoed through the empty locker room.

"Sterling, don't break a bone over a lady," Coach yelled from the tiny side office adjacent to the locker room. "And especially not one bone in particular!" he added with a cackle.

Rhys turned red. Fuck. Even Coach knew he'd been dumped. Was there any way to keep the news from spreading?

Get a team of cute boys to take a vow of abstinence. Who *won't* be talking?

Disclaimer: All the real names of places, people, and events have been altered or abbreviated to protect the innocent. Namely, me.

hey people!

It's midnight, and the first day of school has officially come to a close. Now, some housekeeping: I know a uniformless summer may have left some people rusty on how to make the most of them, so let's take a little time to refresh our memories.

the do's and don'ts of dress-code conduct

The shorter the better, but don't forget to wear *something* underneath your skirt. This is New York, not L.A., and going La Perla–less will only ensure a day of total discomfort. Beyond that, it's risky. And, um, gross.

Nothing looks less sexy than a pit-stained Chloé cashmere sweater, so layer light. And for heaven's sake, don't skimp on the deodorant.

A black shoes–only rule can be manipulated in oh so many ways. It's all about the three *M*'s: Marni wedges, Manolo kitten heels, and Marc Jacobs. There's no better way to express oneself than through shoes. Or, in my case, Choos.

sightings

A moving van outside **J**'s town house. Could our Upper East Side princess be (gasp!) leaving us? . . . **A** balancing two huge bags of antique teacups as she entered a cab. Crumpets, anyone . . . ? **O** chugging blue Gatorade with wet hair, grinning ear to ear as he exited the **92nd Street Y**.

Why so happy, handsome? . . . **R** crying outside an apartment building on Fifth. Getting ready for the interschool production of *Romeo & Juliet*, or living our a real romantic tragedy? . . . **K** buying new Cosabellas at **Barneys**. We all know new lingerie can mean only two things: losing *it* to her **R**, or losing **R** for someone else. . . . **J**'s mom, also at **Barneys**, trying to return last season's Gucci over-the-knee mohair boots. Of course they were a mistake, but you can't expect *Barneys* to pay for your poor fashion choices. Tsk, tsk.

your e-mail

q: Dear Gossip Girl,
I saw **A** getting totally friendly with that weirdo with the tattoos at the Constance assembly. Do you think they're together? Like, *together* together?
—2GIRLTROUBLE

a: Dear 2,
Why, are you jealous?
—GG

q: Dear GG,
Ur column sux. U are some lame-assed poser and IM totally going to find out who u R.
—REALUESGIRL

a: Dear REALUESGIRL,
You (U?) seem to have a lot of misplaced hostility. I will let you know that I am as Upper East Side as they come—and I'm not shaking in my Christian Louboutin eel-skin boots over a badly spelled text message. If you can't handle the truth, maybe you would be better off living somewhere else. Like Weehawken. But let's not fight!
—GG

Now that the first day is over, we can turn our attention to more important matters. Like, who's going to host the first party of the year? All bets are on **J**. Although I've never been the betting type. . . .

You know you love me,

gossip girl

campaign strategies 101

Tuesday morning before school, Avery slipped out of the Carlyle apartment, pleased that Baby wasn't even awake.

"Miss Carlyle." The gray-uniformed doorman nodded briskly to her, and Avery couldn't help smiling. The air smelled fresh, birds chirped noisily, and the sidewalks were glittering with water, even though Avery hadn't remembered a rainstorm. That was what it was like in New York City—each day was a fresh start, the previous day washed away.

And today was definitely a new day. Last night she'd locked herself in her room, putting together invitations to her tea party. She'd written all the invitations by hand on elegant Tiffany & Co. cardstock, and tied each card to the eggshell-thin handle of a teacup. She'd thought it would be fun and unique but now, carrying two huge lavender Bergdorf bags filled with bubble-wrapped china, she wasn't sure. She felt like she was bringing something in for show-and-tell.

Avery approached the corner of Ninetieth Street and spotted a group of junior girls she vaguely recognized from assembly gathered on the steps of a random town house, the preferred smoke-and-gossip hangout of Constance Billard's upper school. The girls were already sucking furiously on their Merit Ultra Lights, even though the first bell wouldn't ring for another half hour. Avery felt a flutter of butterflies in the pit of her stomach, but grinned broadly.

"Hey, Jiffy," she greeted the junior with the smudgy charcoal-lined eyes. Jiffy glanced up from her *W* magazine, which she was furiously marking up with a purple pen. Avery smiled warmly. She knew Jiffy hung out with Jack Laurent, but with her brown bangs hanging straight above her eyebrows and her wide brown eyes, she seemed like the friendliest girl out of all of them.

"Oh, hi." Jiffy pushed her bangs out of her eyes and gave the other girls perched on the stoop a look that Avery knew, from years of giving her own looks, meant, *What the fuck?*

Avery steeled herself and pulled the first invite out of the bag. "I'm having a party after school today. Just some girls, so I can meet everyone and talk about the upcoming school year." Avery cringed. She sounded so ridiculously peppy. "And just hang out," she amended.

Can we bring our teddy bears?

"Ohhh-kaaaay," Jiffy said slowly. Avery handed a teacup to Jiffy and pulled out another one. "Oh, fun!" Jiffy exclaimed as she examined the delicate piece of china and spotted the invite tied to its handle. "Look at this, it's adorable," she said, passing the teacup to the girl sitting next to her, who had eyebrows so blond they disappeared into her forehead.

"I'm glad you like them!" Avery set her bag down on the cracked concrete steps, ready to dole out the rest. Already, a small crowd had formed around her. The Constance girls were loving the invites! She felt like somehow, somewhere, her grandmother was smiling down on her.

"What are those?" Avery heard a voice behind her and whirled around to see Sydney, the weird girl she had been forced to sit next to at assembly yesterday. She was wearing a brown T-shirt that read YOUR RETARDED under her Constance Billard blazer.

"Hi," Avery greeted her awkwardly, still trying to hold the attention of the rest of the girls. "I'm just having a get-together. For the student liaison to the board of overseers thing. Not sure if you'd be interested." She shrugged, hoping the answer would be no.

"Tonight?"

"Yeah," Avery said as she handed an invitation to Genevieve, the large-chested girl who was friends with Jack.

"Thanks." Genevieve took a teacup and shoved it into her orange Longchamps bag, not bothering to look at the attached invite. She threw her cigarette on the ground, dangerously close to Avery's black Morgane Le Fay ankle boots.

"Can I have one?" Sydney asked expectantly, stomping on the remains of Genevieve's cigarette with her vintage Doc Martens.

"Sure," Avery handed a teacup to her, not wanting to be rude. Sydney was a Constance junior, after all, and who was she to judge? She just hoped that if Sydney did turn up, she'd change into slightly more feminine shoes.

With a little less steel in the toe?

"Thanks!" Sydney took the teacup and pretended to sip from it with one pinky raised.

"See you all tonight!" Avery waved to the group of girls, still smiling, and turned to go. She quickly made her way down the street to the blue doors of Constance, wanting to make sure she gave out all the invitations before first period. By lunch, it would be all anyone was talking about.

Sure, they'll be talking about it, but what will they be saying?

b makes some furry friends

Baby yawned loudly in Mr. Beckham's last-period film class, causing other girls to titter. She rolled her large brown eyes at them. Whatever. It was the last period of the day, and frankly, Baby couldn't care less about Woody Allen's *Manhattan*. Hearing Mr. Beckham enthuse about how New York City was an integral character in the film just made her want to stand up and start screaming swear words.

And it wouldn't be the first time.

The movie was so stupid, anyway. She had watched it once with her mother and hadn't been able to stop wondering why someone young and cute like Mariel Hemingway would ever go for a geeky old loser like Woody Allen.

"Do you have something to add to our discussion about the film, Miss Carlyle?" Mr. Beckham asked. He perched on top of her desk like an overgrown bird and grinned lecherously.

Seems like the film gave someone some ideas.

The bell rang. Baby practically pushed Mr. Beckham's skinny butt off the top of her desk, threw her notebook into her lime green Brooklyn Industries messenger bag, and bolted out the door.

She was supposed to begin her Constance Billard punishment by helping Irene, the seventy-three-year-old lunch lady, go through the cafeteria suggestion box. Baby paused for a second and stared into the gorgeous all-mirrors-and-blond-wood cafeteria, tempting herself to see if at the last minute she would cave and try to be a good girl. No way. She turned on her heel and strode down the hallway and toward the big blue doors that led to freedom.

Strike two!

She paused to stare at the bulletin board hanging in the main hall, reading the announcements for different clubs and activities.

PRE-PRE-LAW SOCIETY. *No.*

FLOWER ARRANGING CLUB. *Nope.*

BASKET WEAVING CLUB. *Yeah, right.*

What, no Disillusioned and Missing My Boyfriend Club? Maybe she should be socially responsible like her sister and start one.

"Are you joining anything?" Avery sidled up to her and placed a large lavender shopping bag on the floor. She tucked her blond hair behind her tiny ears and patted her vintage diamond studs.

"Nothing's really my thing." Baby shrugged her tiny shoulders and looked at her sister. Avery was flushed and looked happy. Even her little diamond camellia earrings sparkled a little brighter. "How was your day?"

"So good!" Avery enthused. "I'm having a little get-together tonight at Grandmother's house."

"Does Mom know?" Baby narrowed her eyes. How come Avery hadn't told her about it last night? When she had gotten home, Avery had been in her room, and hadn't even come out when Owen announced he was ordering his first authentic New York City pizza.

"Yeah, it's fine," Avery said quickly. "Anyway, these are the invitations." She pulled a china teacup out of the Bergdorf bag, and Baby instantly recognized the pattern. She had broken one when she was four.

"Thanks. I don't need a teacup." Baby practically pushed it away.

"So you're going to come?" Avery's brow creased.

"Sure." Baby nodded slowly.

"Okay, well, I guess I'll see you," Avery continued uncertainly, as if they were strangers.

Baby nodded and pretended to be engrossed in the red announcement flyers until Avery wandered off. Finally, she headed for Constance's royal blue doors, shoving her hands in her pockets. She felt the corner of something hard and slid the ivory business card out of her pocket and examined it. Had that guy been serious about her walking dogs for him?

And did she have anything better to do?

Baby walked down Fifth until she came to the address on the card. She looked up at the gilt back-to-back *C*'s hanging over the glass doors of the building. Three-foot-high brass letters spelled out CASHMAN COMPLEXES. Baby wrinkled her nose. It was even tackier than she'd imagined.

Seeing *is* believing.

The doorman sat behind an imposing black-lacquered desk, wearing an elaborate blue uniform with gold tassels hanging from his shoulders and across his belly. He was older and looked like he'd been wearing the same uniform since he was sixteen.

"I'm here for this guy." Baby slid J.P.'s wrinkled card across the counter. She hadn't gotten used to doormen yet. They seemed like one of the relics from a different era, like scrunchies or handlebar mustaches.

Don't be so sure about that last one.

"Use the private elevator over on the far left." The doorman smiled in a grandfatherly way, and Baby smiled back. She pushed the button for the penthouse and caught her breath as the elevator *whooshed* twenty-six flights up, to the top floor. The doors opened and she tumbled out into the apartment itself.

J.P. was standing in the middle of a gold-tiled foyer, waiting. He wore khakis and a rumpled blue oxford, and his hair was messy under his Riverside Prep cap, like he had just gotten up from a nap. He smiled at her warmly, scooping up Darwin as the puggle scampered through the arched, gilded doorway. J.P. held up Darwin's tiny paw and waved it at Baby.

"You came," he said warmly.

"I came for this guy." Baby scooped Darwin from J.P.'s large hands and kissed him on his wet black nose. Shackleton and Nemo came running from some faraway room, their nails clacking and sliding as they ran toward her. "How can you not love a face like that?" she cooed, feeling better than she had all day. She placed the puggle on the parquet floor next to his friends. They all looked up at her expectantly, wiggling their butts uncontrollably.

"Have you recovered from the shitstorm?" Baby couldn't resist asking, pleased when she saw J.P. blush. He was the type of clean-cut, high-maintenance guy Avery would swoon over. Baby had always preferred the scruffy, bad-boy types.

Doesn't she mean stoners?

"Thanks for bringing that up," J.P. replied sarcastically. Baby peeked past him and saw room after room, filled with ultramodern and antique furniture all thrown together. Did that door to the left lead to a basketball court? And was it . . . *gold*? Baby thought she saw a hoop.

"'Ello!" A large blond woman entered the room from one of the many mirrored doors surrounding the large entryway. Her platinum highlighted hair was pulled up into an eighties supermodel–style updo. She strode across the floor in her electric blue Prada pumps and hugged Baby, practically suffocating her in a cloud of spicy perfume.

"Welcome. Our house is your house," she said grandly in a heavy Russian accent as she gestured to the rooms with her long, Chanel Vamp–lacquered nails.

"This is my mother, Tatyana," J.P. made the introduction. "Mom, this is Baby Carlyle. She'll be walking the dogs."

"Yes, I am his mother, and he is my beautiful, beautiful son!" Tatyana cried, kissing J.P. and leaving a trail of Chanel Red Splendor lip imprints on his tan cheek.

"Nice to meet you," Baby said politely, resisting the urge to take a picture of Tatyana with her camera phone and send it to Tom. "You have beautiful dogs!" she added awkwardly.

"I know! I love zem like zey are my babies. And they are so great because unlike zees boy, zey *always* need their mother!" She bent over to smother Nemo in a perfume hug, her round butt sticking up in the air.

Baby sneaked a glance over at J.P. He smiled sheepishly and gave her a small shrug.

"*I* always need you." A large, beefy man strode out of a room on the left as if on cue, playfully smacking Tatyana's freakishly perky butt. She giggled. He was wearing a tiny-looking cowboy hat on his Pepto Bismol–colored bald head. He took one of Baby's tiny hands in his pudgy one and aggressively pumped it up and down.

"Dick Cashman," he boomed. He gave Baby a once-over, looking at her dirty white flip-flops and the T-shirt she had worn under her blazer. She had picked it up at a flea market in Cape Cod. It featured a picture of an alligator eating a tiger. "I love that shirt! Great message there—don't feed the alligators: if you do, they'll just bite you in the ass!" Dick cried, grinning.

"Hey, Dad, so this is Baby—" J.P. began.

"Baby? Like, '*Nobody puts Baby in a corner*'? Maybe they wouldn't have to if you actually dressed up!" Dick roared, slapping his knee.

Baby smiled politely, even though she had heard that line fifty million times before, and she didn't even *like* the movie *Dirty Dancing*.

"You'll be looking after the bitches, then?" he continued, patting Nemo furiously on top of the head.

"Uh, yeah," Baby said uncomfortably. She felt like she had stepped onto the set of some bad reality TV show.

The Richest Loser?

"I think Baby should probably get started," J.P. said, handing her three matching, monogrammed Louis Vuitton leashes. "I just have something for you in the kitchen, and then I'll see you out." He smiled awkwardly at his parents.

"Sorry about that," J.P. whispered as he guided Baby through a bright labyrinthine hallway. The enamel-like walls were lined with paintings of green globs that looked suspiciously like boogers. When they reached the ultramodern kitchen, J.P. grabbed a cup emblazoned with the two *C*'s and handed it to her.

"I noticed you left your drink when you chased after the dogs yesterday. It's a chai," he said almost shyly.

"Thanks." Baby smiled, touched. She took a sip. It tasted much better than Starbucks, and a little bit like home.

"I actually don't really know what that is, but I hope you like it," J.P. added. "Raphael, our chef, made it."

"Oh," Baby muttered, pulling the cup away from her lips. Of *course* his chef made it.

And that's supposed to be a *bad* thing?

"I could come with you if you wanted," J.P. offered, still standing in the kitchen door.

Baby took a few steps back. "No, I'm fine on my own," she said definitively. She let out a piercing whistle and the three dogs came running. "See you." She quickly clipped their leashes to their collars and navigated her way back through the booger painting–lined corridor, into the gold foyer, and down the twenty-six flights.

The doorman tipped his patent leather hat as she walked by. "See you again soon, Miss," he called.

And hopefully often!

papa don't preach

Jack sat in a low-slung booth at the Star Lounge in the trendy Tribeca Star Hotel. Even though it was only five o'clock and outside the cobblestone streets were filled with shoppers enjoying the warm afternoon, in here it was dark, with candlelight flickering off the rich oak walls. Jack loved lounges when they were empty; she sort of felt like Mata Hari or some other glamorous spy. She needed the escape from her life, where her father was ignoring her phone calls and it appeared more and more likely she'd have to apply for financial aid for college.

Quelle horrible!

She pulled out a compact and looked at herself critically. Last night, she had been forced to spend her first night in her new room in the garret. She'd slept in a tiny twin bed and had woken up in a pool of sweat because there was no air-conditioning, and the exhaustion showed. She'd liberally applied Crème de la Mer eye cream twice today, but she still had large bags gathering under her eyes.

How very pre-guillotine Marie Antoinette.

Jiffy, Sarah Jane, and Genevieve were supposed to meet her,

but they had all gone home after school to change. Jack knew there was no way in hell she was actually going home for anything other than sleeping, so she had packed a simple, wrinkle-resistant Stella McCartney sheath dress in her giant royal blue Balenciaga city bag. The satchel also housed her dance clothes from her pointe class this morning, where she'd used her anger to absolutely nail her arabesques. She'd changed in the locker room at school, feeling like a total fucking nomad, and had just arrived at the bar determined to get very, very drunk.

She nodded at the twentysomething waiter. His curly black hair fell over his eyes.

"Another Grey Goose and tonic," she demanded, batting her eyelashes. He hadn't carded her before, so it was unlikely he'd card her on her second round.

"Rough day?" he asked knowingly, handing her the drink. Jack nodded noncommittally. A Euro-trashy couple at the other end of the bar were conversing loudly in heavily accented English about whose fault it was that they had gotten themselves kicked out of Pink Elephant the night before.

As Jack idly listened to the couple argue and ignored the waiter watching her, Genevieve, Jiffy, and Sarah Jane burst in, giggling and looking ridiculously dressed up for five o'clock in the afternoon.

"Did you get one of these?" Genevieve handed Jack a white card as she sat down. "I'll have a split of Veuve," she said without looking at the shaggy-haired waiter. "In L.A., Breck and I would always stop at the Chateau Marmont for afternoon champagne," she announced to no one in particular. The waiter quickly stood up and took their drink orders. Jack studied the thick cardstock that Genevieve had handed to her.

COME AND FIND OUT WHAT CONSTANCE MEANS TO ME.

A TEA PARTY TO DISCUSS OUR FUTURE. ADD HONEY AND STIR!

"Yeah," Jack lied. Didn't Avery realize what a major mistake it had been to exclude her? "But are you seriously going? Come on. A tea party?"

"Didn't you think the teacups were cute?" Jiffy asked. "I'd like to go. See what the competition is like."

Jack frowned. "Avery Carlyle is *not* competition," she reminded Jiffy primly as she examined the homemade calligraphy. "Besides, it's not even a real party." Jack took a large gulp of her drink and gestured for another round. She already felt a little tipsy.

"So why not go?" Sarah Jane said suddenly, as if she'd just had a brilliant idea. Her Prada glasses were poised primly on her nose, and she wore a low-cut black Tory Burch tunic that barely covered her behind, clearly going for the sexy-smart look. She took the card out of Jack's hands and studied it. "It's at their grandmother's town house. My mom says it's supposed to be spectacular."

"I have a better idea," Jack said quickly. There was no way in hell she wanted to see Avery's grandmother's *spectacular* town house, which would only remind her of her newfound destitution. "Why don't we just go out? It's the second night of school, it's not like we have anything important to do tomorrow," she reminded them.

"Sounds fine to me," Genevieve shrugged. "Honestly, Avery's tea party sounds pretty boring."

"Exactly. Who the hell wants to drink tea?" Jack took another swig of her drink, feeling her old confidence come back. She always got what she wanted.

Well, *almost* always.

"Should we pre-party at your place?" Genevieve asked.

"No!" Jack cried instinctively. Last year, the best part of the evenings had usually been getting ready in her sprawling bedroom. They would put on her iPod and dance around to old-school Madonna and other cheesy music they would all die if anyone found out they actually listened to. They'd drink champagne, take ridiculous pictures of one another, and try on different outfits from Jack's walk-in closet. Jack had always thought it was kind of immature, but now, she'd do anything to go back to the way it used to be. "I mean . . ." Jack hesitated for a second. "We're renovating."

"Really?" Jiffy's eyes widened.

"Okay, that all makes sense now." Genevieve nodded pointedly to Sarah Jane, who nodded in agreement.

"What?" Jack asked defensively.

"Oh, we just thought we saw a truck outside your house yesterday. It must have been the renovators?" Sarah Jane asked as she swirled the lime in her drink.

"Yeah," Jack said, relieved. "It sucks. Basically, we're gutting the whole bottom floor and we're staying in the attic."

"Why don't you stay in a suite at the Regency or something?"

"You know my mom," Jack sighed, as if that explained everything, even though Jack made it a priority to keep her mother as far away from her friends as possible. "She wants to be on the premises to make sure the decorators don't fuck up."

"I guess we can get ready at my place," Genevieve sighed dramatically. She lived in a modest two-bedroom on Fiftieth and Third with her mom. It was positively tiny compared to Jack's town house, and Genevieve constantly bitched about it, reminding them that her mother was an actress, even though she was just a former soap star now starring in a weird avant-garde musical downtown.

"Okay." Jack motioned to their waiter. Everything had begun to feel deliciously fuzzy. She would go over to J.P.'s after a night of dancing with the girls and maybe something—*it*—would finally happen. "Another Grey Goose and tonic," she enunciated carefully as the waiter approached. It wasn't like she was drunk or anything.

Of course not.

"And the check as well," Jack directed steadily. She pulled her black AmEx out of her Gucci wallet.

"Right away," the waiter said, turning on his heel with the card in his hand. Almost instantaneously, he came back.

"Your card was declined." He handed it back to her. Jack was speechless. She felt Genevieve's questioning stare bore into her.

"I'll get it." Jiffy mercifully pulled her own black AmEx from her green and white Kate Spade bag. Despite her Little-Bo-Peep-goes-on-a-picnic purse, Jack felt like hugging her.

"I was using a different card in Paris. I guess there was a freeze on it or something," Jack lied, her heart pounding. First her dad took her home away and now this? Was she seriously cut off?

"So, where are we going to go? Can we start at Tenjune?" Jiffy asked, naming an obvious club in the Meatpacking District.

"You know, I actually don't want to go out anymore," Jack said suddenly. "I haven an early ballet class tomorrow. But you guys should have fun."

"But it's so early now," Genevieve whined.

Jack didn't bother to give any more explanation. She burst out of the hotel and walked quickly over to Houston to find a cab. The air was hot and sticky and an MTA bus drove by, blowing a cloud of exhaust on her tanned knees. Her Stella McCartney dress billowed upward. Oh God. Could she even *afford* a cab? She felt dizzy and emotional and very, very drunk. She pulled some crumpled singles from her voluminous blue leather bag, knowing they wouldn't be enough.

She spotted a subway entrance and wobbled over, marveling at all the different letters and numbers. The green 6 looked familiar. Didn't that go to the Upper East Side?

She followed a horde of people onto the green line, pretending not to study the map of the stops above her as one guy kept stepping on her foot with his loafer. Finally, after countless stops riding alongside a mariachi band, Jack got off at Fifty-first Street. She hurriedly walked up to the imposing Citigroup building on Fifty-third and Park, where her father's office was. The sun was beginning to set, and it reflected in blues and oranges off the skyscraper's modern steel and chrome tower. The last time Jack had been inside was when she was eleven.

Men and women in crisp business suits hustled through the enormous lobby, and Jack immediately felt out of place in her cocktail dress and blue Balenciaga school bag. "I'm Jacqueline Laurent. My father works on the twenty-second floor. Emerging markets," she rattled off quickly to the large, white-haired man sitting behind a security desk. He quickly picked up an office phone.

"Go on up," the man replied in a thick Bronx accent. Jack walked into the silver elevator, knowing that she had to control her temper. She focused on the weather report playing on the elevator's small TV screen. Tonight would be pleasant, with a chance of a storm.

Just like someone we know.

When she got off on the twenty-second floor, a skinny woman with eyebrows tattooed several inches above her eyes was waiting for her.

"Good evening," the woman said curtly, motioning Jack to follow her into the large office in the corner.

"Jacqueline!" her father announced. He stood up from behind his heavy oak desk and clasped both of her hands with his, but didn't embrace her. Jack looked down at his shock of white hair. She wasn't sure when she had grown taller than her father. He sort of looked like a pudgy Santa Claus rather than a high-powered business executive and former government official.

She smiled, trying not to appear drunk. All this was probably a silly mistake. Maybe her father was trying, in some warped, clueless guy way, to woo Vivienne back—and Jack, her nice canopy bed, and black AmEx card were just caught in the crossfire.

Sure, that seems likely.

"You haven't answered my calls." Her father gestured for her to sit down, and Jack eased into one of the black leather chairs that faced the enormous plate glass windows overlooking Park Avenue.

"You didn't answer my calls, either, Daddy," she said calmly. She smoothed her skirt over her knees and gave him a helpless, lost-puppy look with her big green eyes.

"Your mother didn't tell you what we decided," Charles stated. He walked to a silver coffee service on the opposite side of the room. "Coffee?"

Jack shook her head, seething. This wasn't a casual coffee date. This was her *future*. "Why doesn't my credit card work?" she blurted.

"Why did you leave Paris early?" Charles countered calmly. He poured himself tea in a white porcelain cup, and Jack was suddenly reminded of Avery's stupid party. He took the chair next to Jack's. His intelligent eyes searched her face for answers.

"I . . ." Jack paused. "I wanted to make sure I had time to get back in shape before the internship program. I wanted to get everything in order." Her voice wavered as she lied.

"To get everything in order in the Hamptons?" Charles stated flatly.

Jack blushed. Well, so what? Did she deserve such a brutal punishment? She'd had to take the *subway* for God's sake!

Mother Teresa in the making.

Charles stood up and placed his teacup on the desk with a clatter. "Jacqueline, I'm doing this for your own good. I loved your mother very much. I don't want you to become like her. I want you to know the value of hard work. Until you prove to me that you can handle responsibility and follow through on commitments, I am not financing your lifestyle. I will pay for school and that's it. But not ballet. If you loved ballet as much as your mother thinks you do, then you would have stayed in Paris and finished your course." He smiled and sat down behind the desk again, as if his tough-love speech made up for his absentee parenting.

Jack felt like she'd been slapped. Small tears pooled in the corners of her eyes and she noticed the chip in her maroon nail polish. Her dad *couldn't* just cut her off, could he?

Actually, he just did.

"What about the house?" Jack bleated, not caring how desperate she sounded. Let his two assistants and gaggle of suited minions hear her bawl. Maybe *they'd* take pity on her.

Charles regarded Jack and his face softened momentarily. "I had to get rid of it. It was a huge money drain, and honestly, you and your mother don't need all that space. Of course, you could come live with me and Rebecca and the girls," he offered. "I would love to have you in our family." Jack shook her head wordlessly. Rebecca was only eight years older than she was. Besides, she couldn't just desert her mother. Vivienne would be a mess. She already was a mess.

"I will chalk up the Paris experiment as a foolish mistake if you show me you're responsible," Charles continued, as if he were hammering out a diplomatic negotiation with a particularly belligerent and not especially powerful country. "If you can do that, I'll be happy to support you and your endeavors. Can you do that, Jacqueline?"

Jack *had* to continue ballet. On the slick black stage of Lincoln Center, or on the shiny wood floors of the rehearsal studio, she felt free in a way she wasn't in any other aspect of her life. Ballet made her special, it made her beautiful, it gave her an edge. It made her Jack, not Jacqueline. She locked eyes with her father.

"I have a leadership position at school," Jack countered. What was it called again? "I'm the . . . student liaison to the board of overseers." Or she would be in a few days. She gave Charles a *so there* stare.

"Good!" He clapped his hands together as if this were a cause for celebration.

All that's missing is the champagne. Oops, she already drank that.

"And when did you begin this?" Charles studied the calendar on the side of his desk.

"Next week." She stood in front of the desk like the picture-perfect ballerina she was, her spine ramrod straight.

"So, you haven't officially begun yet?" Charles ventured. He settled one butt cheek on the side of his desk and furrowed his white eyebrows.

"They officially announce it Sunday. At some mother-daughter brunch at Tavern on the Green."

"I'll come," Charles announced gallantly.

"But you're not my *mother*," Jack pointed out. Not only was he going to ruin her life, he wanted to embarrass her at a school function?

"Who's paying your tuition?" Charles asked evenly. "Besides, it doesn't sound like something Vivienne would attend. It's time someone took a real interest in your future, Jacqueline."

"My *future* is ballet," Jack reminded her dad through gritted teeth.

"Well, if you're serious about ballet, then you'll prove you are responsible and I'll write the check. Are we clear?"

Jack nodded, too angry to speak. She couldn't believe the key to her entire future was in her father's brown leather Christian Lacroix wallet—and in the hands of her Constance classmates. If he didn't pay for dance tuition, she'd have to apply for a scholarship, and there was no way in hell the internship program director, Mikhail Turneyev or Turnmeoff or whatever the fuck his name was, would *ever* give her one.

She huffed out of her dad's office, past his skinny bitch of a secretary, who was hovering outside the door listening. She whipped out her cell phone and speed-dialed J.P.'s number, but the phone went straight to voice mail. She was about to blabber on about everything that happened, about how she was officially poor and would probably have to eat totally fattening ramen noodles to survive, and to call her back right away, but then she paused. He'd hate her for being so pathetic. He'd hate her for being poor.

"Hey, it's me. . . . Just give me a call," Jack said simply after the beep. She snapped her phone closed, set her shoulders back, and elongated her neck. *Perfect,* she repeated silently to herself. *Perfect.*

Here's to the power of positive thinking.

tainted love

Home from a ten-mile run after practice, Owen peeled off his sweat-sticky Nantucket Pirates shirt and flung it over the new leather club chair that had appeared in the entranceway. He noticed a new low-slung white linen couch and chairs where the flea-ridden orange couch used to be. It was empty, save for a weird, metallic-looking pillow. Back in Nantucket, even though they'd lived on an acre of land, every night they'd always gathered in the comfortable sunken living room to eat chocolate kisses and share gossip-worthy nuggets of one another's days.

There are plenty of other girls who'd be happy to share kisses with him!

As Owen made his way to his bedroom, the doorbell rang. "I've got it!" he yelled, in case anyone was home. Back in Nantucket, people who came to the door often ended up living with them. One couple, Leon and Gary, had stopped by to ask for directions and had ended up moving in for six months, until they'd decided to move to Amsterdam to cultivate a tulip farm. They still sent four pairs of wooden clogs every Christmas.

"Okay, honey," Edie yelled back, and Owen could hear the

faint sounds of Buddhist chanting from behind the closed doors of her studio.

Owen made his way to the foyer, not bothering to put on a shirt. It was probably just Rhys, there to drop off another Speedo or whatever.

He flung open the door and sucked in his breath. The ethereal, blue-eyed goddess of his semi-pornographic dreams was standing directly in front of him. *Kat.*

Doesn't he mean Kelsey?

They stared at each other for a long, silent moment.

"Hey," she finally said, breaking the silence. "I heard you were living here. My mother was friends with Eleanor Waldorf. You know—the family who used to live here? We're neighbors! I'm just up on Seventy-seventh!" Her voice sounded overly cheerful, and Owen could tell she was nervous. Her silvery-blue eyes scanned his torso and she smiled, a little shyly. Owen picked up his shirt and put it on. It was still wet and clung to his body.

All the better to see your six-pack, my dear.

"What are you doing here?" he blurted out. It was so bizarre to see her framed in the doorway of his new home, after so many weeks of fantasizing about it. But she wasn't just Kat anymore, she was *Kelsey,* and he didn't even know who that was. "Funny running into you yesterday, *Kelsey.*" He had meant to sound sarcastic, but it came out sounding genuinely happy and polite.

Too much time spent around Mr. Manners.

"I guess I should introduce myself. I'm Kelsey Addison Talmadge. I never *told* you my name was Kat, remember?" A slight smile curled her lips, then disappeared as a serious look came over her face. Her skin was gorgeously tan against the deep green V-neck tank top. A hint of her perky B cups winked up at him. God, she was hot.

"I'm sorry. I needed to see you." Kelsey played with a large silver ring on her finger. "I couldn't stop thinking about that night on the beach. But then I felt so guilty, because I'd never cheated before—and never thought I would." Her blue eyes flashed earnestly. "I just really felt something when I met you, but the timing was all wrong and I was scared and we lived in different places. . . . That was why I didn't tell you my name; I just gave you my bracelet. I guess I hoped you would somehow find me," she finished with a shrug. Her eyes were pleading. "I'm sorry I lied. I'm not a bad person, really."

She looked so beautiful and sweet and sincere, and before he knew what he was doing, Owen pulled her into a tight embrace. He could feel her heart flutter against his chest. He put his hand on her cheek and breathed in her apple-scented shampoo.

"I'm glad you found me," Owen said, simply, not quite sure what to do next. Right now, hugging her was even better than all of the dirty dreams he'd been having.

Oh, really?

Owen's iPhone started to vibrate in his pocket. He pulled it out and looked at the display. Just as quickly as his heart had soared, it sank.

"It's a text from Rhys," he said, looking into Kat's blue eyes.

"You're friends with him?" she asked in confusion.

Owen shrugged. He read the text and wordlessly handed the phone to Kat. WANT TO JUMP OFF A FUCKING BRIDGE. WILL SETTLE FOR COCKTAILS. YOU HOME? I'M NEARBY.

A look of concern flashed across Kat's face. "I guess I shouldn't be here," she murmured.

Owen nodded in agreement, even though he wanted nothing more than for her to stay.

"Kat—I mean, Kelsey . . ." Owen corrected.

"I like being Kat with you," she whispered. "We can be whoever we want with each other."

Owen nodded. What she was saying didn't even make that much sense, but it *did* seem romantic.

The downstairs buzzer rang. Kat and Owen froze and stared at each other.

Owen's mind raced. "Wait in here," he said hurriedly, pulling Kat toward Avery's immaculately decorated room, a tasteful blend of beige and white and peony pink that Avery had ordered from some designer as soon as they moved in. He pushed Kat inside.

The buzzer rang again and he leaned in closer. Finally, they kissed. He'd meant it to be a peck, but by the time their lips met, it was urgent and passionate, and he wished he could just close the door and lay her down on the bed and . . .

Right, because that would be the perfect way to christen his sister's new six-hundred-thread-count Egyptian cotton sheet set from Bergdorf's.

His phone vibrated with another text.

AT YOUR DOOR. WHERE THE F ARE YOU?

"I have to go. Wait here until you hear us leave." Owen felt giddy with excitement and guilt.

"What are we going to do?" Kat asked, sounding like the damsel in distress Owen would do anything to rescue.

"We'll figure it out," he said determinedly. He kissed her one more time, and closed the door to Avery's room, his heart pounding.

"Hey, man." Owen opened the front door and grinned at Rhys way too eagerly. Rhys's eyes were red-rimmed and his skin was gray. He looked like he hadn't slept in weeks, even though it had only been a day since Kelsey broke up with him.

"Cocktail hour?" Owen cajoled.

Rhys cocked his head at his blond, tan friend, who was smiling and trying so hard to make him feel better. As if a bad draft beer would make him feel any better. He felt like *dying.* "I was standing outside her apartment for an hour. I saw her go out and walk uptown, but then I lost her, so I decided to come over here. I know I sound like a stalker," Rhys continued.

Owen winced. Kat was probably listening in the very next room. And Rhys did sound pretty stalkerish.

"I don't know where she could have gone."

"You're obsessing," Owen said, not unkindly. He leaned against the tall mahogany doorframe. "She was probably just going to a friend's house or something."

That's one way of putting it.

"I just want to know who's she's with." Rhys shook his head. "She said she'd met someone else. Who could it be?"

"Dude, I don't know," Owen said helplessly. He shrugged, and the sweat-sticky T-shirt suddenly felt extremely uncomfortable against his skin. "Let's go out. Everything always makes more sense over a few beers."

Cocktail therapy, anyone?

tea for two

The setting sun cast patterns of light on the dark blue, late-nineteenth-century Japanese carpets covering the gleaming parquet floors of Grandmother Avery's town house. Avery sat with Sydney Miller. Sydney Miller of nipple-piercing fame. Sydney Miller, the only guest at her tea party.

Just last year, this very room had been featured in *Vogue* after a Drama League party the elder Avery had hosted, and now, with files from the lawyer's office stacked in messy piles on the ground, it looked more like a museum installation that was in the process of being taken down.

Except with fewer people.

"Give me those." Avery pointed to the collection of delicate mini tarts decorated with tiny raspberries that sat untouched on a tray. The pink tray perfectly matched the Chanel suit she had borrowed from Grandmother Avery's closet.

Wordlessly, Sydney handed her the tray. Glasses of carefully prepared homemade iced tea sat untouched on the side table, condensation fogging their outsides. Avery had thought people could take them as they came in, and that serving iced tea would be a cute way to modernize the time-honored tradition of the tea party.

If cute servers came with the iced tea, that is . . .

"I don't think anybody's coming," Sydney said finally as she gazed around the room. The antique Chippendale chairs Avery had dragged over from the dining room were all lined up, facing the small wrought-iron balcony that jutted into the solarium from the second-floor study. Grandmother Avery had had it constructed for its sight lines—when the sun set, whoever stood there appeared to be illuminated. Edie had always scoffed that her mother had gotten the idea after seeing the musical *Evita*. Still, it was dramatic, and Avery had been planning to go up there and give a short speech, and then use the rest of the time to mingle and get to know the other Constance girls.

The doorbell rang. Avery shot an *I told you so* glance at Sydney and her matte-black lipstick, and sprang up from the oversize armchair. She winced in pain as her size nine feet strained Grandmother's size seven Ferragamo pumps.

If the shoe fits, wear it. But if it doesn't fit . . . don't.

She opened the heavy oak door to greet Baby, flanked by three dogs lined up in size order. "Surprise!" Baby smiled mischievously as a large poodle-cross wiggled his butt against Avery's bare leg, grinning and slobbering maniacally. Two tiny puggles were winding their leashes around the bigger dog's legs.

"What the fuck are you doing?" Avery blurted, pushing the dog away with her knee. Was this Baby's idea of a joke?

"Nemo, you freak, didn't you get enough of that in the park?" Baby wrestled the dog away. "I'm just heading back from the park. I was so close, I thought I should stop by. Do you want me to come back after I drop them off?" Baby held up the leashes. The large dog lunged toward Avery's crotch once more.

"No!" Avery cried, slamming the heavy oak door. She sighed wearily.

"Who was that?" Sydney yelled.

"No one," Avery replied woodenly as she reappeared in the sitting room. She grabbed another tart and nibbled on its edges.

"I told you, Bitch Central." Sydney joined Avery next to the dessert tray and popped a whole mini tart in her mouth. Avery could see flashes of her silver tongue ring as she chewed. *At least she came,* Avery thought.

"And there's no booze," Sydney remarked, picking up another tart. "These fuckers are good," she commented, grabbing two more.

"A kegger just didn't seem like an appropriate venue to discuss my plans to run for a school-sponsored position," Avery declared indignantly, pinning a stray lock of blond hair back into her bun. She collapsed onto a peach jacquard–upholstered wingback chair in exhaustion.

"Are you kidding? People would have come for a kegger. A tea party to talk about a school-sponsored position? Do you know how lame that sounds?" Sydney laughed dryly, then saw Avery's hurt expression and softened her tone. "Generally, around here, a party has boys, alcohol, a few girls passed out in the bathroom, and some majorly sketchy hookups going on," she said matter-of-factly. "They didn't do that where you were from?"

"Yeah, but that was *Nantucket*." Avery wrinkled her nose in distaste. She'd assumed she'd left those types of parties behind. Wasn't New York City supposed to be more *sophisticated*? Was that all her classmates cared about? Hookups and drinking?

In a nutshell, yes. Although we're very discriminating about who we hook up with and what we drink.

Sydney nodded and sat down on one of the chairs in front of Avery, as if she were a kindergartener listening to story time. "Why do you think I want to get out so badly? People here are so unimaginative."

"Then why did Jiffy and all those other girls say they'd come?" Avery stood to grab a cucumber sandwich. She couldn't bear to see the food trays looking so full.

"Because they assumed there would be boys and booze and the same type of thing they're used to at every party. Probably one genius was tipped off by the teacups, actually read the invitation, and spread the word." Avery sighed. "Can I ask you something?" Sydney continued without waiting for Avery's answer. "Why do you even want this position so much?"

Avery paused to think about it. She wanted to be SLBO because it seemed like something her grandmother would have done. Then again, maybe people were different in Grandma Avery's time—maybe they had a different idea of what constituted a good party, a good life, a good time. She remembered when Grandmother Avery brought her as a date to a holiday charity ball at the Met. She was six, and had worn a dark blue velvet dress from Bergdorf's. Impossibly tall Christmas trees surrounded the dance floor as Count von Arnim, a dapper Bulgarian royal and a friend of Grandmother Avery, whirled her round and round. She remembered peeking outside and seeing puffy snowflakes fall in the dark expanse of Central Park and thinking that Manhattan was the most magical place in the world. Did that world still exist?

"It's just important," she said softly, twirling the solitaire diamond pendant at her neck. Maybe New York had changed, or maybe she was going about things all wrong.

"Also, the outfit's cute, in this 'I'm on the board at the Met' way . . ." Sydney commented, gesturing to Avery's skirt. "But unless you have plans to host a charity luncheon, you should probably lose the suit."

Avery sighed and took off the beautiful pink suit jacket, laying it against the pink embroidered chair. She pulled the pins out of her hair and shook it out so the blond locks cascaded down her shoulders. She no longer knew what her grandmother would recommend.

"Want to grab a beer?" Sydney offered, making one more trip to the food table. "I sort of want to check out some strip clubs downtown. I'm thinking of doing some sort of independent study on female objectification this semester."

"No thanks," Avery declined, barely listening.

"Okay," Sydney said, unfazed. "Call if you change your mind—I'm starting at Scores!"

She made her way out the door, leaving Avery alone in the already-darkened solarium with the trays full of delicate tarts. Avery grabbed one more and glared, mutinously, at the still-full iced tea glasses, thinking of all the Constance girls who were supposed to be here, drinking out of them. She idly wondered where Jack Laurent and her bitchtastic friends were at this very second. Probably having cocktails somewhere and laughing at her sad attempt at popularity.

Then, just as quickly as her self-pity had come, it went. She stood and tossed the entire tray of tarts into the trash. She wasn't the Queen of Tarts, she was Avery fucking Carlyle, and she'd let those bitches know it.

Off with their heads!

partay part deux

On Wednesday morning, Avery changed into the gross blue and white Constance Billard gym uniform for her first gym class of the year. It was the day after her tea party disaster, and she was determined not to let that little blip color her entire Constance career.

She walked out onto Ninety-third Street, where the rest of the girls had gathered to jog over to the Central Park Reservoir. The gym teacher, Coach Crawford, was swinging a whistle around one finger. She had stringy brownish hair with gray streaks in it and was wearing a way too small tank top that showed off her cleavage. It looked like she had stuffed two grapefruits down her shirt.

"Hey." Avery was surprised to see Baby wearing a Constance Billard T-shirt and athletic skirt, especially since she had skipped French class that morning. On Baby, the gym outfit was so big it looked ridiculous but cool. Avery glanced down at her own uniform. Her T-shirt hugged her chest uncomfortably, making her look like a Midwestern cheerleader. They must have gotten their uniforms mixed up. "How's it going?" Avery asked.

"Another fun class with the Harpies," Baby said lightly. "What could be better?" She nodded at Genevieve and Jiffy. Surprisingly,

Jack was nowhere in sight. Coach led the group down Ninety-third Street toward Fifth Avenue.

"So, I was thinking we should have a party this weekend," Avery decided, glancing at Genevieve and Jiffy out of the corner of her eye. She liked the idea of having a second, real party. She would get Owen and Baby on board, so it would be just like old times, and Avery could use that night to lock in the student liaison votes. "No dogs allowed. But you have to come or else I'll disown you as my sister," she added.

"Sure, okay." Baby nodded, wondering how they were going to have a party when they didn't know anybody yet. The only person she'd really talked to here was J.P. But actually, maybe she could bring him to the party.

"Tall Girl and Shorty! Come on!" Coach growled as she herded the group to the crosswalk, her whistle twirling. *Tall Girl?* Avery sniffed. This was what they called personal attention in private school? There were *certainly* going to be some changes made when she got into power. Ahead of them, Jiffy and Genevieve bounced across the cross-walk.

"Hey, girls. Sorry you couldn't make it to my meeting the other day, but I'm having a party on Saturday night if you're interested," Avery announced, cornering Jiffy as they crossed into the park and the group started to jog up the concrete path to the reservoir. Jiffy's eyes widened.

She glanced at Genevieve, who smirked. "Who's going?"

Baby rolled her eyes and took off down the reservoir path, her hair streaming behind her. How could Avery go from hating these bitches to turning into their total best friends? She had never seen that side of Avery, and she wasn't sure she liked it. She didn't like anything about Constance Billard—or New York, for that matter.

Although the reservoir *was* actually really pretty—there was something dramatic about the skyscrapers towering above an expanse of lush green trees. It sort of expressed all the contradictions of New York: it was modern yet classic, enormous and yet so, so small. Not that she was actually starting to appreciate the city or anything.

Of course not.

"Well, I'm inviting a bunch of Constance girls and then some St. Jude's guys. My brother and I thought it would be fun if we could all hang out," Avery invented as she watched Baby tear down the path as if she really cared about running. The girls climbed the stone steps leading up to the reservoir and paused by the water fountain, pretending to get ready to run.

"You have a brother?" Jiffy demanded excitedly. Avery nodded. It was the same story back in Nantucket. Mention the promise of a boy, and suddenly all the girls came running.

"Yeah, Owen—he's on the swim team at St. Jude's, so a bunch of them will be there too," Avery mentioned casually. She shook her wheat blond hair out of its ponytail and tied it tighter at the crown of her head.

Sarah Jane and Genevieve sidled up. "So, where is the party?" Sarah Jane asked Avery, stretching her leg on wrought-iron fence surrounding the reservoir.

"My grandmother's town house on Sixty-first and Park. I hope you can come." Avery flashed a smile. "My brother is really looking forward to meeting all my new friends."

Avery took off after Baby. She could feel Jiffy, Genevieve, and Sarah Jane watching her curiously as she sprinted around the reservoir, and easily caught up to her sister. Popularity was sort of like fishing: all you had to do was bait the line.

Hook, line, and sinker!

gossipgirl.net

Disclaimer: All the real names of places, people, and events have been altered or abbreviated to protect the innocent. Namely, me.

hey people!

Is it me, or is it suddenly stressful on the Upper East Side? Overnight, people seemed to have gone from happily traipsing up Madison Avenue in their best summer frocks to scurrying back and forth from school, their foreheads knit in Botox-before-thirty consternation. And, as we all know, with stress comes difficulty sleeping. Let's take a look at some common high school nightmares to put our own lives in perspective.

4. **No date for the Gold & Silver Ball.** Your parents should be well connected enough to find someone you can go with, even if it is your second cousin Ned from New Jersey with a halitosis problem (that's bad breath for all you juniors who haven't started your SAT prep courses yet).

3. **Didn't get into a single college.** Well, we all know how that works out for some people. As long as Daddy has enough cash to sponsor a study-abroad winemaking program in France, you should be fine.

2. **Accidentally appearing naked in some horrific location,** like the Metropolitan Museum of Art or on some public transit ad that appears everywhere. Huh. That's actually a *goal* for certain girls . . . so, moving on to the number one fear . . .

1. **Having a party that no one shows up to.** If something this socially debilitating happens, most people would say you should immediately move to an island off the coast of nowhere . . . unless

that's where you already came from. However, if you're like me, you could say screw 'em. Screw 'em all! Which brings me to . . .

the energizer bunny

You know those people who just won't quit? They're the survivors—the Chers of the world, the tireless reality show contestants, the heavyweights who won't go down without a fight. Well, it seems like here on the Upper East Side, we have our very own heavyweight: feisty newcomer **A**. After a disastrous two-woman tea party last night, she's quickly rebounded, and was seen on the steps of a certain three-story brick school building this afternoon, excitedly spreading the word that she'll be having *another* party—this one bigger than the last. I should hope so! Hats off to her tireless efforts. We'll see how well they go over. . . .

sightings

A standing outside Constance Billard with a very scruffy **O**, staging a party-publicity blitz. Is *he* the party favor? Seems like a good strategy to me . . . Her classmates **G**, **SJ**, and **J**, sans their auburn-haired leader, staring at **O** hungrily. Down, girls . . . ! **B** buying a chai latte from **Starbucks** and promptly throwing it away. Have something better in mind? . . . **J** practicing her grand battements in Central Park, looking like she wanted to kick someone. Hard . . . **R** with an awkward goatee and a molester-mustache, trying not to cry. I know bad hair can be traumatizing, but really!

your e-mail

Dear GG,
So, my girlfriend says she's an academic lesbian, and she makes me wear shirts that say things like MY GOAL IN LIFE IS TO KICK THE

PATRIARCHY'S ASS. It kind of makes me uncomfortable. What should I do?
—Emo Boy

a: Dear EB,
If you're into her, I say, wear 'em with pride, even though personally, I think all T-shirts with slogans should be outlawed. And maybe you should start picking out a few T-shirts for her to wear. I like MY GOAL IN LIFE IS TO EMASCULATE MY BOYFRIEND. It has a certain ring to it, doesn't it?
—GG

q: Dear GGI,
I'm calling you Gossip Girl Impostor, GGI, because I don't think you're the real thing. First of all, it's weird that you say you're still around, because I'm pretty sure I know who the real Gossip Girl is and she is off at college. You even sound different. Are you, like, her little sister or something? Did she hand the job over to you? Or did you steal her computer? I bet you kidnapped the real Gossip Girl, and she's tied up in your basement or something creepy like that.
—Nonbeliever

a: Dear NB,
All I'll say on the topic is this: people always question whether Shakespeare really penned all the great works attributed to him. But we'll never know, will we?
—GG (no I)

q: Dear GG,
This girl in my ballet class has missed the past few classes. She's, like, supposed to be the next prima ballerina, but now our artistic director is getting so pissed about her attendance that she might

get kicked out. I think she probably had a nervy b from the pressure and is holed up somewhere eating cookie dough out of the tube. Do you know what's going on?

—Diva to Be

a: Dear DtoB,

Nervy b? Is that ballerina-speak for nervous breakdown? If we're talking about a gazellelike girl with perfect posture and to-die-for legs, she may be holed up, but I don't think she's about to hang up her pointe shoes anytime soon.

—GG

Okay, kiddies. I've found the perfect antidote to the almost-fall blahs—it's the Hotel Gansevoort rooftop pool. It's heated and glass-enclosed, and it's where I'm planning to spend every afternoon. Stop by and say hi!

You know you love me,

gossip girl

b runs with the big dogs

Baby made her way to the Cashman Complexes Wednesday after school, looking forward to some alone time with the dogs. Of everyone she'd met in the city, they were by far the most human.

Because that makes sense.

She spotted J.P. standing outside the building, his three dogs straining on their leashes. He smiled when he saw Baby, and she walked toward him, bending down to greet the eager pups.

"Well, they're all ready for you—they're so excited, it's almost as if they knew you were coming." J.P. smoothed a nearly invisible wrinkle on his olive J.Crew pants. "Mind if I come with you?"

"Kind of," Baby countered gruffly, straightening up. She thought getting back to nature with the animals might help her relax, but not if a pretentious tycoon-in-training was following her. She grabbed the three leashes and began walking ahead of him.

"I've just been stressed out recently. I thought hanging out with the mutts might do me good," J.P. said, walking quickly to match Baby's stride.

"They're not mutts." Baby glared at him. She wondered what spoiled J.P. could possibly have to stress out about, but she decided not to ask. The sun was already beginning to set, lacing the brilliantly blue September sky with streaks of goldfish-colored orange.

"So, Baby, how'd you get that name?" J.P. asked as Nemo stopped to sniff an elm tree on the corner of Fifth near the Frick Museum. The dog's shaggy blond behind twitched eagerly back and forth.

"Baby of the family," she began, giving a condensed version of the story, which she hated. Even though Baby was all for happy-go-lucky, anything-can-happen bohemianism, it was always sort of weird that no doctor in Nantucket had figured out how many babies Edie was going to have. "I was an unexpected surprise. I'm a triplet and my mom thought she was having twins. What about you?"

"My dad worked as a trader at J.P. Morgan Chase after business school," J.P. admitted.

Baby stared at him, then burst out laughing.

"Hey!" J.P. said in mock protest as they crossed into the Park. Ahead of them, the path split in several directions. "I didn't make fun of *your* name!"

"I apologize," she said contritely, pulling the dogs toward the grass. Darwin lifted a leg to pee, and Nemo crouched to take care of his business too. His butt was dangerously close to J.P.'s Jack Spade sandal.

"Shit!" Baby yelled automatically, then burst into giggles when she saw a coil of poop land on the shoe's leather strap.

"Shit!" J.P. repeated, looking down; then he laughed too. He grimaced as Nemo looked up at him innocently. He slid the sandal off his foot and hobbled to the nearest trash can, next to a green and yellow Sabrett hot dog cart.

"You didn't mean it, did you?" Baby cooed down at Nemo as the hot dog vendor glared warily at the drooling dog.

"I think he did. Nemo has *issues* with me," J.P. growled menacingly at the dog, who looked noncommittally back at him with his doleful brown eyes.

"It's not all about you." Baby turned, pulled the dogs back toward the bridle path, then looked back, smiling when she saw J.P. standing helplessly by the trash can with only one shoe.

"Come on—walking barefoot won't kill you." Baby pulled J.P.'s wrist. "As for your dog here, when was the last time he ran?"

"Ran?" J.P. looked down at Nemo blankly.

"See, your owner can't even remember!" Baby said in a playfully accusing voice to Nemo, who seemed to be smiling up at her. She looked over at J.P. "He's bored! Big dog's gotta run!"

Baby marched the dogs toward the fenced-in East Lawn, where people were sunbathing or picnicking, trying to enjoy one of the last warm-weather afternoons. She unhooked Nemo's leash, and he bounded around the perimeter of the grass, woofing maniacally.

"See, look!" Baby looked triumphantly at J.P., who was hobbling across the grass, one shoe on, one shoe off.

"I don't think dogs are allowed off the leash here," he said nervously, gesturing at a green and white sign posted on one of the fences surrounding the lawn.

"Live on the edge!" Baby burst into a run, chasing after Nemo and making barking sounds. J.P. tore off his other sandal and took off after them, stepping on beach blankets as he crossed the lawn. Finally, he cornered Baby and Nemo by an oak tree, where Baby had collapsed, panting, with the drooling dog standing above her.

"See, that's the type of workout they want. Not just marching around the block," Baby grinned up at J.P. The sky looked pretty behind them. Out of the corner of her eye she noticed an overweight pug trying to mount Shackleton. He was panting insanely and looked like his round eyeballs were about to pop out of his fat, smushed face.

"I think you need to have a girl talk with this one," J.P. noted, handing Shackleton's Louis Vuitton leash to Baby. His polo shirt had come untucked and he looked more casual and relaxed than the preppy red shorts–wearing guy Baby had met two days ago.

"And I think you better start wearing closed-toe shoes," Baby teased, leaning back against the oak tree. "So why's a guy like you spending time with a bunch of dogs, anyway?" she couldn't help asking. "Don't you have anybody better to hang out with? Morgan and Stanley? Some possessive girlfriend?"

J.P. shrugged, and eased down next to Baby by the foot of the tree. "These guys are easy to be around." He ruffled Nemo's blond fur. "What about you? Don't *you* have anyone better to hang out with?

"I just moved here, remember?" Baby retorted, pushing a stray lock of wavy brown hair out of her eyes. "Not that there's anyone here I'd actually want to spend time with," she muttered. She dug her heel into the grass.

"Hey," J.P. said seriously. He leaned back against the tree and his warm brown eyes searched hers. "Give New York a chance."

Sounds like he means give *him* a chance. . . .

Baby nodded slowly. Now that she was barefoot in the grass, the city seemed almost nice. If it weren't for the bitchy girls, the awful uniforms, and leaving her boyfriend behind, she might actually like it here.

Well, well. Look who's having a change of heart.

message in a bottle

From: Kelsey.Talmadge@SeatonArms.edu
To: Owen.Carlyle@StJudes.edu
Date: Tuesday, September 9, 9:05 p.m
Subject: Hi

When can I see you again?
xo,
Kat

From: Owen.Carlyle@StJudes.edu
To: Kelsey.Talmadge@SeatonArms.edu
Date: Tuesday, September 9, 9:15 p.m.
Subject: RE: Hi

I want to see you too, but it would kill Rhys.
I'm so sorry, but . . . we can't.

j takes care of business

On Wednesday evening, Jack stepped demurely out of the Cashmans' Lincoln Town Car. Jack, J.P., and the Cashmans were headed to a restaurant Dick had just purchased, Round Table. It was on Charles Street, a cozy street in the West Village that, despite having been filled with celebrity families and investment bankers, still retained the feeling of a bohemian and artsy neighborhood. J.P. looked stunning in his tailor-made suit, his brown eyes sparkling and complementing his ocean blue Hermès tie. Jack couldn't resist leaning into him as they walked in, making sure they were several steps in front of Dick and J.P.'s tacky Russian mom, Tatyana.

Jack stopped by J.P.'s this afternoon, hoping to spend time with him after not seeing him all week. He'd been out walking the dogs, but Dick had invited her to dinner, and now she was supremely glad she'd gone on a Barneys spree the day before school started, because she still had enough Jill Stuart, Phillip Lim, and Miu Miu to last her through the month.

Striding confidently down the cobblestone street, with her handsome boyfriend at her side, Jack was feeling better than she had all week. Avery Carlyle had announced today that she was having a *second* party, but really, Jack couldn't care less. It was actually getting sort of sad. Jack almost felt bad for her.

Almost.

Inside, the restaurant had heavy round oak tables and red leather–covered wing chairs. It looked like the setting for an F. Scott Fitzgerald novel, except for the super-skinny, pouty, all black–wearing waitstaff. They looked like contestants in an episode of *America's Next Top Skinny Bitch*.

The hostess escorted them to the center see-and-be-seen table and presented them with a bottle of Cristal. As Jack took a seat, her Treo vibrated in her emerald green Prada clutch. She slipped it out surreptitiously and glanced at the small screen under the table.

OMG HAVE YOU SEEN AVE C'S HOT BRO! CHECK IT OUT! read the text from Jiffy. Attached was a picture of an attractive blond guy with strong swimmer shoulders wearing a St. Jude's uniform. At the bottom was one line: WE TOTES HAVE TO GO TO HER PARTY!!!

Jack angrily slid her phone back into her clutch. Why the fuck were people so interested in Avery Carlyle and her lame attempts to be popular? There was no way that clueless wannabe even *knew* what a good party was.

Jack took a liberal swig of her champagne to try to calm her nerves. The bubbles danced down her throat, and she felt a tingly warmth spread through her. Avery didn't know what a good party was, but Jack would show her.

How generous!

"I've decided to have a party this weekend," Jack said, an idea forming. And then she had another brilliant idea. She was glad she had always been so polite to Dick Cashman, because this was the moment where it would all pay off. *Perfect,* she chanted to herself.

"You are?" J.P. asked.

"Yes. But I don't know where to have it that will be appropriate. You know, this isn't just a regular party, it's to announce my intention to run for student liaison to the board of overseers. It's a new position at school to uphold private school traditions, so I want somewhere that reflects convention but also modernity." Jack smiled confidently as she parroted Dick's new tagline for the Cashman Lofts, a luxury property in Tribeca that was set to open next month. She couldn't help congratulating herself on her quick thinking. "Cipriani is so overdone, and I don't want to rent out a club, which seems so *sophomoric*," Jack said as she drained her glass of champagne.

Tatyana nodded absently, blinking her vacant eyes and pretending to listen as she sneaked a whole roll into the small dog carrier. It was incredible that Tatyana and Dick had managed to have a kid who was as good-looking as J.P. Maybe that was why they'd only had one kid—they didn't want to hedge their bets.

"Hold on . . . convention and modernity," Dick said, grabbing half a roll and slathering it with butter, ruining the butter pad's delicate, flower-shaped design. Dick stuffed the hunk of bread in his mouth and gestured with the knife. "What about the Cashman Lofts?" His eyes gleamed as he snatched up the rest of the baguette.

"Oh, I couldn't," Jack said sweetly as the waitress refilled her champagne glass.

Yes, she could.

"It'll be great publicity. I'd love to have you kids make a splash. What do you think, J.P.?"

"It's not my party." J.P. shrugged and took one of the rolls in the center of the table.

"It's *our* party, J.P.," Jack giggled, giving Tatyana an *aren't guys silly but we love them anyway* look right before she shot J.P. a *what the fuck* glare. "The lofts sound perfect, Dick." She smiled, still feeling sort of squeamish uttering his name, even after all these years.

"Great, so it's settled!" Dick boomed. "Guess we have lots of things to celebrate, huh? I personally can't wait to try the steak— they're supposed to be getting the cows from the Cashman Ranch, but I'll be the judge to see if those Texas cattle are up to Cashman snuff," he declared jovially. "So, how many people are coming to this little shindig, anyway?" He gestured to the waitress, who quickly walked over, followed by the chef and his two sous chefs.

"Oh, you know," Jack began, not sure if she should lie and say the party was going to be an intimate gathering.

While Dick and Tatyana proceeded to order everything on the menu, Jack turned to J.P. "You could show a little more inter- est, you know," she hissed, annoyed that J.P. was acting so blasé about the party, as if he had better things to do. *Did* he have bet- ter things to do? "And where were you this afternoon, anyway? I've hardly seen you this week."

J.P.'s eyes shifted guiltily around the restaurant. Finally, they landed on Jack's manicured fingernails digging into the white linen tablecloth. "I had to walk the dogs. For my mom," he explained, even though that didn't really explain anything. Since when did J.P. give a fuck about the fleabags?

Just then, Darwin bounded out of his Louis Vuitton carrier and tore across the table to Jack, immediately planting a sloppy kiss on her face. The dog lunged at her again, scratching her cheek with an errant Swarovski crystal that was coming loose from his Gucci collar.

"Oww!" Jack cried. She put a hand to her cheek, shocked when she saw a splotch of blood on her fingers. "J.P.!" she screeched, pushing the dog across the table at J.P. For all Jack knew, she had rivulets of blood gushing down her face.

"You scared him," J.P. muttered, picking up the dog from the top of the table. He cradled him protectively, petting his wrinkled face.

"I am *bleeding*," Jack seethed. People turned to look, waitresses stopped in their tracks, and the head chef stood there looking positively horrified.

"Oh no," Tatyana said, fanning herself with a napkin. Jack pulled her own red silk napkin up to her face and held it tightly, in case she was hemorrhaging. She was practically *dying* while J.P. soothed a stupid *dog* he'd always said he hated.

"Aww, hell," Dick said as the waitress dashed to the back. "Tatyana doesn't do well with blood. You okay, Jackie, baby?" he asked, coming over to her side of the table.

"I'm fine," Jack said through clenched teeth. J.P. wasn't even looking at her. Instead, he was looking at his mother, who was hyperventilating as if she might faint at any moment.

"No, you're not," Dick retorted, and Jack felt one of his pudgy fingers rest on her skin and his yeasty breath near her face. She felt like she was going to throw up. "Honestly, I can't stand those fucking dogs myself, although she didn't mean any harm. It was just one of their damn decorations that Tatyana insists they wear on their collars." He continued to examine her face. "J.P., could you help Jack clean up? I'll take care of your mother."

"Of course." J.P. rose from his chair and held his hand out to Jack. He was the perfect gentleman as always, but Jack thought she detected a note of exasperation in his voice.

Jack's chair made a loud scraping sound as she pushed it back and held on to J.P.'s hand, gingerly walking to the ladies' room and smiling at the rest of the restaurant's patrons. She was injured, but she was going to make it.

Somebody get her a Purple Heart.

all the world's a stage

"I must admit, I don't know what Rhys is planning with the ridiculous costume he's wearing, but I would love to film it for the show," Lady Sterling said confidentially to Owen on Wednesday evening. Rhys had sprinted out of the locker room and asked Owen to meet him as soon as possible. He hadn't said anything about *costumes*, though, and Halloween was weeks away.

Lady Sterling ushered him into the expansive foyer. "Owen, dear, please do tell your mother I would love to see her. So glad she's come back to the fold, as they say!" She clicked down the hall, humming to herself.

Rhys appeared at the top of the red-carpeted stairs. "Glad you could make it, man!" he greeted Owen enthusiastically. He was wearing a cheap, light green suit that looked like it had come from the sale rack at Kmart. A patchy mustache was taped to his already stubbly face.

"What are you up to?" Owen demanded nervously. Did Upper East Side boys enjoy playing dress-up?

Only when it involves Upper East Side girls!

"I told my mom this was a swim team initiation. It's a little complicated," Rhys explained cryptically. He gestured Owen to come upstairs. His bedroom was cluttered with heavy antiques, making it look more like a guest room in a British manor house than a sixteen-year-old boy's room.

"First, clothing," Rhys said, holding a powder blue suit up to Owen.

Owen shook his head in disbelief. "You have to explain what that suit is doing in your closet." The suit was so stiff, it looked like it could stand up on its own. Owen held it up and looked at himself in the mirror in Rhys's white-tiled bathroom, then noticed the shelves of neat products lined up in size order over the sink. He picked up a red tube called You Rebel by Benefit and sniffed it cautiously. What was it for?

Rebellion, obviously.

"The suit? It's something my mom won from some charity auction. They auctioned off a complete *Saturday Night Fever* wardrobe." Rhys shrugged.

"Okay, good." Owen walked back into the bedroom, relieved Rhys hadn't actually bought the suit. "So what am I supposed to do with it?"

"Well, you're going to put it on, and we're going to take a walk over to Kelsey's apartment. Eees the perfect disguise," Rhys said in a weird accent that sounded like he had drank six tequila shots after having his wisdom teeth removed. He pretended to scratch his balls and smiled broadly. "Dude, I just need to know what guy she's with," he explained in a normal voice.

"And then you're going to take him on in pants that are twenty-three sizes too small?" Owen asked, looking at the hem of Rhys's ridiculous pants. They were about six inches too short.

"No, it's just that I don't want her to recognize me," Rhys

said, as if it were the most logical plan in the world. "You said you'd come. Dude, I'll buy donuts," he offered.

Owen looked into Rhys's imploring eyes, thinking about the e-mail Kat had sent him yesterday. God, he wanted to see her, but Rhys had actually cried into his beer the other night. What else could he do? "Okay," he nodded, even though he knew it was a very bad idea.

"Thank you," Rhys said, now all business. "So, I have this," Rhys began, pulling out another fake mustache from a heavy chest of drawers. The hairs had matted together in several places and looked like a collection of mating spiders.

"This is supposed to go near my mouth?" Owen demanded. The hairs on the mustache looked suspiciously pubelike.

"Yeah." Rhys grabbed it back and squirted a thin trail of a gluelike substance on it, then passed it back to Owen.

Owen shook his head and attempted to paste the nasty moustache to his upper lip. Next he changed into the awful suit. *I'm doing this for my buddy,* he reminded himself as he pulled the tight powder blue bell-bottoms over his striped cotton boxers.

"'Bye Mom!" Rhys yelled to Lady Sterling when they were at the front door. She was sitting in the living room, listening to loud bagpipe music while watching the dailies from *Tea with Lady Sterling.*

"If we're doing this, I need some liquid courage," Owen said, leading the way to the bodega they'd bought beer from before. They made their way past the wilted daisies sitting in buckets of muddy water and went straight to the back refrigerators. Owen picked out cans of Colt 45 and Olde English. The cans made wet spots on the sky blue fabric of his nasty suit.

The deli guy rolled his eyes at his costume, and Owen flashed him an embarrassed grin. Even though Rhys's plan was weird and stalkerish, it was also kind of hilarious.

"For the road." He handed Rhys a sweating can in a brown bag as they exited the bodega and walked past the town houses over to Fifth. The sidewalks were filled with moms and strollers, but no one gave them a second glance.

He cracked a can open for himself and chugged it, appraising his friend. "You do know how gay we look, right?"

"Yeah, you can be the boyfriend I met in Miami, okay?" Rhys laughed, but Owen could tell he was distracted.

They reached the corner of Seventy-sixth Street and crossed Fifth Avenue. They sat down on one of the concrete benches lining the high stone wall that separated Central Park from the street. From here they had a perfect view of the large apartment building Kelsey lived in, just across the avenue.

"I promised donuts." Rhys walked to the metal coffee cart on the corner. Owen surveyed his surroundings. The air had the promise of fall in it, and Owen noticed one lone maple leaf slowly make its way to the ground, where an overzealous five-year-old wearing a dinosaur-imprinted hoodie stepped on it.

"So, I'm guessing your buddies in Nantucket didn't make you dress up like Borat and stalk their exes." Rhys plopped a paper bag into Owen's lap. He slid companionably next to him on the wood bench.

Owen grabbed a cruller from the bag. "I actually didn't really have any guy friends in Nantucket," he admitted. He blushed a little, wondering if he'd revealed too much. "I mean, I guess I was just busy with girls and stuff."

"I always wished I could be more like that," Rhys said thoughtfully, taking another swig of Olde English. "I've always just liked one girl at a time." He gestured to the apartment building, where a formidably tall doorman was standing at rapt attention. Ten stories above, a sheer lilac curtain fluttered in an open window. Owen wondered if it was Kat's room, and how much time she and Rhys had spent there together. If Kat had cheated on him that summer, probably not that much, he thought. But then he felt bad for even thinking it.

"It's the small things I miss," Rhys said after a moment, self-consciously pulling down the legs of his pants, so they covered at least part of his ankles. "Like, she would always bring me Gatorade after practice. I know that's stupid. It was . . . just nice." Rhys scratched at his pant leg, embarrassed. He liked Kelsey because she brought him *Gatorade*? Rhys hoped Owen didn't think he was a total loser. He'd already dragged him all the way out here and made him wear a ridiculous costume.

Owen nodded politely, not taking his eyes off the window. As much as the topic made him uncomfortable, a part of him was curious to know more about Rhys and Kat. How long had they gone out? How far had they gone?

A group of middle-schoolers carrying skateboards walked by. They stared at Rhys and Owen and burst into laughter. Owen cringed, ready to take the suit off and forget this whole stupid thing. But then he realized, *This is what guy friends do. They're there for each other.*

Pube mustaches and all.

"I can't believe I'm telling you this, man," Rhys said. "But I guess since you're my boyfriend and all . . ." Rhys cracked a half smile. "Kelsey and I never did it. I wanted it to be special," he finished quietly, staring straight ahead.

"Oh." Owen paused in surprise, mid-bite, then took another

bite so he'd have time to think. So Kat hadn't lied on the beach when she'd said it was her first time. Owen wasn't sure if he should feel guilty or relieved. Or overjoyed. Or ready to kill himself because he was such an asshole.

"Well, maybe this was the best time for a breakup. You know. The fall is full of fresh starts and . . . and the best way to get over someone is to get under someone new?" It came out sounding more like a question than he'd meant it to. Maybe if Rhys got over Kat—*Kelsey*—he would be fine?

"Have you ever been in love?" Rhys asked, ignoring Owen's raunchy suggestion and looking deep into his eyes.

"Oh my God, you're so fucking gay," Owen laughed, hoping to lighten the mood. It was way too serious a conversation to have with the guy whose dumpage misery he was responsible for—especially in a polyester suit.

"Seriously. Like when all you want is to hold the other person. Like you can't stop thinking about them in the morning and at night, and dreaming about them," Rhys gushed, looking totally sincere except for the mustache that was half falling off his face and hanging over his teeth.

"Yeah," Owen agreed. He did know that feeling. He felt it for the same girl.

"I thought we'd get married someday. Have kids, you know?"

"Are you sure those pants won't make you infertile?" Owen asked, desperately trying to change the subject.

"Fuck you," Rhys said good-naturedly, taking another swig of his beer.

They turned back to the green-awninged building. A flash of blue appeared. It was a girl.

"Shit! It's her!" Rhys dropped the can of beer in his lap in panic. He grabbed it and put it on the ground next to him before any more could spill on the starchy green material of his suit. He already looked like he'd peed his pants.

Way to go deep under cover.

Kat was wearing a form-hugging blue dress, totally oblivious to their presence. She started to cross the street, her tan legs hurrying across before a car came.

"She's coming this way! Fix your 'stache," Rhys whispered furiously, brushing off his pant leg with one of the tiny white napkins from the donut bag.

Owen did as he was told, straightening his mustache and feeling the scratchy whiskers against his face as Kat walked closer and closer. She was twenty feet away, then ten, then five, and it seemed impossible that she wouldn't recognize them.

"Ahhh, yeah, baby. So, I'm thinking we can have our commitment ceremony on the beach, just the two of us, and then partay!" Rhys blurted out in a terrible accent. He turned to face Owen, a wild look in his eyes.

"Can you confirm my six-thirty pedicure today?" Owen heard Kat's lilting voice two feet away from them as she walked past, holding an arm up to hail a cab. He watched her blue dress swirl around her knees. A taxi pulled up almost instantly, and she got inside.

Rhys and Owen waited in silence until the taxi was out of sight.

"Aww, yeah, baby!" Owen yelled, high-fiving Rhys. It had been a close call. Kat had almost seen them. "These disguises are fucking awesome!"

"Nothing happened." Rhys shook his head despondently.

"Well, she wasn't with a guy, right?" Owen clunked his can

of beer awkwardly against the one Rhys was holding. "Listen, I'll help you find a new girl. You know, just someone to have fun with. Take your mind off things," he added hopefully.

Rhys took a swig of Olde English and tried to ignore the dull pain in his heart. Maybe Owen was right. Maybe he did need to find a new girl. Actually, the more he thought about it, the better it sounded. As soon as Kelsey saw him with someone new, she'd be so jealous she'd beg him to come back. A smile spread slowly across Rhys's face. It was such a perfect plan. "You're right," he said, feeling better than he had all week. "Thanks, man."

"No problem." Owen watched Rhys's face light up, feeling pretty good himself. He'd clearly overestimated how broken up Rhys was. Rhys had been through the worst of it, and just getting him out there, meeting some new girls and having a good time, would do the trick. Soon Rhys would be over Kat, and she and Owen could be together. Everyone would be happy. Owen was so excited he couldn't resist giving Rhys a beery hug.

"Get the fuck off me, dude," Rhys burped cheerfully.

Next on *Tea with Lady Sterling*: my gay son's big fat gay Key West wedding!

j is shaken, not stirred

Jack rode the M4 bus up Madison to J.P.'s apartment late Thursday afternoon, trying not to touch any possibly germy surfaces, silently cursing her father for leaving her so destitute she couldn't afford cab fare. She and Genevieve had gone to Bergdorf's after school to buy party outfits, but Jack had quickly discovered that shopping knowing she couldn't buy anything was like being on Atkins, surrounded by pastries.

There was no way Jack could have gone home, where Vivienne had been chain-smoking Gitanes in bed for three days straight, wearing an eye mask and speaking loudly on the phone in French to pretty much anyone who would listen, including the second of Charles's three ex-wives. Jack hated all of the pathos and ennui of it, which she knew her mother secretly loved. Vivienne had even suggested that Charles was right, and that Jack *did* need to learn how to suffer. Well, fuck them.

Once she saw the sign for Sixty-eighth Street through the driver's window, she pressed the dirty yellow tape strip for the bus to stop, holding her hand away from her body in case she contaminated herself. She shook out her auburn hair and walked regally down the bus's black rubber steps, hoping the Cashman Complex doorman didn't happen to be looking down the street. She bounded into the ornate entrance, her black Tory Burch flats thwacking against the polished marble floor, and nodded confidently to the doorman.

"Miss Laurent," the doorman acknowledged as he waved her in. Jack felt a wave of relief. It wasn't as if she *looked* poor. She pushed the button for the private elevator and hurriedly stepped in, eager to feel J.P.'s arms around her.

Frances, the Cashmans' unsmiling maid, let her in. Jack glanced around the entranceway at the shiny black marble floors, the huge plate glass windows, the gold umbrella stand. She used to cringe at the penthouse's mishmash décor and tacky pieces, wishing that J.P.'s family could be more *subtly* rich. But today the opulence just felt overwhelming. She tried to steady herself as she climbed the spiral staircase that led to J.P.'s top-floor bachelor pad.

"Hey." He was wearing a red Lacoste polo and pressed Ralph Lauren chinos. He smiled, irresistible dimples forming in both cheeks. "You're looking pretty. Did I get it right?" J.P. teased as he ushered her into his bedroom and closed the door. Every time she saw him—floppy brown hair with a perfect side part, intelligent brown eyes, chiseled jaw, and a body made for rugby or squash—Jack felt like everything was right in her world. He was the prince to her princess. And this weekend they'd be hosting a party, showing all the world how *together* they were.

"Are you okay?" J.P. asked, brushing a lock of auburn hair off her face.

"Fine," Jack lied. "Just stressed out with ballet." She ignored the momentary flash of guilt that shot up her stomach. J.P. had fallen in love with her before she got all moody and depressive and poor. She needed to be the girl she was just a few days ago. That was the girl he loved. And surely she'd be that girl again soon.

She hugged him, inhaling his usual scent of Ralph Lauren Romance, and then gave him a slow, smoldering kiss. She took a step toward the bed and slowly unbuttoned her cardigan, locking her green eyes with J.P.'s brown ones and giving him what she hoped was a sultry, come-hither look.

Just then, the door flew open and Dick Cashman burst in. A skinny, bespectacled male assistant trailed behind him, wearing cowboy boots that matched Dick's.

"Holy mother of hell!" Dick twanged when he saw Jack hastily pull her cardigan around her shoulders. "I'll let you kids get decent!" He slammed the door as Jack hastily smoothed her blouse. It wasn't like they were *doing* anything.

Not yet, anyway.

"I guess I should see what Dad wants." J.P. shrugged and opened the door.

"I'll come," Jack groaned. It would be supremely slutty to just hang out in her boyfriend's room after being discovered in a compromising position. She pretended that she was Grace Kelly. Surely the Prince of Monaco's father had walked in on her and the prince back when they first hooked up, right?

Would that have been the afternoon Princess Grace drove off a cliff?

"So, about the crapper," Jack heard Dick's voice boom from down the hall as he gave his assistant the grand tour. "NASA designed it. Normally, they're only on space shuttles. I saw a documentary about them and thought, 'Fuck me, I'll buy one!'

Custom made just last week!" J.P.'s father loved to buy ridiculously expensive toys and useless gadgets. But, unlike her father, at least *he* supported his wife and family.

"Hey, Dad," J.P. interrupted as he descended the steps from his suite into the foyer. Jack lingered up above. Even from ten feet up, she could see Mr. Cashman wink at his son. Jack buttoned her cardigan all the way up to her neck, trying not to feel embarrassed.

"Sorry about the interruption," Dick chuckled, striding toward J.P. His male assistant's cowboy boots made loud clicking sounds on the newly polished floors. "But I wanted to show you what the dogs dragged in." Baby Carlyle, her high cheekbones streaked with dirt, peered from behind Dick's bulk.

Surprise!

"Hey!" Baby greeted J.P. enthusiastically. She pulled her tangled hair into a ponytail on top of her head and grinned mischievously. "Sorry I'm late to pick up the dogs, but I found the best place for them to run. It's Fort Tryon Park in the Bronx, and it's awesome. Nemo would love it! I was just telling your dad about it."

"Sounds great for the bitches!" Dick Cashman leaned down to pet Nemo. "Want to take the chopper up there?" Dick offered.

"No!" J.P. said awkwardly. Jack narrowed her green eyes at Baby, who hadn't even noticed she was standing at the top of the stairs. What the *hell* was that skinny nobody doing in her boyfriend's apartment?

"Okay, well, whatever you kids want," Dick Cashman sounded disappointed as he tromped away toward the labyrinthine hall that led to his office. His assistant practically ran after him.

"Thanks!" Baby smiled affectionately at Mr. Cashman's

retreating back. She hadn't known what to make of J.P.'s dad at first, but the more she talked to him, the more she loved how random and tacky Dick was. Even though he was one of the wealthiest men in New York, at least he was having fun with his money instead of just using it to make other people feel bad.

"So, you're here to take the dogs?" J.P. asked stupidly. He sounded weird, and the peach fuzz on the back of Baby's neck stood on end in warning. She looked up to see Jack Laurent at the top of a spiral staircase, glaring down at her. She wore a cashmere cardigan buttoned high up her long, graceful ballerina's neck. She radiated evil.

Jack slowly descended, her chin held high, and stood beside J.P. proprietarily.

"Oh, uh, Jack, this is Baby. She's been helping out with the dogs."

"We've met," Jack said icily, narrowing her eyes. When J.P. had said he was walking the dogs yesterday, had he been walking them with *Baby Carlyle*? Was *that* what he had been doing all week after school? "And we have the dogs taken care of today," she added coolly.

Look out, pups, you're about to see a catfight!

J.P. coughed and took the leashes away from Baby. "Yeah, sorry for not telling you sooner," J.P. said, but he didn't make eye contact. Shackleton whined. "Is it all right if you get paid tomorrow?"

Baby looked from J.P., who was staring straight down into Nemo's tangled fur, to Jack, whose arms were folded across her chest.

"Sure, that's just fine." Baby's voice dripped with sarcasm. She saw exactly what was going on, and if he wanted to play that game because he feared the wrath of his alpha girlfriend, she wasn't going to stop him. "I'll stop by tomorrow for the check." She stomped off, surprised at how hurt she felt.

As she emerged from the Cashman tower, Baby pulled out her cell to dial Tom, and wished for the millionth time that she was there or he was here. It clicked to voice mail immediately and she hurried downtown in the growing darkness, wondering why she suddenly felt lonelier than she had all week.

Poor Baby.

"So your dad *hired* Baby Carlyle?" Jack asked sweetly, once J.P. put his drooling, smelly labradoodle and pugs in the dog playroom all the way on the other side of the apartment. She walked over to the terrace and opened the sliding doors. There was a cool breeze and she could see people walking in and out of Central Park. She belonged up here, not in some musty garret full of castoffs. Her heart slowed down. Everything was *fine*.

Doesn't she mean *perfect*?

"Yeah. To walk the dogs. Is everything okay?" J.P. asked as he sat down at one end of the low-slung, ultramodern calfskin couch. The Cashmans' study was a huge, multilevel room with tall bookcases full of gilt, unread first-edition volumes. The walls were flanked with statues and frames of varying sizes, mismatched so that a Chagall hung next to a Seurat, which hung next to a portrait of some medieval dude with a scepter and doves flying around his way too small crown.

Jack turned away from the terrace and walked over to the hammered steel wet bar. She knew she could always call Roger, the butler, to pour them drinks, but it was so much more romantic to mix them herself. She felt very Upper East Side wifey, welcoming her husband home after a long day.

"Are you sure Baby Carlyle is okay?" Jack demanded, splashing Bombay Sapphire and tonic in two highball glasses.

"Why wouldn't she be?" J.P. shifted on the couch, watching Jack swirl the concoction.

She smiled sweetly as she handed him his drink. "She's in one of my classes at Constance. Apparently she's mentally unstable. Her sister said she had some type of problem." Jack shrugged casually, taking a seat on J.P.'s lap.

"She seems fine," J.P. answered, sliding Jack onto the couch.

"Looks can be deceiving." Jack tried to sound unconcerned but really, inside she was sort of freaking out. Why the fuck wasn't J.P. ravaging her right now? Did J.P. want to walk dogs with some fashionless, skinny nobody like Baby? And why were the Carlyles trying so hard to ruin her life?

She took a sip of her drink and examined the heavy crystal glass she was holding. Her surroundings suddenly seemed so opulent. The gold everything she'd never even noticed before suddenly felt so out of reach. It just wasn't fair. A frustrated tear began to slip down her cheek. She wanted to punch something.

Doesn't she mean someone?

"Are you okay?" J.P. asked. "Look, Baby was just walking the dogs. It's not a big deal."

"I'm not crying over *her*," Jack wailed. "It's just . . ." She really was losing it.

"What, then?" J.P.'s eyes searched her face.

"There was just this dress," she invented, realizing how stupid she sounded as soon as the words left her mouth. But she couldn't admit that she was threatened by a dog walker. Or tell him that her friends couldn't stop talking about Avery Carlyle's brother. Or about her father not paying for ballet. About her melodramatic mother and her musty garret apartment. After all, who wanted to be seen with a poor *loser*?

But crying over an imaginary dress is okay?

"A dress?" J.P. pulled his hand off her back. "You're *crying* over a dress?" he asked in disbelief.

"I'm not crying!" A small tear slipped down her cheek.

And the Oscar goes to . . .

Jack gazed at J.P.'s broad, handsome face, wanting him to understand. But she still couldn't bring herself to tell him the truth. She wiped her tear away with a pearly pink–manicured finger. "I wanted to wear it to the party," she added.

"What does it look like?"

She furrowed her brow thoughtfully. "It's . . . pink," she said, thinking of the frilly dress the five-year-old who'd moved into her town house had been wearing. "With puffy sleeves. And a white sash."

"Okay," J.P. said slowly. "Barneys?"

"Yes." She snuggled into him. Just being near him made her feel so much better.

"I'll get it for you. But you shouldn't worry so much about the small things." J.P. pulled her tightly into his strong chest, and Jack rubbed her cheek against the soft cotton of his polo shirt. "If you keep stressing over the small things, the big things will kill you."

You think?

b makes a hasty exit

For the fifth and hopefully last day in a row, Baby put on the hideous Constance Billard seersucker skirt and waited in the enormous, uncluttered kitchen for Avery and Owen to walk to school. She wasn't sure why she had even bothered to stay in New York this long. J.P. had been the only person she had met who made it seem like maybe, just maybe, the city would be different, and now she'd discovered he was the same as everyone else.

"So, I got a call from Mrs. McLean at Constance Billard. You skipped some sort of service hour?" Edie walked into the kitchen wearing a flowy white skirt, with blue Bic pens holding her hair into a semblance of a bun.

"Yeah, it was a stupid misunderstanding," Baby said breezily. She didn't want to go into detail. It would be so much easier dealing with all of this once she was back in Nantucket.

"Mmm-hmmm," Edie agreed. "I can imagine Mrs. McLean would be more strict than what you're used to, but really darling, swearing in French? Can't you think of more creative ways to get in trouble?" She sat down on a stool next to Baby, stroking her long, tangled brown hair. "If you need to shake things up, do it right." Edie nodded sagely, stood up, and floated out of the room, like some sort of psychedelic fairy godmother, off to dole out advice to the next wayward person who needed it. Baby paused. Had moving to Nantucket all those years ago been Edie's way of shaking things up?

She sighed, looking around their expansive new kitchen. Back at home, the kitchen was always a gathering place, but so far no one had even cooked here. She sat on one of the sleek metal bar stools lined up by the sleek black granite counter. She pulled her hair into a sloppy side ponytail and hit speed dial 1 on her cell.

"Hey, Babe," Tom said in his sleepy-stoner voice. It had been her favorite thing to wake up to during the summer.

"Hey!" She tried to sound upbeat as she grabbed an orange from the carved teak bowl on the counter and poked through the skin with her thumb.

"Morning." His voice was gravelly. She could hear his car horn beep and wished he were turning the corner of her street in his dusty Cougar, ready to drive her to school.

Baby sighed. The last morning they'd spent together, they'd been up all night. Last Friday, they had lasted all of five seconds at a crowded club in the Meatpacking District. After making a hasty exit, they'd giggled as they ran across the avenues, stopping in Gray's Papaya on Sixth to share a hot dog and then making out under an awning by the Coffee Shop in Union Square. By the time they began to make their way home, the sun was rising and they'd gotten free muffins from a friendly vendor at the green-market. It all seemed so long ago.

"So, what crazy adventures have you gotten yourself into, hippie girl?" Tom asked. Baby bit down on a section of orange. It was embarrassing to admit that so far, the highlight of living in the most exciting city in the world was walking some spoiled Upper East Side kid's dogs—for free.

Not exactly the glam life.

Just then, Avery and Owen burst into the kitchen, talking excitedly.

"Okay, write down your list of people. Swimmers in green pen. Actually, any athletes in green pen. Everyone else in blue." Avery amended, frowning at a clipboard as if she were working the door at Bungalow 8. All she'd been able to think about for the past two days was her second party and how much better it was going to be than her first. First of all, there would be actual alcohol, and second of all, there would be boys—the two key ingredients to winning over all the Constance girls.

Amen.

Baby turned to the corner so she wasn't interrupted. "Not too much is happening here. The usual, I guess. So, what's going on with you?" she asked, trying to keep the conversation light.

"Hey, hold on. . . ." There was static at the end of the line. Baby held the phone closer to her ear. Everything in Nantucket just felt so . . . far away. "Sorry, I'm actually picking Kendra up right now so I sort of have to run. I'll miss you tonight."

"Why can't you have the party on Saturday night? I could come then," Baby pleaded.

Avery stopped mid-sentence with whatever she was saying to Owen, something about getting his teammates to be extra friendly. She wrestled the phone away from Baby and put the little Nokia to her ear.

"Tom? Yeah, Baby won't be coming up for the weekend. She has a party she has to attend here on Saturday. Looks like it'll just be you and your bong." Avery grinned wickedly.

"Give it back!" Baby hissed at Avery as she yanked the phone away. "Sorry about that. So, can you change the party to Saturday?" she asked, lowering her voice. She hated to sound like she was begging, but she'd rather spend eight hours traveling on a gross Greyhound bus to be by his side at the bonfire than go to Avery's trying-to-fit-into-Bitch-Central soiree.

"Oh man, I totally would, but everything's set. We've got the kegs, we've got the food, and it's all ready, you know?" Tom said. In the background she could hear a car door open and slam.

"I guess so," Baby replied woodenly, not really understanding why Tom couldn't just move the party. What else did the Nantucket kids have going on Saturday night? Baby slowly put her orange down, surprised at herself for thinking that. It was as if she'd absorbed the bitchy attitudes of the girls around her.

Didn't we tell you it was contagious?

"Hey, Babe, I gotta go," Tom said abruptly. "Have fun and stay out of trouble." He hung up. Baby listened to the silence on the other end of the phone for a few seconds, then slowly put it back into her messenger bag.

"So I already told all the guys about it, and they're totally down for the party," Owen stroked his new blond goatee. He grabbed Baby's orange and dug out a few sections. He looked surprisingly good with his half beard, like an actor in a Shakespeare film.

Or a pirate. All he was missing was a peg leg.

"You're having a party?" Edie drifted back into the kitchen at the sound of chattering voices. "Where will it be?" she asked, leaning on the countertop and absentmindedly rearranging the fruit into a haphazard pyramid. She was no doubt thinking about the summer solstice party she'd hosted last year, where everyone had ended up in a drumming circle on the beach.

If you substitute "black-tie gala" for "drumming circle" and "beach" for "town house," it's *sort of* the same thing.

"Well, I was hoping to do it at Grandmother's house," Avery began, knowing her mother wouldn't say no. She'd toyed with the idea of renting out a club and had even visited a few Meatpacking District hot spots. But then she realized clubs were for people whose apartments were too small to have *real* parties, and Grandmother Avery's town house had already been home to so many historic soirees. Besides, who didn't love a house party?

"That's a terrific idea!" Edie clapped her hands together, her ever-present turquoise bracelets jangling. "I'd love to invite some people—when are you thinking?"

"Saturday," Avery admitted, adjusting her jewel-embellished gray Marc Jacobs headband in her thick blond hair. Even though Jack Laurent had announced that *she* was having a party that same night, Avery was not about to change her plans. It made her all the more determined to throw the best party the Upper East Side had ever seen, and show Jack once and for all that she meant business.

Edie's face fell. "But that's the opening night of the chinchilla exhibit. I got together with one of my old friends, Piers Anderssen? He's now a Brooklyn experimental artist, but he just went with it. He turned his whole apartment into an indigenous rain forest that will be open to the public on Saturday night. I need to be there."

"That's okay!" Avery said quickly. She loved her mom, but her eccentricities had been weird enough in crunchy Nantucket. Besides, it wasn't going to be a mingle-with-parents-as-you-sip-tea kind of party. She'd already tried that approach and wasn't going to make the same mistake again.

"Okay." Edie frowned. "It's nice to hear you kids are already fitting in."

"Thanks, Mom." Avery kissed her mom's peppermint-scented cheek and motioned for her brother and sister to follow her out the door to school.

It was weird to walk to school together, Baby thought as they got into the elevator. It reminded her of elementary school.

"So, back to the party," Avery said as the elevator doors opened into the lobby. "I really need to know who's taken and who's available and—"

"You know what? I need to stop and get some juice. I'll catch up with you," Baby said when they were outside. She didn't want to listen to Owen and Avery chatter about the stupid party.

"Are you sure?" Baby saw a flash of sisterly concern run across Avery's face, but it quickly disappeared. "Okay, see you later." She shrugged.

Baby bought a lukewarm tea from a street cart on Fifth and loitered until she lost sight of them. She deliberately walked uptown slowly and entered the Constance doors just as the first bell rang. She walked into French class a few minutes late, without even stopping by her locker to grab her textbook. Madame Rogers already hated her, so the chance she would be called on was next to nothing.

"Vous êtes très en retard," Madame Rogers said sternly. *You are very late.* She didn't even look up from the board, where she was explaining the subjunctive.

"Doesn't she mean retarded? Look at her shirt!" Baby heard Genevieve whisper to Jiffy.

Even Avery didn't look up.

"Je m'excuse," Baby muttered, walking over to take a seat by the windows.

"Vous devez vous rendre dans le bureau de la directrice." Madame Rogers stood in front of Baby's desk. *You must go to the headmistress's office.* "You cause disruption or you don't bother to show up. You're not welcome in this class anymore," she said firmly. Baby looked up. She hadn't been expecting to be kicked out of class, especially when she hadn't done anything. Her face burning, she stood, ready to stomp down to Mrs. M's office.

"Comment dit-on loser?" Baby heard Jack whisper as the door closed. Baby shook her head. Forget about waiting for three strikes—she was out now. She walked down the hall to the deserted lobby, practically slamming into Mrs. M.

"Baby, it seems we had a miscommunication and you didn't quite understand that our student service hours are mandatory. I want to remind you that they are. I'm looking forward to seeing you this afternoon." Mrs. M smiled at her with her warm brown eyes, still giving her the benefit of the doubt. If Baby didn't hate it so much here, she would almost like Mrs. M. But she knew what she had to do.

"I won't be able to make it. *Ever.*" She didn't turn around to see the look of shock on Mrs. M's face as she walked toward the door. "Sorry." Once the door closed behind her, she skipped down the steps and let out a piercing whistle. A cab screeched to a stop as all the girls in the first-floor classrooms turned to stare out the window.

"Port Authority," Baby said smoothly to the cabbie, rolling down the window. Mrs. M had arrived at the top of the imposing Constance stairs and was staring down at her. Baby gave her a small wave, then leaned her head back against the leather seat.

That's one way to make an exit!

gossipgirl.net

hey people!

The first week of school is over and it's time to regroup. Maybe you had a fashion faux pas, maybe you've already made a fool of yourself in class, or maybe you were so hung over you didn't even make it to class. No worries. Who doesn't make a mistake once in a while? (Except maybe me.) Take the weekend to enroll in a crash course in reputation rehab.

You know how in the women's magazines we pretend not to read, there are always articles titled "Get a Guy by the Fourth of July" or "Ten Steps for Perfect Skin"? I'm not promising anything. It's not like we can erase the past, so if you *did* commit a faux pas, you're going to have to live with that for years to come. But if you do what I say, maybe you won't have to eat lunch hiding out in a bathroom stall for the rest of your high school career.

1. Find a member of the opposite sex and start a hot-and-heavy relationship—very publicly. There's no better way to make people forget one juicy piece of gossip than by giving them another to talk about.

2. Damage-control your style. Keep wearing whatever you're wearing—originality is key—but always keep some standards. Make sure you always smell good (there's plenty of room for deodorant in your locker!) and have great shoes, even if you're wearing mom's seventies castoffs.

3. Party like a rock star. Become the person everyone wants to hang out with. That shouldn't be too hard, right?

And speaking of partying, we have two soirees on our hands. Inquiring minds want to know which one I'll be attending. Well, just like buying a beachfront bungalow on St. Barths, it's all about location. Throwing a bash at a club gets you attention, but do you honestly really care if the kids in Duluth, Minnesota, are jealous of you because they saw the pics on Gawker? Remember, the Internet doesn't forget, so sometimes discretion *is* key. Then again, you're pretty much guaranteed that someone will end up hooking up on your bed. The best of both worlds would be, of course, to throw your bash at an exclusive hotel that hasn't yet opened to the public. Never-been-slept-on beds with five-hundred-thread-count Egyptian cotton sheets, a fully stocked bar, and no rules? Does it get any better?

In a word: no. Which is why the ever-crafty **J** has scored the above option—at *the* most talked about complex in New York. It's an all-green building complete with recycled-rainwater waterfalls in all rooms. Going green has never been hotter. Count me in!

And count one homespun New England girl *out*. Iced tea and spectacular architecture can't compete with eco-chic. **A** better forget about her party and hope for an invite to **J**'s. Or she could just console herself with a nice cup of tea. . . .

sightings

R in the self-help section of the **Barnes & Noble** on Eighty-sixth, reading *You Just Don't Understand: Women and Men in Conversation*. I could make myself available if he needs an interpreter. . . . **A** and **S** in the computer lab. Looking up lesbo porn, you two . . . ? **B** on the Greyhound to Boston. Leaving so soon? Who's going to walk the dogs . . . ? The pierced, tattooed **S** again at **Toys in Babeland** at a "Literate Smut: How to Read Erotica" lecture. Sounds educational!

q: Dear GG,

Why are you always hating on **A**? Are you **J**? Or *B*? Actually, I heard **N** spent some time in Nantucket this summer. I bet you're just a scorned lover and that's why you have it in for **A**. Even if you're not, it's weird that you don't mention all those people you were so obsessed with for so long.

—Curious

a: Dear C,

Sorry to disappoint, but I am neither **J**, **B**, nor **N**. And while I'll always have a special place in my heart for **N** and his glittering green eyes, I've got two new obsessions: **R** and **O**. Keep up, people. Times change.

—GG

q: Dear Gossip Girl,

I live on the West Side and I was taking the bus home late from a study session and I saw this group of preppy guys with bizarre facial hair sprinting across the transverse toward the duck pond. What the hell?

—Study Girl

a: Dear SG,

You were at a study group till late? It's the first week of school! Unless you're studying the anatomy of a specific male, you need to lighten up or it'll be a loooooong school year. As for what you saw . . . well, it *is* almost a full moon, so it's either werewolves or some lame sports-team initiation. Next time, ditch the study session and investigate!

—GG

q: Dear Gossip Girl,

I just moved to the city with my three kids, and I've hardly seen them since I got here. Back in my day, we were going out to Studio 54 and hanging out with Andy Warhol and the rest of the Factory—making art! Now everyone just seems to be running around, trying to hook up with each other. Where's the creation?

—KEEPTHEARTINHEART

a: Dear KTAIH,

Don't be so down on our generation. We put our hookups on the Internet so other people can watch. Life as art is very hot.

—GG

q: Dear GG,

I'm having a party this weekend. Want to come? Everyone else is coming and I'm going to have a Dance Dance Revolution competition.

—PARTAYLIKEAROCKSTAR

a: Dear PARTAY,

Tempting, but I think my social calendar is a little bit full this weekend. From what my sources tell me, there's not one but *two* great parties shaping up that I simply must attend. Good luck at the competition.

—GG

Oops, I'm late for my ginger-rub massage at Bliss. Keeping up with you people is exhausting! See some of you (all the important ones, anyway) at the super-exclusive party at the most luxurious new property in Tribeca. Hint: I won't be wearing super-tight pants, a cowboy hat, or toting any furry friends.

You know you love me,

gossip girl

if not now, when?

From: Kelsey.Talmadge@SeatonArms.edu
To: Owen.Carlyle@StJudes.edu
Date: Friday, September 12, 3:00 p.m
Subject: Now?

o waxes on love . . . and other things

"You ready?" Rhys came over to the row of lockers after swim practice on Friday. He was fully dressed, his brown leather Tumi messenger bag slung over his shoulder. Owen furtively slid his iPhone back into his pocket. He'd just received an e-mail from Kat, and even his fingertips were tingling just thinking about her. "I made an appointment for us," Rhys said mysteriously.

"Okay." Owen raised his blond eyebrows suspiciously, remembering their stakeout from the other day. He instinctively looked at Rhys's bag, as if expecting to see a starchy seventies suit or a bushy fake mustache peeking out through the zipper.

"So, my times this week have sucked," Rhys began, pausing when he saw Chadwick and Hugh walking out of the locker room together. Chadwick's mustache seemed to have irritated the oozing crop of acne by his nose, and Hugh's bushy beard made him look like a brown-haired version of the fisherman on the frozen fish sticks box.

Come on, who doesn't love a guy in foul weather gear?

"Man, I've gotta break the streak." Hugh lewdly stroked his beard and glared at Rhys. "Dude, if you don't hook up with a chick, I'll do it for you. I'm serious." He widened his eyes crazily.

"It'll happen, man. " Rhys nodded confidently.

Owen smiled inwardly. *Atta boy.* The power of positive thinking.

"Anyway," Rhys continued once Hugh and Chadwick were out of earshot, "I think for Coach to take me seriously as captain I need to streamline a little bit." He whispered, as if he were relaying top-secret information.

Owen wondered if he was talking about one of those weird diets Avery was always on, like the one where she had to only drink water with cayenne pepper and lemon juice for a week, but then got so hungry that she went to the Nantucket Bake Shop, bought a Boston cream pie, and ate the whole thing.

"Would you go waxing with me?" Rhys asked as they walked out of the Ninety-second Street Y and into the sticky late-afternoon heat. "I'm really sucking right now, and I'm thinking the hair is really slowing me down," he added. Owen stopped in his tracks. He knew some guys liked to shave before big meets at the end of the season, but during the first week of practice? And *waxing*? It sounded really painful.

"This place is supposed to be really good." Rhys pulled out a wrinkled pamphlet from his messenger bag and handed it to Owen. "The results last for up to four weeks without any stubble," he explained, sounding like he was quoting the purple and pink paper in Owen's hand. "It's much better than shaving."

"Don't you mean much gayer than shaving?" Owen retorted. Using fruity products in the shower was one thing, but actually paying money for a service that sort of sounded like torture made Owen seriously uncomfortable.

"I'll treat you," Rhys pleaded. Owen paused. It wasn't like he had anything else to do this afternoon, and hanging out with Rhys would keep him from giving in and seeing Kat. God, being good was hard.

And being bad is so much more fun.

Owen rolled his eyes but found himself softening. "Okay, fine. But if you start waxing your eyebrows or getting facials, I'm going to have to stage an intervention," he said with a smirk. He glanced at Rhys's even complexion and realized that Rhys probably did get facials.

"Dude, this isn't about upkeep, this is about swimming," Rhys protested, taking the flyer from Owen and putting it back into his bag as they walked south down Lexington.

"Whatever you say," Owen agreed good-naturedly. He noticed two girls walking down the street wearing white polo Seaton Arms uniforms and elbowed Rhys sharply.

"Great," Rhys nodded, smiling. He didn't even notice the girls, who had paused on the other side of the street, waiting to cross.

Owen shook his head. He was *hopeless*.

"I made us appointments for three-thirty, so we should probably take a cab." Rhys stepped off the curb and boldly flagged one down. He gave the cabbie a Midtown address. Owen slid in beside him and looked at his arms thoughtfully. He had never really noticed his arm-hair before. It was white blond and pretty inoffensive.

"Here we are," Rhys said, sliding out of the cab and handing the driver a twenty. "Keep the change," he muttered as they walked through the doors of the J. Sisters Salon.

"You have appointment?" A stern-looking woman in her

sixties surveyed them. Her hair was pulled back so tightly her eyes looked as if they were going to pop out.

"Yes, the name is Sterling," Rhys announced confidently. Wordlessly the woman gestured behind her to a tiny lilac and pink waiting room.

They took seats on the petal pink leather couch and Owen flipped through magazines, glancing at *W* while they waited for Rhys to be called in. The couch was incredibly comfortable, and Owen felt surprisingly relaxed. No wonder girls loved going to the spa. They were playing the same type of relaxing, flowy, Enya-type music his mother listened to while doing yoga, and the air smelled great: a combination of lavender and cinnamon.

"Ricey?" a tiny, strong-looking Brazilian woman in a blue uniform demanded in a lilting voice, poking her head into the room. Her forearms were huge, as if she could bench-press two hundred, easy.

"Go get 'em, honey," Owen called as Rhys followed her into one of the waxing rooms. He looked down at his Adidas slides and noticed a patch of thick, curly brown hair on his big toe. He experimentally tugged at one of the longer ones and was surprised at how much it hurt. Thank God he was only there for moral support.

"Are you done with that?" A tall brunette with her hair cut in a cool, asymmetrical bob that skimmed her chin gestured toward the magazine in Owen's hand. Owen looked up and realized they were the only two people in the waiting room. She stood above him, and Owen's eyes were immediately drawn upward to her chest. She was pretty, with toned, volleyball-player arms and a graceful collarbone. Not to mention some really terrific boobs.

"Of course," he said, handing her the issue of *W.*

"Thanks." The girl took the magazine and sat down next to him, her tanned calf briefly grazing Owen's hairy leg. Owen pulled back self-consciously.

"Do you come here often?" She raised one perfectly groomed eyebrow at Owen suggestively. One of her eyes was blue and the other was brown, but it somehow made her look quirky and cute rather than freakish.

"No, I'm just here with my buddy, Rhys. We're on a swim team," Owen explained. She would be cuter if her hair weren't hanging in her eyes, he decided.

"Really?" she asked, a smile playing on her coral lips. She pushed her hair back from her face as if reading his mind. "So what does that mean?"

"Well, the extra hair can kind of slow you down in a race," Owen began. "So if you want to get faster, you can shave off a ton of time by streamlining," he parroted back Rhys's explanation.

"That's fascinating!"

Owen couldn't tell if she kidding or not. He tried to imagine himself kissing her, his lips pressed against her coral ones, but couldn't. He heard a *riiiiiip* sound from the other room, and that's when it came to him: he should try to hook her up with Rhys. It was perfect—they could go waxing together.

The couple that waxes together stays together.

Owen smiled and turned on the charm. "Yeah," he said. "It was Rhys's idea. He's an amazing swimmer. He's the captain of our team," Owen announced proudly.

"Captain, huh? What school? I go to Darrow," She named the small, redbrick hippie school down in the village where seniors were taught in the same classroom as kindergartners. Edie had been raving about it until Avery found their crappy college placement list online. Only one kid had gone to an Ivy League school in the last five years.

The girl stuck out her hand and tucked her legs behind her on the violet couch. "I'm Astra. Astra Hill."

"Owen Carlyle. Nice to meet you," he said. "And it's not like he's some dumb jock. He's fucking brilliant. Like, probably the smartest guy I've ever met," Owen went on randomly. He was thrilled to see a flicker of interest in Astra's mismatched eyes.

"How long have you known him?" she asked. With the soft music playing in the background and their hips practically touching on the cozy velvet couch, it felt like they were on a date at one of those restaurants that seated couples side by side.

Owen thought back. "About a week." He self-consciously touched the scruff of beard he was growing in solidarity with Rhys. "It seems like so much longer."

"God, you must really like him," Astra noted, looking a little disappointed. "Do people know?"

"Know what?" Owen was confused.

"About you guys?"

"I guess so," Owen said in confusion, not sure what she meant. Behind the desk the receptionist was flipping through a magazine and surreptitiously listening to their conversation.

"That's great," Astra said. "You know, I always thought these Upper East Side schools were so snobby and limited, but that shows that there's really hope. Maybe you guys could come speak to our Queer and Questioning group over at Darrow. We're always looking for people to share their experiences." She nodded encouragingly.

"Sorry?" Owen asked. He'd been distracted by Astra's cleavage busting out of her yellow sundress.

For research purposes only.

"I mean, I just thought that St. Jude's might not want to have such an out and proud couple leading the swim team. But I think that's great!" She sounded like she was praising a three-year-old for having done an exceptionally good job at putting his shoes on the right feet. She took his hand and squeezed it. "I call myself flexual, because I don't want to label my sexuality and possibly limit an experience. You know, I really admire your bravery. . . ." Astra trailed off, looking searchingly at Owen's face.

"Oh, it's . . . we're not . . . gay!" Owen stammered, feeling the tips of his ears turn red against his white blond hair.

"Oh," Astra said. She flopped back against the velvet seat and let go of Owen's hand.

"But . . . I mean . . . Rhys has a lot of feminine qualities." Owen tripped over the words. He meant that if Astra wanted a gay boyfriend, Rhys was even better than a gay boyfriend because he was, well, *not.* It just didn't make sense when he tried to say it out loud.

"What do you mean?" Astra asked, her words clipped.

"I mean, he's just my buddy," Owen said, deciding to fall back on the truth. "Rhys just got out of a long-term relationship so he's a little fragile."

"Oooh, that's terrible," Astra cooed earnestly. "Why did they break up?"

"Oh, just the usual. They, uh, wanted different things." Owen tugged at the collar of his white-collared shirt. The room suddenly felt twenty degrees hotter. There was a stifled cry from one of the back rooms. He hoped Rhys was okay in there.

"Are you single?" Astra raised her eyebrows suggestively.

"Nope. I mean, not really. One of those complicated situations."

He could feel Astra's eyes boring into him. *Lock it in, Carlyle,* Owen thought as he willed himself not to think about Kat's curvy body in his arms. He had to talk Rhys up so this Astra chick would forget about her flexuality and realize that Rhys had everything she wanted—in one convenient package!

Somebody's got a calling in online dating profiles.

"Rhys could have any girl he wanted, but he's just a one-woman guy," Owen continued. It was so awkward to pitch another guy's great qualities. He really did sound kind of gay.

"I like that. A one-heart, one-love man." Astra nodded in approval.

Rhys emerged from the waxing room, looking completely pale, his skin blotchy under the lopsided, Super Mario–style stubble that stood out against the head-to-toe smoothness of the rest of his skin.

"I just need to sit down." He collapsed in the seat next to Owen. "And drink a bottle of hundred-proof vodka." He smiled weakly, not noticing Astra.

"Your friend is a big baby," the waxer said disgustedly, pointing at Rhys and handing him a small patterned Dixie cup of water from the cooler in the corner. "But look at the improvement!" She pulled up his white Lacoste polo to reveal red, perfectly hairless skin on his chest, then slapped him, creating a painful white hand mark. Owen winced.

"Oh, poor baby," Astra cooed. "Want to come with me to Pinkberry? It's important to have a positive sensation after a negative one, you know?" Rhys smiled at Owen, and Owen gave him a discreet thumbs-up.

"That sounds great, actually," Rhys nodded. "Rhys Sterling," he said, extending his hand. Astra took it eagerly.

They began to talk, and Owen pulled out his iPhone. *Soon,* he e-mailed Kat. An e-mail immediately flashed back: *Can't wait.*

Owen smiled. Waxing was awesome. Totally fucking painless!

"You." The Brazilian woman pointed at Owen and beckoned him into a lilac-painted back room.

Until now. *Rrrrip!*

the secrets-and-lies issue

Jack climbed the stairs exiting the subway at Union Square on Friday afternoon. She was on her way to Peridance, where there was an afternoon professional-level barre class that only cost seventeen dollars a pop, or sixteen dollars each if you bought a book of ten. She was determined to stay in shape, even if it meant taking bargain-basement classes at grimy downtown studios. Her phone rang in her pocket as she crossed Sixteenth Street.

"Hello?" she answered curiously. She hadn't recognized the number.

"Dick Cashman here!" a voice boomed. Jack hadn't spoken to J.P. at all today. He'd been moody and silent for most of dinner last night, and Jack had made up for it by allowing Dick to refill her wineglass a few too many times.

"So, you kids are all set for tomorrow night. We've got the bar up and running and a special section of rooms just for you. You should be good to go, Jackie baby!"

"Oh, that's too much," Jack cooed appreciatively.

Too much is never enough.

"No problem, love helping out the ladies in my life. Now just don't burn the place down. Insurance, you know." He hung up and Jack turned to walk in the opposite direction, back to the uptown subway. Who gave a fuck about ballet? It wasn't like missing a few days of classes would matter. Besides, it was the weekend and she'd had a very rough week. There was an adorable pair of gray suede Manolo boots at Barneys, and she still had a gift card from her last birthday. She deserved a present.

Feeling relieved, she hardly even noticed the subway ride back uptown. It was going to be so much fun to host a party with J.P., like the true power couple they were, and would be forevermore.

BITCHES, WHERE ARE YOU? she texted Jiffy as she emerged from the subway, feeling giddy. Coming to the Upper East Side from anywhere else in the city had always reminded Jack of the moment in *The Wizard of Oz* where everything turns Technicolor. On the Upper East Side, the sidewalks seemed brighter, the buildings seemed shinier, and everything just seemed better.

That's because it is.

JACKSON HOLE, Jiffy texted back, which happened to be the grossest diner in all of Carnegie Hill. The air felt cooler all of a sudden, and Jack pulled her black Ralph Lauren cardigan around her shoulders. Fall was her favorite time of year. It was a season for renewal, and her life was slowly getting back on track.

She got to Jackson Hole on Second Avenue and Eighty-third Street, where Jiffy, Genevieve, and Sarah Jane were crowded into a booth in the corner. "Party time tomorrow night, ladies," Jack grinned, shooing the middle-aged waiter away without ordering anything. This was not the weekend to get fat.

"Where is it again?" Genevieve asked. She flipped her blond

hair over her shoulder. Her white Calvin Klein blouse was buttoned up almost to her neck.

"Cashman Lofts, in Tribeca." Jack grinned wickedly at them. In a way, she was grateful for pathetic Avery Carlyle and her attempts to become popular. She was the kick in the butt Jack needed to stop crying over her misfortunes, get her shit together, and reassert her dominance over the social scene.

"And I'm not having it at my house, because I don't want you puking vodka cranberries on my mother's bed." Jack narrowed her catlike green eyes at Genevieve. "Again," she added, remembering how last year Genevieve had hooked up with another one of her father's lame young actor connections who'd been in town for some experimental play reading. She'd gotten totally drunk and puked all over Jack's bathroom. It was disgusting.

"Whatever, it's not like you never got drunk," Genevieve retorted as she bit into a large onion ring. The grease on the plate glinted in the late afternoon sun that streamed through the windows. Suddenly, Jack felt voraciously hungry. She grabbed two onion rings and shoved them into her mouth, enjoying the salty taste.

"Could we maybe stop by Avery's party first?" Jiffy rolled a slightly deflated cherry tomato around her no-dressing green salad and then popped it into her mouth. Jiffy was perpetually on a diet to get rid of the five pounds that stood between her hips and her 3.1 Phillip Lim jeans.

"Of course not." Jack felt a wave of annoyance. Why were they even talking about this girl? "Who actually wanted to go?"

"Well, she has a hot brother." Jiffy shrugged.

"Okay, so you go and hook up with the hot brother. Report back to us." Genevieve pulled a Marlboro Red out of her

Longchamps hobo bag and lit up. She looked around, daring anyone to reprimand her.

Just then, Avery Carlyle herself walked by, enormous Dean & DeLuca bags swinging on her slender arms. She looked as carefree as ever. Jack narrowed her eyes. How could she possibly look so calm when her social demise was so completely imminent?

"Avery!" Jack called commandingly. Avery turned, her blue eyes opening wide in confusion. Her face reddened for a second, but then she squared her jaw and marched over to the table.

"Jack." Avery steeled herself and stood at the table. Anyone would think that they were all friends, a perfect picture of the New York City private school world. She surveyed the four girls, pleased when Jiffy at least gave her a small half smile. Maybe they *could* all be friends? She smiled warmly back. All this situation required was some grace and poise, even though she felt Jack's hostility. What was Jack's problem, anyway? It wasn't like Avery was out to steal her boyfriend or anything.

Because really, who would do that?

"Avery," Genevieve dripped sweetly. "So glad to see you."

Avery was suddenly reminded of a documentary she'd seen about shark attacks; they surround their prey before tearing them apart.

"So, where are you off to?" Jack asked. "Don't you have something to steal or some Constance community service to go to? Oh, right," she pretended to remember. "That's your sister."

Avery smiled sweetly, keeping her cool. "I was just picking up a few things for my party tomorrow night. I would love it if all of you came." She looked directly at Jack. She could feel her heart thumping in her chest, but her voice was steady. Grandmother Avery would have been so proud of her grace under pressure.

She saw Jiffy nod, and felt a glimmer of promise. If she could get Jiffy, maybe the other girls would follow.

"I know that in Nantucket you were Miss Crab Queen or whatever, and don't worry, you'll probably still hold that title here," Jack began. Genevieve and Sarah Jane giggled. Avery flushed. Back in eighth grade she'd been crowned Miss Nantucket Lobster Queen. How had Jack found out about that? "And I got the memo that your grandma was a big deal in the fifties. We all saw the costume retrospective at the Met three years ago. Who cares? Go write a Rizzoli art book about her or something, but stop trying to be her." Jack stood up so that the two girls were facing each other, eye to eye.

Avery seethed. Fine, Jack could be a bitch to her, but to make fun of her dead grandmother? She felt her eye begin to twitch, a warning sign that tears were about to flow. "The party is at eight. Here's the information." She coolly handed out the printed flyers Sydney had helped her make in the Constance Billard computer lab during lunch. She had to admit, they looked fun, edgy, and totally professional—much better than her teacup gimmick.

"Saturday?" Jack pretended to study the purple and white flyer. "As you've undoubtedly heard by now, I'm having my own party that night, otherwise I would have loved to come. But you and Sydney will have fun together, I'm sure." Jack took a celebratory onion ring from Genevieve's plate and chomped on it, blinking at Avery with a bored smile.

"Have fun at your party, Jack," Avery said calmly, amazed at her poise. "If any of you change your mind, you've got the info. See you." She stalked off, ignoring the giggles behind her. She made it half a block over to Park Avenue before the tears began to fall.

Avery leaned against a sandstone building to collect herself. When she looked downtown, she could see the graceful arc of the Chrysler building reaching up to the sky. She squeezed her eyes shut, the tears blurring her vision so that all the buildings radiated light. Grandmother Avery wouldn't just give up. She'd turn up at Jack Laurent's party looking fabulous and poised and steal all the desirable men from Jack and her friends. Or she'd make sure the party never happened in the first place.

Avery marched determinedly downtown to the empty town house and booted up her computer, realizing how stupid it was not to own a fucking BlackBerry. Nantucket social engagements could be planned in a day planner, but here, she needed something immediate. She logged onto the Constance Billard home page and searched the directory for the address of Jack Laurent, half hoping it would be in some godforsaken place like Queens or the Upper West Side. Instead, the address was listed as Sixty-third between Fifth and Madison—right by her grandmother's house.

She flew out of her building and practically ran down to Jack's. She rang the doorbell, pressing her pale pink–polished finger against the bell over and over again. Finally, a little girl wearing a silver tiara and a flouncy purple tutu over a patterned Oilily dress came to the door. Her pale blond hair was pulled into a neat braid down her back.

"Is Jack home?" Avery asked sweetly, hoping she had the right house.

"Who's Jack?" the girl asked in confusion. Avery stared at the girl's light blond hair and realized that she looked nothing like Jack. She felt her face turn red again.

"Jacqueline Laurent?" Avery asked in confusion. "Is your mother home?"

"Is Jack the name of the lady who lives in the attic?" the girl lisped, chewing on the end of her flaxen braid with her one front tooth.

"I don't think so. . . ." Avery trailed off. *The attic?*

A tall, stunning woman wearing high-waisted gray Theory pants and a crisp white Ralph Lauren button-down came to the door. Her flawless skin made her look like she'd stepped out of an Estée Lauder ad. She squinted at Avery in the late afternoon sun.

"I'm sorry," Avery said in her most sophisticated voice. "I'm looking for Jacqueline Laurent. She gave me this address."

"We just moved in. She lives upstairs now," the woman said shortly. She pursed her collagened lips and eyed Avery up and down disparagingly before exhaling a deep, dramatic sigh. "It's a rather unique situation that I can certainly tell you I didn't sign up for. Satchel can show you where she is, but in the future, I will remind Jacqueline and Vivienne to inform their guests of their proper address," she said crisply.

"Okay, " Avery agreed, confused. What other address could they possibly have?

"Satchel, baby, can you show this nice lady upstairs?" the woman asked, dropping to eye level with the girl and over-enunciating her words. Satchel nodded solemnly, as though she were used to her mother making everything sound like a press statement.

Satchel held out a tiny, sticky hand for Avery and led her through the apartment, bypassing a huge kitchen with two Sub-Zero refrigerators, an ornate dining room and living room with Louis XIV furniture, and past two mahogany staircases spiraling upward toward the back of the house. The town house certainly looked more put together than the Carlyles' new apartment had when they'd first moved in. They'd torn through all the boxes hap-hazardly on their first day, when no one could find Rothko and Edie had been convinced someone had packed him by accident.

"I just started kindergarten," Satchel said importantly as they traipsed through room after cavernous room. "It's good but it's hard. We only have one nap time and one snack, but I have seventeen friends!" she said proudly.

"Wow, that's a lot," Avery said, using her *I really don't talk to little kids very much but I'm going to try to sound enthusiastic* voice. "I don't have as many friends as you." Admitting that made Avery feel instantly lame.

"How many do you have?" Satchel pressed.

Avery remembered back to kindergarten, when it was all so easy. There had only been twelve kids in their class, so she and Owen and Baby had pretty much ruled the social scene, despite the weird organic snacks their mother always packed for them. When had everything become so complicated?

"I have twenty-five friends," Avery said, making up a number. She couldn't believe she'd just lied to a five-year-old. Luckily, Satchel wasn't even listening, and scampered ahead of her, sliding on her lacy pink socks.

"Here it is," she said solemnly, opening a door and pointing to a rickety set of wooden stairs. "I would be scared to live in the attic," she added in a whisper.

"Me too," Avery agreed. She stared at the nondescript white door that was clearly some sort of servants' entrance. This was where the infamous Jack Laurent lived? Did her friends know? If it hadn't all been so bizarre, Avery would have laughed.

"Can I go now?" Satchel asked. Avery nodded, hand poised to knock on the door.

"Will you be my friend?" Satchel asked seriously, before leaving.

"Sure," Avery smiled.

"Yay! I'm going to tell my mom I have eighteen friends!" Satchel yelled, carefully holding on to the railing as she walked down each step.

Avery started to knock on the door, slowly at first, then more incessantly. The door resounded hollowly. Finally it opened, and there was Jack in pink Juicy sweats and a white Michael Stars T-shirt. Her mouth dropped open when she saw Avery.

Jack started to close the door in Avery's face, but Avery held it firmly open. Jack's heart thudded in her chest, but she tried to maintain her poise. *Perfect, perfect, perfect,* she chanted to herself and tried stare Avery down with an ice princess glare.

"What are you doing here?" she asked coldly.

"I wanted to drop by to let you know I've canceled my party," Avery said very slowly, dripping with fake friendliness. "Since it's silly for us both to have one on the same night." She tried to peek beyond Jack to get a sense of what the apartment looked like. A scratched hardwood hallway flanked by ugly blue bookcases led into a small, yellow-painted efficiency kitchen. Beyond that Avery could see a living room with dusty blue couches that looked like they'd been involved in an L.L. Bean factory explosion. A cracked Pottery Barn umbrella stand holding a broken black umbrella stood by the entrance.

"Okay," Jack spat back, "I know you want to be my friend, but, honestly, this is a little bit pathetic." Her voice rose nervously despite herself.

"So, this is where you live? It's nice. You must hang out here all the time with Jiffy and Genevieve." Avery made her voice perky, because this was just too good. With its dim light and slanted ceilings, it would be a realtor's nightmare to spin the space into anything other than what it was.

Um, an attic?

"Not like it's any of your business," Jack said haughtily, "but my mother and I are currently in the process of redecorating. We want to make sure everything is handled correctly, so we're staying here rather than at a hotel. It's *temporary*." Jack emphasized the last word, wishing it were true. She saw that Avery didn't look convinced. "One of the workers must have let you in."

"A little girl let me in. She said she lived here," Avery said slowly, wanting to corner Jack and force her to admit her lie.

"Well, I guess she was trying to pretend to be someone she wasn't. Just like some people I know." Jack refused to open the door any further. They were both standing precariously on the top step. Avery could feel a splinter from the unfinished stair railing try to wedge itself into her pinky.

"That's funny, because I spoke with her mother too...." Avery let her voice trail off leadingly.

Jack opened the door a crack and leaned against the wooden doorframe, unable to believe this was happening to her. Avery knew everything, and unless Jack wanted her to run her self-important mouth off to all of Constance and beyond, she would have to cave. A little.

The way the floors are caving?

Jack sighed. "I was just talking with my boyfriend and we agreed it would be much more convenient for us if we had our party in October." Jack sniffed. "So if you still wanted to have your thing tomorrow night, that would be fine."

Avery nodded noncommittally, even though her heart already felt like it was doing a victory dance in her chest.

"I'll tell my people to come," Jack continued. "Does that sound okay?"

"Okay," Avery agreed, trying hard not to smile. She wondered if they would hug and make up.

Kiss, kiss, *kiss!*

"See you tomorrow?" Jack narrowed her eyes, hoping it sounded more like a threat than an affirmation. The last thing she needed was Avery Carlyle suddenly thinking they were friends. Already, an idea was beginning to form in her head. Avery could have her amateur house party. Maybe everyone would come and it would be totally out of control. They'd trash old Dame Avery's *spectacular* town house!

"Of course." Avery smiled sunnily. Now she could *really* get started with her plans. "See you tomorrow!" she trilled, and trotted down the stairs and out the side entrance.

Avery breathed deeply as she emerged onto Madison Avenue, letting the crisp fall breeze whip through her thick blond hair. She couldn't help smiling. Grandmother would be so proud. By next week, she'd be the new toast of New York. Just what she'd always wished for!

You know what they say: be careful what you wish for. . . .

there's no place like home

Baby stepped off the ferry on Friday night and inhaled the scent of the sea-salt air, the wind tousling her wavy brown hair as she made her way up the dock. She pulled off her itchy Constance Billard blazer and threw it into the ocean, where it bobbed on top of the water for a few moments, then sank out of sight.

Baby stood next to the tollbooth that led to the line for the ferry and waited for someone to ask her where she was going. On the island, everyone hitched, and she felt much more at home flagging down a random car than a New York City cab. Within two minutes a rusty red Dodge pickup with a missing headlight stopped and a cute twentysomething guy wordlessly opened the passenger door, motioning for her to get in. This was what she loved about Nantucket: it was a real community, and when you needed something, people were friendly.

"Coming from Boston, huh?" the guy asked as she closed the heavy truck door. He was wearing a faded gray UMass T-shirt, and his skin was ruddy pink from the sun. He looked like a lobster.

Watch out for the claws.

"Not really," Baby replied, looking down and realizing how absurd she must look in her uniform skirt.

"Okay, so where are you off to?"

Her phone beeped, and she looked down with annoyance. J.P. He'd called three times since she'd been on the bus. Couldn't he just find another dog walker? Or maybe his girlfriend could take the dogs out for him? No, that would mean changing out of her bitch suit for five minutes, which was impossible. She picked up the phone and answered in annoyance.

"Hey, I'm done with the New York experiment," she began, not waiting for him to speak. "I'm back on Nantucket, so you should just find a new dog walker, someone who can accommodate you better with cheaper rates." She hung up before she could hear him say anything. What would be the point?

"Ex-boyfriend?" the driver asked.

"Absolutely not," Baby said, jamming her phone into her faded green Jansport so she wouldn't even have to think about it. She gazed out the window at the sprawling farms and tidy New England colonials in muted shades of white and gray. Home. She was finally back home again.

"Well, I'm getting off around here, so thanks for the ride!" Baby chirped as they rounded a familiar corner.

The driver pulled over and she hopped out of the car on one of the side streets near Tom's house. It led directly to the beach, and she half sprinted down the uneven wooden steps to the sand, her messenger bag thumping against her back. She could already see the bonfire near the water and paused for a second at the sight of all her NHS classmates stumbling around in various stages of undressed drunkenness.

Baby made her way down the beach and recognized Lucas

Anderson, one of Tom's friends, before she heard Tom's familiar half snort, half chuckle that sounded like a guinea pig being squeezed. He only made that noise when he was really high. Tom and Lucas were sitting on a damp piece of driftwood, apparently unaware that the tide had risen up to their ankles. Lucas was wearing Birkenstocks over thick, oatmeal-colored socks and was picking out the same four chords of "Free Falling" over and over again. A three-foot-high bong constructed of plastic soda bottles sat between them like an old friend.

Time to run, not walk, back to civilization!

Baby walked quietly over to them, stepping over the driftwood and shivering in her underwear as she sat next to Tom.

"Baby?" Tom blinked a couple of times as he tried to determine if she was real or just a stoned illusion.

"I'm here," Baby said simply. She leaned back into his arms and let his fingers tickle her gently. He took her face and guided her mouth to meet his. He smelled like Tide and the ocean and a little bit of pot. His pupils were huge, but Baby wasn't annoyed. She felt a little high too, just from being around him. It just felt so good to finally be back in the only place she wanted to be.

"I can't believe you're here," Tom said incredulously in his stoner voice. Lucas just stared at them, his mouth agape.

"Let's go for a walk," she suggested, half dragging Tom away from the log. The sky was pitch-black, but the moon created a path of light across the inky water. Baby took Tom's hand in hers, her whole body tingling with excitement.

"So, are you here for the weekend?" Tom asked, taking a joint out of his pocket and lighting it.

"For this weekend and the foreseeable future!" Baby smiled at him, swinging his arm giddily with hers.

"Okay," Tom said slowly. He stopped and ran his fingers through her tangled hair. "So where are you going to stay?" he asked, in between kisses.

"The guest cottage," Baby said, as if it were obvious. She and Tom would live together, happily ever after.

Aren't fairy tales grand?

"What about school?"

"It's only been a week. I'm sure I can get caught up," Baby said playfully, though she was sort of annoyed. Why couldn't he just enjoy having her here?

"Okay," Tom said again. "What do you want to do?"

Did she need to spell it out? She squeezed his hand as they half ran back to the small weather-beaten cottage where Tom lived with his brother, and climbed up the rickety stairs to Tom's bedroom. He set his iPod to Al Green, and Baby wrapped her thin arms around him, feeling like nothing in the world could be more perfect.

Let's get it on . . . ooh baby, let's get it on. . . .

"Hey," Baby said as she pulled Tom into her.

"Hey." Tom nuzzled her hair. Baby's heart leaped as he pulled her down onto the bed.

His arms felt warm and strong around her, and she felt like she might burst with happiness. She was home, back with Tom, after what felt like an eternity of being so far away from everything she knew and loved. "I love you," she said simply, because there was nothing else to say.

"You too," Tom muzzled her neck sleepily. He giggled, and then his giggles turned into those annoying guinea-pig noises.

Baby sighed. Maybe he'd gotten so high with Lucas because

he missed her so much and had to do something to drown his sorrows?

Or maybe he's just a typical stoner boy who has a very special relationship with his bong.

They lay back in the bed and she pulled the cover over them. Tom immediately collapsed into the pillow, his eyes closed. "Do you want to take a nap or something?" Baby asked, even though Tom's breathing had already evened out into deep snores. She sighed again and snuggled into his back, listening to the gentle lapping of the waves in the distance.

The next morning, Baby woke up to the sound of her phone ringing.

"Ugh," she murmured sleepily, seeing her sister's name on the display. She silenced the phone and sat up, looking around Tom's room. Why wasn't Tom in bed with her? She threw on his sweatshirt and padded downstairs. The sweatshirt was warm and soft and smelled like Tom.

She looked out the window and spotted him, standing next to Kendra's beat-up white XTerra. Kendra was in his arms, and his right hand, with the thick silver ring Baby had given him, was clasped around Kendra's hip. Baby felt a cold shot of fear rush through her. Tom was speaking earnestly to Kendra, and a flash of anger crossed Kendra's face. Baby opened the door slightly. The rusty hinges creaked.

"She's back," she heard Tom say defensively. Baby sat down on the concrete steps and hugged her knees to her chest. She had chills, even though it was warm outside.

"What? For the weekend?" Kendra sounded like she had snapped out of the stoner haze she had been in for the past two years. Her voice was sharp and clear and incredibly angry. Baby felt like she couldn't breathe.

"I don't know for how long. But I love her." Tom's voice rang out in the early morning air. Somehow, even those three words weren't enough to warm Baby up.

"What about us?" Kendra asked accusingly.

Us? The last Baby had heard, Kendra had been sleeping around with some UMass dropout who was working as a crab shack cook.

"You're my friend, but Baby is my girl," Tom insisted. Baby could see Tom's arm circling Kendra's narrow hip, as if he was going to pull her into a kiss. "Just give me time to sort this out," he pleaded.

With that, Baby stood. Tripping over her feet, she stormed back inside, slamming the door behind her.

"Shit!" she heard Tom call out.

"Baby!" Tom's older brother, James, was standing bleary-eyed by the sink as Baby came hurtling inside. "You're back!"

Baby grimaced. The room was filthy, with clothes lying untouched in a pile and a half-eaten slice of pizza congealing in its own grease on the counter.

Tom appeared in the doorway, panting from sprinting after her.

"Oh man, you guys are going to have it out." James opened the fridge, pulled out a gallon of Tropicana, and drank it straight out of the container. Then he sat down at the table, looking up at them expectantly.

"What the hell was that?" Baby said evenly, her eyes locked on Tom.

"It was nothing," Tom said, shooting a pleading look at

James. "It was just . . . Kendra. Baby . . . Baby, just listen to me." He grabbed her wrist, and Baby pulled away, feeling his stupid ring against her skin. She didn't want him to touch her. "Nothing happened," Tom whispered urgently.

"Yeah, right," Baby spat. "How could you do this to me?" she demanded plainly. This type of stuff happened in New York to people like Jack Laurent and J.P. Not to her, and not in Nantucket.

Tom bit his lower lip with his front teeth, but didn't say anything. "I'm going," Baby said finally, breaking free from his grasp.

"See, you're always leaving me," Tom said accusingly. "I was lonely, okay? I missed you, and Kendra was there. If you hadn't left, this wouldn't have happened," he finished.

She glared at him once more and stormed out. The back door slammed behind her.

Baby ran toward the beach and hurtled herself into the ocean, where her tears mingled with the salt water. At least she wasn't in Manhattan. At least she was home.

And home is where the heart is . . . not.

gossipgirl.net

Disclaimer: All the real names of places, people, and events have been altered or abbreviated to protect the innocent. Namely, me.

| topics | sightings | your e-mail | post a question |

hey people!

NEWS FLASH: My sources tell me **J**'s much-anticipated bash has suddenly and inexplicably been *canceled*. **J** is encouraging anyone and everyone to go to **A**'s bash instead. Is this a newfound alliance? Or is something more devious going down?

sightings

J and **A** signing for a large delivery at **A**'s grandmother's town house from that liquor store on Second. With **A**'s real estate and **J**'s connections, this could be quite a party partnership. . . . **R** walking up Fifth Avenue, holding hands with a mystery girl. Too bad **K** was at a Seaton Arms tennis tourney and couldn't see him. . . . **O** walking by a bodega on Madison, stopping to smell the . . . apples? Does someone have a fruit fetish . . . ? **A** hiring decorators to put up hundreds of lights in her grandmother's solarium. I don't think the decorations matter when half the guests are guaranteed to be passed out, but props for trying. . . . And **B** . . . nowhere. Anyone? Because **J.P.**'s dogs—and **J.P.**—have been walking around with their tails between their legs.

your e-mail

Dear GG,
I live on Nantucket, and when I was running on the beach this morning I found a Constance Billard blazer washed up on the shore. Isn't that a private girls' school in New York City? What happened?
—Nantucket Nectar

P.S. If you ever come to Nantucket, my Dodge has fully reclining seats, if you know what I mean.

a: Dear NN,
Hmm, I certainly haven't heard about any Upper East Side tragedies, but I only have *this* island covered. Could it be that one of our own has decided to end it? I can think of a certain bohemian beauty who's been awfully moody ever since she got here. . . . As for the visit, thanks, but it takes way more than the promise of fully reclining seats to make me leave Manhattan.
—GG

q: Dear GG,
I totally know who you are. You're probably, like, a Constance teacher who's just working on this tell-all novel to embarrass everyone. Right?
—Novel Girl

a: Dear NG,
A of all, I'm far too interesting and fashionable to ever be a teacher, and B of all, if I had wanted to write a novel, don't you think I'd have done it by now?
—GG

After a summer of boring we're-going-to-college parties where everyone pretended to be BFFs even though they really hated each other, I'm just itching to get back to the start-of-school parties, where Riverside Prep boys can mingle with Seaton Arms girls, Constance B girls can make out with St. Jude's boys, L'École girls can hook up with each other, and plenty of drama is guaranteed to occur. It's the first party of the year, and I, for one, can't wait to witness some scandalous behavior. *Et vous?*

You know you love me,

gossip girl

good things come to those who wait

From: Owen.Carlyle@StJudes.edu
To: Kelsey.Talmadge@SeatonArms.edu
Date: Friday, September 12, 3:00 p.m
Subject: Re: Now?

Kat,
Come to my sister's party. Can't wait to see you. . . .
Love,
O

party like a rock star

"We really did it!" Avery squealed, throwing her arms around Owen in a drunken, sisterly hug.

Owen ruffled her wheat blond hair and grinned drunkenly back at her. "Yeah, we did," he agreed with a grin. He glanced around the party, searching for someone. "Hey, I'm gonna grab another beer. You want anything?"

"I'm fine." Avery waved a hand. She'd had four drinks already, and everything was bathed in a happy, golden haze. She couldn't believe how well the party was going. Grandmother Avery's solarium was a blaze of twinkling lights that reflected off the marble floor. The small glass-enclosed pool was filled with bikini-clad L'École girls, the kitchen with St. Jude's and Riverside Prep boys doing shots, and the dining room with Constance girls eyeing the St. Jude's guys. Avery didn't know everyone's names yet but couldn't have been happier.

Owen ruffled her blond hair one last time and disappeared into the frenetic mass of bodies.

"Hey." Jack Laurent sidled up next to Avery, appearing as if out of nowhere. She wore a tight royal blue Proenza Schouler dress and towering Miu Miu platforms that made her a full two inches taller than Avery. She was holding the hand of a very cute, aristocratic-looking guy. "Great party, Avery!" Jack leaned in to give Avery a kiss on the cheek.

Mwah, mwah!

"J.P. Cashman," the guy said, holding out his hand. Avery took it, batting her eyelashes. "I know your sister. She's been walking my family's dogs. Is she coming tonight?" he asked convivially. Jack stared daggers at him.

Avery nodded, noticing now how good-looking J.P. was. Why had Baby never mentioned it? Then again, Baby always went for stoners like Tom, not pretty, Upper East Side billionaires-in-training. She probably hadn't even noticed.

"I got you another drink." Jack handed Avery a Tanqueray gimlet, and she took it gratefully. "I thought you might need one—it's so hard to be a hostess *and* take care of your own needs, especially when it's such a great party."

Avery grinned, too tipsy to detect the hint of sarcasm in Jack's voice. Jack had been true to her word, and dozens of kids Avery had never even met were now crowding into the solarium. The caterers Avery had insisted on hiring from Masa had long since gone, and Grandmother Avery's white couch was full of half-eaten California rolls and half-naked couples. She smoothed out a wrinkle in her black Marc by Marc Jacobs satin hostess dress, feeling like quite the hostess herself.

"Thanks so much for coming!" Avery spontaneously pulled Jack into a hug. Maybe it was the millions of tiny lights installed all around the room, but Jack somehow looked different tonight. Even her freckles weren't as irritating as they'd always seemed. She squeezed Jack's arm as she carefully polished off her wine and then took a sip of the cocktail Jack had made for her.

Didn't Grandmother Avery ever warn her about mixing her drinks?

"Of course! I hope you have lots more parties in the future. I'd be happy to help with all of them. And I meant to say it before, but good luck with the election tomorrow." Jack smiled warmly at Avery as she tugged J.P.'s hand to lead him away.

"So how come you're not wearing your new dress?" J.P. asked as they surveyed the crowded room. J.P. had been true to his word and had given her a pink princess dress, exactly as she'd described it. But it was absurdly frilly, with layers of bubble gum pink taffeta, and she would've looked like a giant cupcake in it.

"What, you don't like what I'm wearing?" Jack deflected the question, gesturing to her body-hugging sweaterdress. J.P. knew better than to say she didn't look good, so the point was pretty much moot.

"No, you look great," J.P. conceded. "But remind me again why you canceled the loft party?" he pressed. His brown eyes scanned the crowd as if looking for someone. "I mean, you were the one who said you didn't want a house party. My dad had everything ready. He was disappointed."

Jack shrugged. Couldn't he just let it go? And did he have to sound so disapproving? "I changed my mind," she said lightly, and lifted her face up for a kiss. She wished she could tell him that she really didn't have a choice. Avery Carlyle held her social universe in the palm of her hand, and unless Jack stopped her, her entire life would be over.

Jack turned the stereo up, and Kanye thumped through the house. "That's better." She flicked off the lights, plunging the room into sexy, dim shadows that played off the floor-to-ceiling windows.

She started to make her way to the kitchen to pour Avery a shot, but J.P. grabbed her arm. "It's pretty noisy in here—want to go chill outside?" he yelled over the pounding music.

"I want to drink more first!" she yelled back, shaking his arm away and continuing in the direction of the kitchen.

"Fine, I'm out of here," J.P. replied shortly. "Enjoy the party." He walked quickly through throngs of people grinding downstairs and out the front door.

Wonder where he's off to in such a hurry . . .

Jack rolled her eyes. Fine. J.P. could be lame. She was on a mission to give Avery Carlyle exactly what she deserved. Starting with another drink of something that did not mix well with wine or gin.

Across the room, Owen watched Avery gulp down her gimlet, a shot glass in her other hand. He was about to tell her to slow down when he noticed Rhys in a corner, sitting on an antique chair with the girl from the waxing place perched on his lap. They looked like they were ready to make out any second. Owen couldn't believe how well his plan was working. He gave Rhys a discreet nod of approval.

"Who's that?" Avery followed his gaze. "Is that couple having sex on Grandma's chair?" Avery stormed over, her drink sloshing onto the floor. Owen was laughing at his prim-but-plastered sister when he felt someone tap him on the shoulder.

The scent of apples filled the air.

"Hey," Kat whispered, her blue eyes dancing mischievously. She was wearing the same tight black halter dress she'd worn the night they met. Had she chosen it on purpose?

Wear the same outfit to two parties? I should hope not!

Owen glanced nervously at Rhys. He shivered, a mixture of adrenaline and fear coursing through him.

"It looks like he's doing better." Kat discreetly gestured toward Rhys and Astra, and Owen nodded.

Kat nodded thoughtfully, then smiled so sexily Owen stopped worrying about Rhys. Then she bit her lip. "Do you think I should say hi to him?" she asked, looking up at Owen for approval.

"I guess." Owen felt his heart pounding in his chest.

"And then maybe I could find you later?" she whispered near his ear. He felt her hot breath on his neck. He nodded wordlessly and waited, unable to breathe, as she stepped away from him and marched over to Rhys.

"I thought that swimmer dude and that Seaton Arms girl had broken up," Jiffy whispered across the makeshift bar to a very dateless Genevieve as they both watched Kat enter Rhys's sight line. Jiffy was wearing a pair of Citizens black skinny jeans and a black Diane von Furstenberg bubble dress that looked more like a Lands' End tent. Genevieve shrugged and poured a liberal splash of vodka into her crystal tumbler.

"Hey, Rhys." Rhys looked up and his eyes widened in surprise. She looked amazing in a tight black dress that showed off her athletic shoulders and thin legs. He practically shoved Astra off him. She was nice and all, but he had really only been interested in her to make Kelsey jealous. Which, apparently, had worked.

"Hey." Rhys grinned back, standing up to face her.

"I'm Kelsey," she said, holding out her hand to Astra.

"Astra." She stood and smiled politely back, brushing the wrinkles out of her silver Tory Burch tunic.

"I just wanted to say how lucky you are to have met Rhys.

He's terrific," Kelsey said to Astra, as if Rhys weren't in the room or, oh, her ex-boyfriend of only a few days.

Rhys's smile faltered. Something was wrong. She should be breaking down and crying and running off right now, at which point he would apologize to Astra, chase after Kelsey, and they would spend the rest of the evening cuddling in his bed, whispering *I love you*'s and *I'm sorry*'s. In the morning they'd eat lemon scones and laugh over how silly and overly dramatic their "breakup" had been, glad to have a funny story for their children someday.

And in what world besides a Hilary Duff movie does this actually happen?

Astra smiled as she tried to grab Rhys's arm and pull him toward her. He took a step away, his eyes locked on Kelsey's face.

"So, how'd you two meet?" Kelsey asked in her slow, melodious voice. It sounded like she was actually interested. And then it occurred to him: Kelsey was totally over him and couldn't care less if he hooked up with Astrid or Astro or whatever the hell her name was.

Rhys felt like he was moving underwater as he walked away from the two girls without another word. He had to get out into the fresh air. As he walked, he grabbed a bottle of Citron vodka and practically slammed into Owen, who was standing impassively by the doorway.

"Hey, you okay, man?" Owen asked in concern. He had purposely placed himself far enough away so he couldn't hear the conversation between Rhys and Kat, but from the wild-eyed look on Rhys's face, it hadn't gone well.

"No," Rhys choked. The room was too hot and too crowded. He felt like he was about to explode just standing there. Not really knowing what else to do, he jumped into the pool, splashing everyone. He stood up in the water, still holding the bottle of Citron, his button-down and jeans completely drenched.

"Hey!" Avery boomed, swaying on her Louboutin heels.

Jack grabbed her arm and escorted her toward Genevieve, Jiffy, and the Tanqueray. "Looks like you need another drink!"

"Hey, are you okay?" Owen leaned over the pool. A group of half-naked L'École girls looked on, pretending to be very interested in the patterns of ash their Gauloises cigarettes made as they flicked them in the water.

"No," Rhys sputtered. He stood in the three-foot-deep water and pushed his dark hair out of his eyes. Tears mixed with chlorine on his face. "Kelsey . . . She's . . . she's *fine*," Rhys sputtered, pulling himself out of the water. "It's really over."

"Well, who cares? You've got Astra! She's smokin'!" Owen tried to pump his buddy up as he passed him his own glass of straight Ketel One.

Rhys shook his head and pulled himself out of the pool. "Dude, I can't do this. I'm fucking wet!" He looked down as if he had just realized this. "I need to leave now."

Owen looked at Rhys, dripping wet and clearly on the verge of full-on sobs, and felt unspeakably guilty. He'd thought Rhys was really starting to get over Kat, but maybe he'd only thought that because he wanted it to be true.

"You probably need to stay here with your sister, right?" Rhys asked in a monotone, answering his own question.

Owen put down his drink, considering. Rhys was his friend. But Kat was . . . Kat.

"Yeah. I'm sorry, man," Owen apologized, feeling like shit. "Are you sure you don't want to stay?" he asked halfheartedly, looking at Rhys's drenched limited-edition black John Varvatos Converses.

"Yeah," Rhys choked, hardly able to get the word out. His feet made a squishing sound with each step as he put the pool, the party, and the love of his life behind him.

Maybe he should try a new look. I hear bushy mustaches are all the rage. . . .

a's law—whatever can go wrong, will go wrong

"So, I really like Owen Carlyle," Jiffy Bennett remarked, half passed out on Hugh Moore's lap in a reclining chair next to the pool. "But, you know, I'm open to anything tonight." Hugh's brown eyes widened in anticipation as Jiffy threw her thin arms around his bulky neck.

The party had been raging for the past four hours, and now, past 1 a.m., it was starting to really heat up. The pool was full of girls in La Perla bras and panties that left nothing to the imagination, especially in the water. The liquor cabinet had been completely ransacked, and Avery had spent the last hour enthusiastically hugging everyone she encountered and trying to remember their names.

Which is difficult when you're so drunk you can't even remember your own.

"Hey, you know that right now, if you do anything, it's not consensual," Sydney yelled up to Hugh as she climbed out of the pool, wearing a white tank top and boy shorts that had turned practically transparent. Hugh looked overwhelmed to have one girl climbing on top of him and another standing nearly nude in front of him. He was momentarily mesmerized by Sydney's numerous piercings.

"Think about consent is all I'm saying." Sydney glared at Hugh and stalked off.

Over in the solarium, Avery was sitting on the sofa, surrounded by dozens of new friends. *Take that, Satchel,* she thought drunkenly, thinking of the five-year-old who lived in Jack Laurent's house. Grandmother Avery would be so proud of her. She was about to win that election—which would totally be in the bag once everyone picked up the gift bags on the way out. She'd had necklaces made at a darling custom-design shop on Prince Street. A = SLBO was written out in tiny, delicate script in white gold, so it looked ghetto-fabulous in a sort of downtown, cash-meets-trash way.

Hasn't she ever heard of campaign buttons?

"I'm so glad we're friends now," Avery told Jack, enunciating each word carefully. The whole night, Jack had been at her side, getting her more drinks, suggesting everyone do shots, starting a game of Never Have I Ever in the pool, and keeping a steady playlist of great music blaring through the speakers. Avery hugged her new friend. Jack was awesome. She couldn't believe how wrong she'd been about her.

"Me too, Ave," Jack said, extracting herself from Avery's tight grip. "I'll be right back."

She made her way out the town house's front door and onto the stoop. It was quiet out here, except for the thumping of Justin Timberlake's "What Goes Around Comes Around" behind her. Unlike Avery, she had only had a few drinks, and the cool September air completely did away with any residual buzz.

Jack pulled out her Treo and dialed 311, New York's government information and complaint line. She listened to staticky Frank Sinatra hold music as she looked up at the blue-black sky.

"Hello, this is Marion, how may I help you?" a bored-sounding woman on the other end of the line finally answered.

"Hi, I need to make a noise complaint," Jack said sweetly.

"Address?" the woman asked in a raspy voice.

Jack looked at the iron plate screwed onto the oak door of the building. "Sixty-four East Sixty-first Street." She smiled as she heard the bass thumping through the door. By tomorrow, Avery Carlyle would be a complete nobody.

Hope she's enjoying her last drink . . .

"Okay, ma'am, we'll have someone investigate." Marion hung up and Jack quickly scurried into the party, turning up Nas on the Bose dock as she collided with a nearly naked Sydney, wearing only boy shorts and a sheer tank top. She stalked over to the corner of the pool and yanked a semi-conscious Jiffy off Hugh Moore's lap.

"We've got to go now," she snapped.

"But Hugh and I were just getting to know each other!" Jiffy protested as Hugh smiled lasciviously, stroking his half beard.

"You don't want to get to know him, trust me," Jack said, still trying to yank Jiffy into a semi-standing position. Just then sirens wailed outside and there was an authoritative knock on the door.

Avery walked to the door, smiling and holding two bottles of rum. She looooved parties, especially when people were still coming this late. But as she yanked open the door, instead of cute St. Jude's boys, she saw one short, squat woman and one super-tall, thin man, both clad in New York City Police Department uniforms. *Ohmigod.* Avery stood speechless.

And drunk.

"Noise complaint." The short brunette officer held up a badge. Kids began streaming out the front door, eager to escape before their parents found out. The taller, male police officer shut the door and stood in front of it, causing a tide of people to rush back to the living room, where someone thoughtfully turned the music off and the lights on. Avery could see cups all over the floor and mysterious puddles in different areas. For a second, she imagined how trashed the upstairs must be and then snapped to attention. Obviously the cops weren't here to see if the house was a mess.

"Whose party is this?" the female officer, whose tag read OFFICER BEECHER, asked, looking around. Without the music, people had gathered into groups of twos and threes. Hugh had taken Grandmother Avery's rare edition of *The Collected Works of Shakespeare* off the shelf and was reading a monologue from *Othello* in a baritone voice. Officer Beecher raised an eyebrow at him, then looked back at Avery.

"We're just having play rehearsal." Hugh shrugged, trying to save Avery.

How sweet.

"It's my party," Avery said, trying to make her voice as authoritative as possible. She set the two bottles of rum down on the settee, hoping the officers hadn't noticed. Owen came up behind her.

"Shit," he whispered and put his arm around her protectively.

"Do you have ID?" Officer Beecher asked. Avery shook her head miserably. She could hear her heart pounding in her ears. They couldn't arrest her, could they?

"Okay." The male police officer frowned. "Do you have a party permit?"

"This is my grandmother's house!" Avery said shrilly.

"Okay, well, we received a noise complaint. Where is your grandmother? Is she here?" Officer Beecher asked.

"She's *dead*!" Avery wailed. Both officers rolled their eyes.

"Well, according to what we have here, the house is the property of a Meyers and Mooreland law firm. Unfortunately, until we speak with the owner of this house, we need to arrest you for trespassing. Put your hands behind your back."

Avery's heart flew into her throat. She wasn't a criminal.

"Look, officer. I'm her brother . . ." Owen began, but neither of the officers seemed to hear him.

"It won't hurt," the male officer said as the cold metal snaked around Avery's wrists and locked with a sickening clank.

"Okay, party's over," the female officer announced to the crowd. It wasn't necessary. Everyone was already running in all directions.

"After party at my place!" Hugh yelled into the melee. Both officers led Avery out the door and into the back of the police cruiser. The red and blue lights cast an eerie glow over the deserted street. Avery heard her own desperate sniffles as she shuffled down the regal brownstone steps and toward the cruiser.

"You don't really need to wear those." The male officer gave Avery a sympathetic look as he unlocked the handcuffs and helped Avery into the backseat. Avery nodded gratefully, flexing her hands. She sat back in the police car, her head thumping numbly. She fingered the custom-made necklace she had worn under her dress for good luck. As the car came to a halt at a stoplight, she pulled it off to examine it.

The letters read A = SLOB in elegant cursive.

Avery stared at it, then broke into noisy, wracking sobs. She might as well get thrown in jail forever, because her life at Constance and the Upper East Side was absolutely and completely *over.*

"We've got a live one," the male officer sighed.

Wait till she hurls all over them.

a prefers french cuffs to metal. . . .

Dazed, Owen watched his sister get driven away in a police car. He pulled out his cell and called his mother, feeling bad for bothering her on the opening night of her big Brooklyn rodent exhibition.

"Owen?" Edie answered, sounding kind of pissed. The roar of laughter and clinking glasses echoed in the background. Edie was obviously having way more fun than they were.

"Hi, Mom." Owen cringed. Part of the reason Edie let the triplets do whatever they wanted was because things like this didn't happen to them.

"I received a phone call from the police about the party. The precinct is right there, so I told them you and Baby would come for her."

"Sorry, Mom," Owen mumbled. Where *was* Baby, anyway? He hadn't seen her all night. Or last night, for that matter.

"Call me as soon as you all get home."

Unable to locate his tiny rebellious sister anywhere, Owen made sure the guests had scattered, and locked up Grandmother Avery's house. Then he jogged down to the police precinct, just a few blocks away.

He felt nervous when he first walked in, but quickly found that the precinct was less like *Law & Order* and more like the Nantucket police station he'd once visited on a school field trip. One cop sat behind a heavy wooden desk. A grainy black and white television was on in the background, its sound interrupted every so often by a staticky noise from one of the police radios. The female officer who'd arrested Avery sat in a chair by the holding cell, filing her nails.

Avery sat in a corner of the cell with her ankles crossed, crying hysterically. She held her wrists together in her lap as if they were still encased in invisible handcuffs. On the opposite wall of the cell stood a toilet and a small, grimy-looking sink.

"Wipe your nose, honey," the female officer called to Avery in a bored voice. Avery sobbed incoherently, her entire face red and wet with tears and snot. Owen was mesmerized. He had never seen Avery like this, not even the time when she was second-runner up for Miss Lobster Queen Junior in the seventh grade. Not even when they were little.

"My family has the most powerful lawyers in the city," Avery slurred, not noticing Owen. "I also really have to pee, but I am *not* using that toilet, and if I got a urinary tract infection, I could sue, you know." She rattled the bars for dramatic effect.

"That your sister?" the police officer asked Owen. "You can take her home. We spoke to your mother. She knew about the party, so there are no trespassing problems."

Owen grinned, relieved they weren't in any trouble. He knew he should feel bad, but seeing prim and proper Avery sitting in the drunk tank was kind of hilarious.

"Hey, Ave!" he yelled, his voice echoing across the concrete and linoleum. She looked up. Owen pulled out his iPhone and snapped a photo of her behind bars for posterity.

"Don't worry, Miss Blondie has a great mug shot she'll be thrilled to submit to her yearbook," the cop behind the desk laughed.

The female officer unlocked the door to the cell, and Avery tripped into Owen's arms. "Owen, you saved me," she slurred.

"Okay, we're going home. Say goodbye to the nice police officer," Owen couldn't resist teasing.

The officer behind the desk looked almost sad to see her go. It must have been an entertaining evening.

Owen navigated Avery into a cab. "Seventy-second and Fifth," he said. He noticed the cabbie staring at Avery in alarm. Her face was smeared with makeup, her eyes were bloodshot, her nose was running, and her mouth hung open in a gaping, drunken way, as if just breathing took enormous effort. "She's fine," he assured the driver.

"I'll make siren noises if it will make you feel at home," Owen laughed. Avery fell onto his shoulder and began to snore.

Tsk, tsk. What would Grandmother say?

The cab pulled up to their twenty-story stone apartment building, and Owen helped navigate Avery to the green-awninged front door. Out of the corner of his eye he saw Kat sitting on the wooden bench to the right of the entrance, in the shadows of the landscaped bushes.

"Hey," Owen whispered. "I'll be down in a second."

Owen dragged Avery into the elevator, hauled her inside the penthouse, and lifted her onto her perfectly made bed. He pulled off her shoes and practically sprinted to the elevator, out the door, and to the bench downstairs.

"Hey," he whispered, suddenly feeling exhausted.

"Is she okay?" Kat asked, twirling a strand of caramel-colored hair in her fingers.

"She will be, eventually," Owen shrugged. "Her pride's going to be more hurt than anything." He noticed goose bumps forming on Kat's slender arms and wanted so much to wrap his arms around her. "Are you cold?"

"A little," Kat admitted. She pulled her knees up to her chest, suddenly looking like a vulnerable little kid. "I thought I'd never see you again after Nantucket," she said with a small smile. The doorman looked over at them, then turned away.

"Let's take a walk. I'll bring you home," Owen said gruffly. Kat stood up and Owen saw her reaching her hand over to him. He crossed his tan arms over his thin gray T-shirt so she couldn't grab his hand. If she did, then he wouldn't be able to do what he had to.

"It was a fun party," Kat continued as they made their way up Fifth Avenue. The street was empty, except for the doormen flanking each building. "I was glad to see Rhys with someone."

Owen felt a lump form in his throat but began walking faster, trying to walk Kat home before he began kissing her all over again. He could feel the heat from her body. He made himself think of Rhys, heartbroken and soaking wet at the party. Rhys needed Kat, and there was no way Kat would go back to Rhys if Owen was still in the picture. He steeled himself and looked straight ahead. They were almost at her building. He stopped and took her hands as they stood on the corner. The sign said DON'T WALK, but it didn't matter, since there were no cars around.

Owen looked into Kat's silvery blue eyes and took a deep breath.

"What?" she asked.

"The night in Nantucket didn't mean anything. I know you want me to have feelings for you, but I don't. It was just . . . a one-night stand," he lied. He couldn't believe how assholic the words sounded when he actually said them.

"You don't mean that," she said steadily, her blue eyes boring into his. Owen tore his hands away and crossed his arms over his chest again.

"I do. It was a one-night stand. I don't have feelings for you," he repeated, then quickly turned and began to walk down the street in the direction of his apartment.

"Wait."

Owen stopped walking and turned around. Kat's eyes glinted. She held her hands on her hips like an Amazon warrior. She wasn't crying. Actually, she looked more pissed than broken-hearted. "So everything you said—"

"Get over it," Owen spat, trying to channel Avery when she was acting annoyingly self-righteous. He dug into the pockets of his Diesel jeans and pulled out the Tiffany ID bracelet, feeling its familiar grooves as he handed it to her. He couldn't resist closing her fingers over it before he turned and walked the five blocks back to his building, the image of Kat's confused, pleading eyes burning a hole into his brain.

He nodded woodenly to the doorman and walked toward the elevator. His own heartbroken face stared back at him from the shiny mirrors lining the lobby.

If everything went according to plan, soon Rhys and Kat would be back together, and they would both be happy. As for Owen, he was ready to find out what else Manhattan had to offer.

Ladies, the line starts here.

don't you wish your girlfriend was fun like b?

Baby tossed and turned uncomfortably on the sand on Sunday morning, trying to stay asleep. She had spent all of Saturday on the beach and had eventually fallen asleep by the water. Her summer hammock had been taken down by the family friends Edie had invited to take care of the house, so she ended up finding an old sleeping bag in the shed and dragged it down to the water's edge. Finally, she was able to cry herself to sleep. The last thing she wanted to do was wake up and start crying all over again.

She wiggled her butt into a small depression in the sand and squeezed her eyes shut, blocking out any rays of light. As she drifted off, she felt a warm tongue licking her face. *Tom?* she thought as her large brown eyes popped open. Instead of her contrite ex-boyfriend, she gazed at Nemo's blond, enthusiastic, very furry face.

"What are you doing here?" she demanded in astonishment, petting Nemo's fur. She wondered if this was some weird, subconscious post-breakup dream, but Nemo felt very real to her.

"Well, you know, big dog's gotta run."

Baby shielded her eyes from the sun with her hand and saw

J.P.'s face break into a wide grin. He wore green pants with tiny frogs and fish embroidered on them.

She extracted herself from the puffy red sleeping bag and stood up, brushing sand from her Constance Billard uniform skirt. She wasn't sure whether to laugh or cry or just pull J.P. into a hug. Instead, she narrowed her eyes at him and put her small hands on her tiny hips.

"Big dog's gotta run on my beach?" she challenged. A flush of red rose up J.P.'s face.

"He missed you," J.P. said simply, watching Nemo lick her tiny ankle with abandon. "The dogs didn't want you to leave."

Baby knelt down and buried her face in Nemo's soft fur. He panted appreciatively in her ear.

"Well, your *girlfriend* certainly wanted me to leave," Baby retorted, her head still buried. She wasn't going to make this easy for him. A wave crashed noisily against the shore.

"That's sort of why I came," J.P. said, suddenly sounding serious. He stuffed his hands into the pockets of his frog-embroidered pants. "I'm sorry I was an asshole to you the other day. With Jack," he clarified. "You didn't deserve that."

"Can you apologize for your pants, too?" Baby's face suddenly broke into a smile. She pushed her stiff, salty hair back behind her ears. Who even bought, much less wore, *critter* pants? In a way, it was almost as who-gives-a-fuck as her own style. The morning sun beat down on her face, and for the first time in twenty-four hours she felt warm all over.

"Anyway, the reason I'm here is . . . will you come back to New York?" J.P. asked tentatively. "I mean, the dogs need you," he finished brusquely, coloring a little.

Baby paused, gazing out the expanse of ocean licking into the sand. Could she leave her tiny island paradise? She thought of the party she had missed last night and felt a wave of sadness that she had so thoughtlessly left Avery and Owen and her mom. She missed them. She turned back to J.P., looking at her so hopefully, and looking so *good*. Maybe New York wouldn't be so bad after all.

"You brought the chopper?" she asked.

"Yeah," he admitted. Then he pulled out two rumpled tickets from his pocket. "But I also bought ferry tickets. My dad needed the chopper this afternoon," he explained. "I thought we could take the long way home."

Baby didn't know what to say. Cashman Junior stopping at the island's tiny ferry terminal to buy tickets?

"There's a car waiting in Boston," J.P. said. "Unless you want to take the bus?"

Baby grinned. "Not necessary," she said, feeling like she wanted to laugh and cry at the same time. She was going home. To a new home. And this time she was actually a tiny bit excited about it.

Hmm . . . wonder why?

a gets everything she ever wanted

When Avery woke up she was lying fully dressed in last night's clothes, on top of her pink bedspread. It was almost noon, she had a pounding headache, and her blond hair was matted to one side of her head. She felt like she had been run over by a truck.

Good morning, Miss Drunky.

She swung her legs off the bed and trudged slowly to her bathroom, desperate for water to get rid of the old-sock taste in her mouth. She opened the door to the adjoining bathroom and almost screamed when she saw herself in the mirror. Her black dress was hopelessly wrinkled and had a weird, scummy stain on the bodice. There was a small chain of bruises around both of her wrists. Terrible images from the previous night flooded her memory. She remembered getting drunk. The police lights flashing. The smell of throw-up on the ivy surrounding the town house as she was escorted out by the cops. She leaned in closer to the honed Carrera vanity and stared at her reflection. She looked like death. Death with a gold necklace on it. A necklace that read SLOB.

"Good morning, sunshine," Edie trilled, walking into her

bedroom wearing an all-white jumpsuit that made Avery's eyes hurt. Edie threw open the gauzy green curtains and opened the window, leaning out and breathing deeply. Avery closed the bathroom door and dove back under her covers before her mother could see what a mess she was. Yes, her mom was always preoccupied, but not so much she wouldn't notice Avery was in worse shape than the free sculptures Edie picked up off the street.

"How are you feeling?" Edie asked lightly, but there was concern in her voice.

"Not good," Avery croaked, gripping the covers.

"Want to tell me about it?" Edie sat down on the silky pink duvet cover, stroking Rothko, who had come to say good morning. He nuzzled Avery's covered feet with his whiskered nose. Edie looked at Avery expectantly. "Actually, you know what?" She stood and wandered out of the room, coming back a minute later with nine red candles. She set them up on the white antique dresser Avery had brought over from Grandmother Avery's house and lit them one by one.

"This is to wish you luck this year in school, and remove all the bad energy from last night. I heard what happened."

Avery poked her blond head out from under the Frette duvet, wondering just how much her mother knew.

"I have to say I'm disappointed. Not so much with you three, but more with the whole police system. It seems that things are just different here than when I was growing up." Edie's blond brow furrowed as she lit the candles. Avery sat up and looked at her mother in amazement. That was it?

The candle flames moved back and forth in the morning breeze. "I should have done this earlier, but I've been so busy." Edie sighed apologetically.

Avery hid her face under her monogrammed pillowcase. She didn't want to deal with her mother's mystic incantations, not today. Couldn't her mom just be helpful and bring her an Advil?

Or a Bloody Mary?

"Actually, where's Baby? I'm sure this would help her as well," Edie said thoughtfully. Avery sat up. Where *was* Baby? She had never even shown up at the party last night, and had ignored all Avery's texts.

"Um," she began brilliantly. She pulled her cell phone from under her pillow. Had she slept on it? Ugh. There were no messages from Baby, only one from Sydney.

KILLER PARTY—I KNEW YOU HAD IT IN YOU! Avery buried her phone under the covers again. If the Constance Billard freak thought it was a great party, her social life *must* be over.

"Where is she?" Edie pressed. "I didn't see her this morning."

"She's at . . . a protest," Avery babbled, not sure where the lie was coming from. She thought of Sydney. "About . . . wallabies in captivity. Like at the zoo." Wallabies? Was she still drunk?

Quite possibly.

"Oh!" Edie said. "She must have taken my conversation to heart!"

Avery looked at her mother, surprised.

"She's found a cause," Edie explained vaguely, waving a turquoise-laden hand.

"I guess so," Avery mumbled.

"But then she won't be at the brunch," Edie observed, sounding disappointed. *And I just lost the only other vote in the election,* Avery realized. As if it even mattered after last night's disaster.

"I've so been looking forward to reconnecting with my old high school friends. Although, come to think of it, we never really got along in high school," Edie sighed. "Will you be ready in ten minutes?"

When Avery dragged her unshowered, Lilly Pulitzer dress–wearing self out of a cab and into Tavern on the Green behind her mother, her stomach had only slightly settled and her head was still pounding. The lights at Tavern on the Green were twinkling, and the girls were all assembled in the Crystal room, which had huge floor-to-ceiling windows and felt a bit like a greenhouse. The room was filled with round, white linen–draped tables topped with arrangements of lilies and white orchids, and pure sunlight streamed through the windows. Normally, it would have looked pretty, but viewed with a hangover, the whole setting seemed like some sort of torture device. Around them, girls wearing enormous Gucci sunglasses stumbled over to the linen-covered table where the SLBO votes were being cast. There, a Tiffany blue box with a hole cut in the top was overflowing with ballots—all of them no doubt calling for Jack Laurent to be SLBO. Avery wondered if she should even bother to put her own vote in and decided against it. That would be too, too pathetic.

"I wonder if I should talk to Mrs. McLean about setting up some sort of artistic endowment from your grandmother's trust," Edie mused, looking around the room. She was clad in a flowy blue dress she had hand-dyed herself. "It would be great to encourage creative expression. Everyone here looks the same." She frowned in disappointment at the crowd of hungover, sunglasses-wearing, simple sundress–clad girls.

Edie guided Avery toward the round tables, looking for their place cards. "Edie Carlyle!" A skinny brown-haired woman accosted them. "Gwendolyn Bennett." She held out one hand dripping with gold Cartier bangles. "I have to say you look as . . . artistic as ever," she said, looking Edie up and down. "And this must be one of your daughters?" Avery smiled tightly as Gwendolyn scrutinized her through small, rodentlike eyes.

"Oh, hello, Gwendolyn. I remember you so well," Edie pulled the woman in and kissed her on both cheeks. "This is Avery. My other daughter, Baby, is at some sort of wallaby protest. Apparently they're treated just dreadfully in zoos. Can you imagine?"

"Taking up the cause as ever." Gwendolyn was saccharinely sweet, and Edie mashed her lips together in a thin line. "My daughter, Jiffy, is in school with both your daughters, and I've heard so much about them, I feel as if I know them." She smiled down at Avery, who grimaced. She'd known coming to this event would be a disaster. Couldn't she just die in peace? She excused herself and walked into the adjoining room, where girls were nursing mimosas and whispering quietly amongst themselves.

"So, I heard she was so totally hammered at her party that she ended up peeing herself," Jiffy murmured, sitting at a table next to Sarah Jane and Sarah Jane's rail-thin mother, whom Avery recognized from countless fashion websites.

"I know." Sarah Jane nodded. "And I heard she's probably going to jail, but, like, her mom doesn't know how bad it is yet. They're trying to find a lawyer, but no one will even touch the case." Sarah Jane's tiny gray eyes darted over to Avery, who walked by them with her head held high. She wished she hadn't donated all her NHS sweatshirts to Goodwill as soon as she had found out she was moving, because she kind of wanted to move back to that quiet island where nothing happened, lock herself in the attic, and raise emus.

Groups of girls were walking over to the election table, presided over by some frizzy-haired sophomore. Avery casually walked past the table, but even the sophomore glared at her as if Avery would contaminate the elections if she came too close.

"Oh, there you are." Edie put her arm around Avery's shoulder and mercifully led her away from the ballot box. "I found our table, and some of the other ladies there are absolutely fascinated by Baby's work with wallabies. Would you mind going over and speaking to them?" Avery rolled her eyes miserably, trying not to recoil as an army of black-vested waiters delivered heaping plates of daffodil-colored scrambled eggs to each table.

She sat down, trying not to retch on the silver-plated tableware and crisp, ivory-colored napkins. Beside her, Edie was animatedly talking to some truck-shaped girl's mother about indigenous animals. A tiny, ancient woman wearing a black knit St. John suit stepped up to Avery, scrutinizing the dorky name tag taped to her chest.

"You must be Avery Carlyle's granddaughter," she said in a raspy voice. Avery could feel droplets of spit land near her ear as she whirled around and nodded. She doubted her grandmother would want to be related to her anymore. The woman smiled pleasantly.

"Muffy St. Clair." She extended her hand to Avery. "Your grandmother and I got into a lot of trouble back in our day. It was up to her to keep the city interesting. I certainly hope you follow in her footsteps," she said, clinking her glass of Veuve against Avery's Pellegrino. Even thinking about alcohol nearly caused Avery to heave.

"Thanks." Avery smiled awkwardly.

"See?" From a few tables away, Sarah Jane poked Jiffy hard in the ribs. "She's trying to become BFFs with the alumni board so they'll let her stay at Constance."

Genevieve's mother, Blanche, sidled up to them. "Poor girl," she murmured. "And look at her mother." She pointed over to Edie, who was making a beeline for Mrs. McLean. "She's trying to beg for her daughter to stay in school. So sad, really." Blanche escorted Genevieve up to the bar, where they both ordered Ketel One, straight up.

Avery looked around for a friendly face and noticed Sydney angrily sitting next to a black-clad, incredibly buttoned-up-looking woman with collarbones jutting out from under her navy cashmere sweater. Jack Laurent was seated beside a ruddy, older man in an oatmeal-colored linen suit and a baby blue shirt, looking at his Rolex and tapping his foot. He looked terribly out of place, since it *was* a mother-daughter brunch.

Muffy St. Clair took the stage, with Mrs. McLean assisting her every white vintage–Ferragamoed step. She tapped the microphone, which let out a loud screech.

"Welcome, Constance students, alums, and parents, to the annual mother-daughter brunch. To begin the festivities, it is an honor and a privilege to announce the winner for the student liaison to the board of overseers." Muffy scanned the audience. "Back when Constance Billard was first founded, it prided itself on a tradition of excellence. Constance students are looked to as pillars of grace, poise, and intellect," she began slowly. People in the crowd resumed muffled talking. Avery covertly took her mother's mimosa, wanting to get started on numbing the pain before Jack Laurent's name was called. She took a sip and nearly yakked.

"The student liaison will ensure that this excellence continues long into the future," Muffy continued. The room became hushed once more. Even the waiters stood back from the tables in anticipation. Mrs. M smiled tightly, anxious to get the brunch over with. Muffy slowly pulled out her reading glasses from her quilted Chanel purse and slid one wrinkled finger under the envelope flap. "And the winner is a name I know all too well." Avery looked up sharply and saw Jack take her linen napkin from her lap and place it on the table, poised to stand in acceptance.

"Avery Carlyle." Muffy's face broke into a broad grin. Avery looked around the silent room, completely stunned. A moment passed, then Edie put her fingers in her mouth and gave a piercing wolf whistle.

Avery stood up and walked to the stage as if in a dream. She looked out into the sea of faces as the crowd murmured and began to clap.

"If you're half as high-spirited as your grandmother, I'm looking forward to a wonderful year," Muffy said in a crackly, high-pitched voice and winked at Avery. If she hadn't been afraid of breaking one of Muffy's brittle bones, Avery would have hugged her. Instead, she shook her hand vigorously and grabbed the mic. "Thanks!" she squeaked, looking out to the crowd. "I'm thrilled to lead the Constance Billard community!" Then she clattered down the steps, feeling like she was floating.

"Oh my God, congratulations." Sydney squeezed through the crowd to meet Avery at the side of the makeshift stage and hugged her tightly. "The necklaces? Fucking genius!" Sydney squealed, holding her A = SLOB necklace up. It caught the light from outside, and Avery looked around, noticing similar sparkles from every table. "You made such an exit last night. You're a fucking rock star!"

Avery squeezed her eyes shut, her hangover suddenly gone. This wasn't a dream. Her party had been a success, albeit in a crash-and-burn type of way, and girls were wearing her necklaces. They really *did* like her! Maybe her stomach *could* handle one little glass of champagne.

Or a bottle. Keep the rock star image up.

"Congratulations, Avery," Mrs. M boomed into the microphone.

Jack abruptly scraped her chair back from the table, thinking she might be sick. "What?" she murmured, almost involuntarily.

"I thought they were announcing *you* for this position, Jacqueline," her father whispered angrily.

"I—" Jack's voice came out in a squeak.

"Call me when you're really ready to stop playing games, Jacqueline. You lied, and I'm disappointed in you." Her father walked out, nearly colliding with a waiter holding a full tray of champagne. Jack glanced up at Avery, waving to everyone as if she had just been crowned Miss America.

Jack looked around, but no one seemed to be on her side. Even fucking Jiffy was wearing the A = SLOB necklace, half obscured by the ridiculous Hermès scarf she'd tied around her neck. It looked like a weird leash.

This was absurd. Jack got up and stormed out of Tavern on the Green, practically careening into some bagpipe player outside. She made her way out of the park and onto the street, hailing a cab on Central Park West, headed straight to J.P.'s.

MEET ME OUTSIDE YOUR BUILDING, she texted as the cab wove through Central Park to the East Side. She was so mad her hands were shaking. She couldn't believe she'd lost that stupid position and couldn't wait for J.P. to console her. At least *he* wouldn't disappoint her.

Jack felt calmer and her fingers stopped trembling once she saw J.P. standing outside the massive modern apartment tower.

One of his stupid dogs was with him, and he was wearing those ugly critter pants she always made him take off.

"Hey!" Jack called from the cab. "Do you have cash? I forgot my purse." She gave him a pouty look and watched him fumble through his wallet.

"Here you go," he mumbled to the cabbie as Jack stepped out of the cab.

"So, what's going on?" J.P. asked, stifling a small yawn. Jack narrowed her green eyes. What was *his* problem? *She* was the one who was tired. Tired of her fucking shitstorm of a life.

"I had a bad morning," Jack began. "And I don't understand why you left me alone at that awful party last night," she whined. "What are you going to do to make it up to me?" She'd meant for the question to sound sexy, but it came out sounding more like a customer relations complaint.

"Actually, I'm sort of busy." J.P. stepped back, pulling the dog's leash tight so that it wouldn't jump all over Jack.

"Doing what?" she asked, looking around. It was 1 p.m. on a Sunday—what could he possibly have to do?

Besides her?

"And why didn't you answer your phone last night? I'm supposed to be your girlfriend." Her voice rose several octaves. Did *no one* care about her?

"Sorry, Jack. This just isn't a good time—"

"You're supposed to take care of me!" Jack cut him off, wanting to shove him hard. "You're supposed to be there for me when I need you."

"Listen, Jack, we need to talk," J.P. said, frowning. Behind him, the September sun glinted off the modern building.

"Oh, so you want to talk now? How convenient. Because you

know, I wanted to talk to you all last night, after you fucking left the part. . . ." J.P. grabbed her wrists. She glared at him, sure he was going pull her close and put his lips on hers just to shut her up. She was so not in the mood. Or maybe she was. Whatever. But then he didn't try to kiss her after all.

"I can't do this anymore," he said finally, letting her go.

"What?" Jack felt an icy shiver of fear run through her stomach and wondered if she was going to throw up.

"You're so demanding, and I just can't do it anymore." J.P. looked exhausted as he scooped up the dog. It let out a little bark. "Look, I've had a long day. You need to just go—we'll talk more later." He hailed a cab and held the door open for her. "Here's money for your fare," he said, pulling a twenty out and handing it to Jack. She wanted to rip the bill into shreds and throw it back into his face, but she took it. She had to.

"But—"

"But nothing," J.P. said, closing the door behind her.

Jack didn't say another word. She felt sad, small, and totally pathetic. As the cab began driving down Fifth, she spotted Baby Carlyle on the corner, wearing one of J.P.'s Riverside Prep T-shirts and walking his two puggles into one of the stone entrances flanking Central Park.

Jack choked back her angry tears as the cab cruised downtown to her tiny garret. She was going to make the Carlyle girls' lives a living hell.

Because, as we French speakers know, hell is other people.

three's company

Sunday evening, Baby sat on her makeshift hammock on the penthouse terrace wearing a pair of tiny terry cloth shorts and a 1990 Grateful Dead World Tour T-shirt. She gazed up at the dim stars. The sky didn't look at all like it did in Nantucket, and when she looked south, the stupid Cashman Complex blocked any view of the moon. But in the darkness, and in a totally capitalistic way, the interlocking *C*'s were almost pretty.

She leaned back again, feeling more exhausted than she ever had. The more she thought about it, the more she couldn't believe she had stayed with Tom for over a year. She'd thought he was authentic, but he was just a player in bong water–soaked clothing. She ran a finger over the thick twine of the hammock. It was weird that her life was so much more disordered now than it had been a week before, yet she felt much calmer.

The door opened, and Owen stepped outside with a six-pack of Coronas. "You want one?" He opened the bottle with his teeth and handed it to her.

"Thanks." Baby sat up and hugged her knees to her chest.

"Are you okay? You seem a little sad." He sat down on the

hammock next to her, and it sagged under his hundred-and-eighty-pound frame, almost touching the ground.

"I went back to Nantucket yesterday. Tom was with Kendra." She said it matter-of-factly. It didn't even hurt to say it.

"Whatever. She's a total skank," Owen said knowingly, remembering the time he and Kendra had hooked up in New Hampshire on a freshman ski trip. "And I never really liked Tom that much," he mused, scratching his almost-full beard.

"It's okay," Baby said, leaning back. With his oatmeal-colored socks and pizza crust–filled cottage and homemade bong collection, he *was* kind of a loser. Why hadn't she ever noticed it before? "So, did I miss anything here?" Baby asked. She couldn't believe she had decided to hang out with Tom instead of going to Avery's first big party and holding her hand during the election. She had been more self-obsessed than Avery ever was.

"Avery got thrown in jail." Owen shrugged, swigging his beer.

"No way!" Baby breathed in disbelief. She wasn't sure whether to believe him or not. The image of Avery in jail was sort of funny, though. "Is she okay?"

"Better than ever," Owen continued, taking out his iPhone. "But apparently they don't party Nantucket-style here." He flipped through his photo album until he came to the picture of the red-faced, tear-streaked Avery behind bars. It was so pathetic it was hilarious. Baby burst into laughter. She couldn't believe she'd missed it.

"Owen, you promised you would destroy that!" Avery screeched, appearing behind them. She grabbed his phone and quickly pressed delete. She was wearing tight blue Nantucket volleyball shorts and Tom's barn-red sweatshirt. "I was cold," she said by way of explanation, noting Baby's look. "It still stinks, though."

"We broke up. You can have it." Baby shrugged.

Avery's eyes widened. Was *that* what Baby had been doing this weekend?

"So, I thought you had a hot date with that lady police officer tonight?" Owen interrupted. "Y'know, do each other's hair, give each other tattoos?"

"Shut up," Avery said good-naturedly as she grabbed a Corona and expertly hit the bottle against the metal railing to open it. "Oh, and I have something for you." Avery fished in the pocket of her sweatshirt and pulled out the A = SLOB necklace she had saved for Baby. "I won that school leadership thing at school," she announced, a broad grin spreading across her tanned face. She *still* couldn't believe it.

Baby hugged her sister proudly. Avery's silky, just-washed blond hair cascaded over her tiny shoulders. She deserved to be SLOB or SLBO or whatever the hell it was called. Good for her. Then Baby remembered her three strikes. Would she even be allowed back at Constance?

"I don't know how to keep up with you two." Owen leaned back in the hammock, smiling playfully. It felt good to be hanging out with his sisters. There was never this much drama with guys.

Oh, come now. Methinks he doth protest too much.

"Hey, what about you, Goody Two-shoes? Have you even hooked up with a girl since you got here?" Avery demanded, squeezing her butt between her siblings on the hammock. Now that she had the SLBO position, she could once again stick her lightly freckled nose into her siblings' lives.

"Not yet. Biding my time. You know, doing things the Carlyle way," Owen replied, not looking at her. He glanced up Fifth Avenue almost longingly.

"Well, your friend was cute," Avery said, remembering the dark-haired guy Owen had been hanging out with at their party. She took a sip of Corona, then remembered her resolution to detox this week and put it down on the terra cotta–tiled terrace.

"You see, I've been spending time making cute friends." Owen weaseled away from Avery's investigation.

"Well, I propose a toast." Baby stood up and lifted her Corona into the air. Avery and Owen stood up beside her. "To New York!"

"To New York!" the Carlyles shouted, their voices echoing in the evening air as they clanked their Coronas against each other.

Hear, hear!

gossipgirl.net

Disclaimer: All the real names of places, people, and events have been altered or abbreviated to protect the innocent. Namely, me.

hey people!

Cheers! So we've got a new student liaison, and let's hope she gets some changes made—like extra free periods and double lunches and triple photography. How else will you find time to go home, hook up, take a shower, and make it back to discuss *L'Étranger* in AP French? Maybe she can also swing for her sister to get re-enrolled in school . . . or maybe not.

Unfortunately, **A** doesn't have all the answers—and you won't find them in the back of your AP Calculus textbook, either. Here's what I still want to know:

What's up with **J** and **J.P.**? Are they on a break, Will-and-Kate style, or have the prince and princess on this side of the pond broken up forever? And where does that leave **B**?

Will **R** and **K** reunite? Is **O** destined to be lonely, or will the lover boy from Nantucket live up to expectations? And is he really just a player, or is he looking for love?

Too bad not everybody's feeling the love: **J** is on the warpath. Something tells me **A** and **B** better watch their Marni-clad backs. And maybe the rest of us, too . . .

And then the last question: aren't you glad I stayed? And aren't you glad you're along for the ride? It's going to be another wild and wicked year, and I'll give you the dirt on everything worth knowing. I give you my word. And you know that's at *least* as good as a platinum, no-limit AmEx.

You know you love me,

gossip girl

One week after their arrival,
the Carlyle triplets are already the Upper East Side's
most talked-about new residents.

Baby has a secret crush.
Avery has a secret plan.
And Owen has a secret love.

But when everyone's watching and whispering,
it's hard to keep secrets. . . .

Look out for the second novel in

gossip girl
the carlyles

You Just Can't Get Enough, coming October 2008

Five Spectacular Stories.
One Ah-Mazing Summer.

THE CLIQUE
SUMMER COLLECTION

MASSIE
Available now

DYLAN
Available now

ALICIA
JUNE 3, 2008

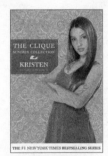

KRISTEN
JULY 1, 2008

CLAIRE
AUGUST 5, 2008

Spend your summer with THE CLIQUE!

poppy

Welcome to Poppy.

A poppy is a beautiful blooming red flower
(like the one on the spine of this book). It is also
the name of the new home of your favorite series.

Poppy takes the real world and makes it
a little funnier, a little more fabulous.

Poppy novels are wild, witty, and inspiring.
They were written just for you.

So sit back, get comfy, and pick a Poppy.

poppy
www.pickapoppy.com

gossip girl

THE A-LIST
THE CLIQUE

the it girl
POSEUR